THE
NEW
GIRLFRIEND

BOOKS BY SHERYL BROWNE

THE
NEW
GIRLFRIEND

SHERYL BROWNE

Bookouture

Published by Bookouture in 2020

An imprint of Storyfire Ltd.
Carmelite House
50 Victoria Embankment
London EC4Y 0DZ

www.bookouture.com

ISBN: 978-1-83888-038-5
eBook ISBN: 978-1-83888-037-8

For Maggie
With special love to my brother, Dave, who was there for her. And
to Maggie's children, Rachel and Anthony.
She loved you all fiercely.

PROLOGUE

Alone on the station platform, Josh huddled further into his coat and tugged his collar up against the freezing rain. His train was overdue, running late, he supposed. Such was his luck lately. If it could go wrong it did, spectacularly. Everything he touched seemed to fall apart. What he'd done to make the women in his life hate him he still didn't know. He breathed in hard, his throat feeling raw from the spirits he'd tipped down it after his teaching colleagues had left the retirement do he'd felt obliged to go to this evening. Bad idea. It had only brought his problems into sharp focus.

Reeling, he heaved out a sigh and checked his watch. It would help if he could see the bloody thing. He closed one eye and squinted at it. Christ, he felt bad. He'd felt rough when he'd woken up that morning, having drunk more than he should after the gut-wrenching conversation with the woman who'd thwarted his every attempt to support her. Trying not to think about it, at least until he'd spoken to his stepfather, he moved further towards the one light on the platform that hadn't been smashed, checked the time on his phone and then attempted to read the text his stepfather had sent him. Adam had agreed to meet him at Worcester station. He was a decent bloke, whose opinion Josh valued. He knew he could trust him not to relay anything back to his mother.

He could barely read the text, feeling disorientated as the words swam out of focus. He hoped he wasn't going to pass out. Lying on a railway station platform in sub-zero temperatures, he'd probably freeze to death before the train arrived.

Had the train he was waiting for been cancelled? He checked the app, succeeding after two fumbling attempts, only to find that it had. *Great.* There was no way now he would make his connection at Birmingham. So what did he do? He could hardly walk to the centre of Birmingham in this state. He debated whether to call Adam and ask him to come and fetch him. Adam would be okay about it, and it would mean they could talk on the way, but Josh was loath to ask him to drive out here after being at work all day. Deciding it was probably his only option, he was about to call when he saw another text from him.

Do you want to message me when you're at Evesham? I'll set off as soon as I get it.

There's a problem with train times, Josh texted back. *Will call you.*

He'd just selected Adam's number when his phone rang.

Dammit. His heart rate ratcheting up as he realised who it was, he was about to answer when something dark and sleek darted past his feet, almost causing him to jump out of his skin. Christ, what the hell was that? If it was a rat, it was a big bugger. His heart palpitating, he inched cautiously towards the worn yellow band at the edge of the platform and peered over. He sighed with relief when he saw two alarmed green orbs blinking up at him. It was a cat. A black cat, lucky if it crossed his path. Definitely not a rat. He laughed shakily as the cat, clearly as spooked as he was, imparted its feelings with a feral hiss, then leapt back up onto the platform in one swift move and slinked warily past him.

Jesus. He'd be imagining werewolves next. Taking a breath, he hit return call, praying silently as he did. He was half expecting it to go to voicemail, but she picked up. 'You called me,' he said, his stomach knotting.

'To tell you I'm deleting your number,' she replied curtly. 'There's no point you ringing and texting me, Josh. We've said all we have to.'

'*You* have,' he retorted, disbelieving. He had a lot more to say, if only she would give him a chance. 'Why are you doing this?' he asked, anger churning inside him when she didn't reply. 'Look, I'm trying here. Can we not both just act like adults, given the situation?'

'Perhaps you should try looking at the situation from my point of view,' she suggested. 'I'm going.'

'Don't,' Josh said, swallowing back a knot in his throat. What in God's name was he supposed to do if she wouldn't listen to anything he had to say? 'Look, can't we at least meet up again? There has to be some way we can—'

He heard the wild mewl of the cat a split second before he lurched forward. A sharp jolt ripped through him, jarring his bones agonisingly as he landed on the unforgiving tracks. White-hot pain searing down his spine, he tried to raise his head. Couldn't. *Shit!* Icy fear gripped his stomach as he heard a train approaching. He had to move. Now! Careless of the grit and gravel biting into his cheek, he brought his hands up, attempting to get some leverage. His gut twisted as he noticed the crimson stain flowering beneath him, felt the warm stickiness of his own blood. Christ, he had to get off the fucking tracks. Desperation clutching his chest, he tried to call out, but nothing escaped his throat other than a muted rasp.

Help me. He blinked at the phone, which lay tauntingly just out of his reach, and dragged in a harsh breath. The tracks hissed. Not a lucky black cat. Not for him. Deadly steel snakes vibrating beneath him, reverberating inside him. He heard the gurgle as he gulped back the coppery taste in his mouth. Felt the terrifying rumble of thunder beneath him. Heard a scream. Someone, somewhere, calling out.

CHAPTER ONE

Cassandra

July 2019

Cassie had wanted something upbeat in place of the traditional hymns, to reflect who Joshua was. She'd decided on something by a French band he'd been into since he'd heard their demo tapes on the internet. Tears stung her eyes as she recalled how he'd shown her a YouTube clip, explaining to her that it was electro-swing, and then promptly waltzed her around the kitchen. Sitting in the church, where she was somehow supposed to say goodbye to her son, she glanced sideways at Adam, grateful for the solidity of him, of their marriage. She wouldn't be able to get through the service if it wasn't for him, this dependable man who loved her unquestioningly – though she wondered whether he would still love her if he knew all there was to know about her.

Her heart aching unbearably, she clung to his hand as one of Josh's friends from work recited the short poem she'd asked permission to read as a tribute. Adam squeezed her fingers as she listened to the girl's tremulous voice: "'Do not stand at my grave and cry; I am not there, I did not die.'"

It wasn't true. She squeezed Adam's hand back, acrid grief crashing through her. Josh wasn't here. And she needed him to be. She needed to see him, to reach out and touch him; her child, who'd come so unexpectedly into her life, filling the void inside her. He'd saved her, his tiny body comforting her when she'd been so bereft. Where was he now?

Adam wrapped an arm around her as fresh sobs racked her body. She bowed her head. She couldn't look at the coffin. Her chest heaving, the tears spilled unchecked from her eyes onto the order of service on her knees.

She felt his arm slip from around her after a second, and wondered how he would contain his emotion as he delivered the eulogy. He'd loved Josh as if he were his own. He'd always been there for him. Cassie knew he was berating himself now for not being there when Josh had needed him most. As if he could have been. He couldn't make himself believe that Josh had fallen onto the tracks and died such a horrific death because he'd drunk too much. The colour had drained from his face when the police had speculated about suicide. It was inconceivable, he'd told them categorically. Josh wasn't conflicted or depressed. He'd texted him from the station, he'd pointed out. Showing them the text had swayed them back to their former assumption that he'd fallen accidentally, possibly landing awkwardly and sustaining an injury. His blood-alcohol concentration had been high, they'd eventually confirmed. There wasn't much else left of him to establish cause of death, other than the obvious trauma caused by the train.

Still Adam was determined that he couldn't have fallen. Josh had texted him, he'd repeated quietly as they'd left the inquest.

Feeling his pain, Cassie closed her eyes as he began: 'Standing here today to say goodbye to our son, Joshua, is one of the hardest things I've ever had to do.' She heard his voice crack as he spoke, and her heart bled for him. His face was pale, she noticed, incongruous with years of outdoor work; his expression taut. He was struggling, fighting to maintain his composure.

'As Josh grew from a boy into a teenager, I could see the man he would become,' he went on falteringly. 'Strong, dependable, macho when he needed to be on the rugby field but never afraid to show his caring side.' Pausing to swallow, he stopped and glanced at the ceiling.

'He loved his music and his sport,' he continued shakily. 'Lived for his canoeing. Casting off the shackles of everyday life, as he referred to it. Getting back in touch with himself through nature. I'll never forget the time he pointed out that I was perhaps a little too close to nature to be enjoying the experience. He was right. A novice and upside-down in a canoe is not a great place to be. Josh never took credit for it, but I think he saved my life that day.'

He paused again, pinching the bridge of his nose hard. 'He urged me to get back on the horse.' A sad smile curved his mouth. 'We often went canoeing together after that. We would spend hours talking about life, his plans for the future. I'm a builder by trade, it's all I've ever known. It's not up there as far as high-powered careers go, but on one of those trips Josh told me he was proud of me, proud of the fact that I run my own company, provide people with jobs and teach them a trade. I couldn't have been prouder of *him* at that moment. Our teenage son was growing into a man right before my eyes.'

As Adam hesitated again, Cassie felt her brother shift in his seat next to her, ready to take over should he be too overcome. Knowing that Adam wouldn't want that, she pressed her hand to Tom's arm, urging him to stay.

'He confided that he wanted to be a teacher,' Adam managed after a second, his voice choked. 'Wondered what I thought. He was concerned I'd be disappointed that he didn't want to join me in the business, I think. I told him that Cassie and I would both be proud of him. It was a perfect vocation for someone with a caring soul and a natural instinct to help others.

'He had so many plans. One of those was to take Cassie and me to a concert to see his favourite band, whose music we chose today because it was so much a part of who he was. There was one song he played over and over. It talks about every day being a miracle, helping one another and connecting back with people. We didn't realise until he'd gone what a miracle every day we had with Josh was. He laughed a lot, loved people, loved life. He wasn't the kind of person who would hunker down and wait for the storm to pass; he danced in the rain. Remembering his enthusiasm and desire to live life to the full, seeing the many friends he made, I know in my heart he wouldn't want us to hide away in our grief. He would want us to celebrate his life by remembering the good times and living ours.'

He stopped, looking directly at Cassie. Even from yards away, she could see the anguish in his eyes. He was as broken as she was. How could he not be? To begin with, she hadn't felt she could go on, hadn't thought she deserved to. Josh had left because of her, because of the silly argument they'd had. She would never forgive herself for that. Now, though… Imagining Adam trying to deal with grief twice over, the torture he would suffer, undoubtedly blaming himself again if she chose what seemed to be an easier option than trying to live without her son, she knew she could never do that to him.

'Goodbye, Josh,' he said unsteadily. 'You were the best son anyone could ever have. We're not ready to lose you, but we have to let go. Wherever you are, stay safe in the knowledge that we love you.'

Cassie wanted to run as the curtains began to close, not away from her boy's coffin, but towards it. She was scared, terrified for him. She couldn't bear the thought of him going through this on his own.

It was her brother who stilled her. 'Come on, Cas,' he urged her, his arm sliding around her shoulders as she stood, only to feel the muscles in her legs grow weak. 'Josh will always be with us in our hearts.'

How? Cassie stifled a sob as she leant into him. How could he be in her heart when he'd taken it with him?

She felt Adam's arm around her as they made their way to the exit. 'We have to thank his friends,' he said softly. 'But if you're not up to it…'

Cassie drew in a breath. It stopped short of the raw pain in her chest. 'I'm fine,' she murmured, wiping futilely at the tears on her cheeks. She had to do this. Seeing so many of Josh's friends here today, she'd ached with a combination of fierce pride and stomach-wrenching sorrow. She had to thank them personally, meet the young people who'd shared his life and were also grieving the loss of him.

Standing outside the church, she made herself smile as she and Adam went through the formalities, shaking hands with people, many assuring them how loved their son was. The look in one girl's eyes as she approached them, a young man supporting her, tore a fresh wound in her heart. She was obviously distraught.

'I'm so sorry,' the girl whispered, hugging Cassie fiercely for a brief second before pressing a hand to her mouth and turning away.

The young man with her fed her into the arms of another woman, who led her away towards the toilets, and then turned back to shake Adam's hand. 'I'm sorry for your loss, Mr Colby,' he said, his own eyes shiny with tears he was clearly working to hold back.

Smiling briefly, Adam nodded his appreciation. 'Thank you…?'

'Ryan Anderson,' the young man supplied. 'I was a couple of years above Josh at school. Jemma… my wife… she knew him too. He was a good mate, looked out for people, you know?'

Cassie smiled, though it felt like there were a thousand shards of glass inside her. She knew that was true. Growing up, Josh was always surrounded by friends who thought the world of him. 'Your wife and I have met briefly,' she said, swallowing back her tears. 'Thank you both for being here for him, Ryan.'

'I'd better get Jemma home.' Ryan nodded after her. 'She's not feeling too well.'

'She's clearly very upset.' Guessing her baby was due soon, Cassie smiled understandingly. 'Please thank her for me, and pass on my best to her.'

'I'll make sure to,' Ryan promised.

'His rugby coach is here,' Adam said, indicating the man as Ryan turned away. 'I'll just go and acknowledge him.'

Cassie smiled gratefully, guessing he would know what to say to him. Glancing around, she caught sight of a girl with long flame-coloured hair standing hesitantly by the churchyard gates. Noticing her looking in her direction, she wondered whether she might be about to approach her, but the girl looked away, gazing around as if searching for someone. She seemed very young, her face pale, without any apparent make-up. She was heavily pregnant, her thin cotton smock dress accentuating her bump. Cassie's breath caught in her throat as she noticed the cross-body bag she was wearing.

It was Josh's. She'd bought it from John Lewis for his birthday. She was sure it was the same one. The girl had obviously known him well, if she had his bag. Cassie's heartbeat quickened and she took a step towards her, then stopped as Adam pressed a hand to her arm. 'He's coming on to the reception,' he said. 'How are you holding up?'

'Coping. Just,' she assured him with a small smile. 'I was wondering who that girl was.' She nodded back to the gates, but the girl had gone.

CHAPTER TWO

Twelve weeks since Josh's death. Twenty-four years since the day he was born, the day that had started out as the bleakest day of her life and had turned into the best. Cassie stared at the alarm clock she kept by her bed. Wished she could will the hands back. She'd thought she would leave the hospital empty-handed; instead she'd left with a miracle. How could she continue going through the days, marking them off on a calendar, when there seemed to be no purpose in life, no future worth facing without him?

She hadn't realised her time with him would be so short when she'd brought him home, examining every perfect inch of him before placing him in his pretty white cot. She'd vowed to love and protect this child until the day she died. She hadn't lived up to her promise. Josh had been snatched away from her. It was karma, Cassie was sure of it.

She listened to the sounds of life going on around her: cows mooing in the fields that backed onto the house, pre-milking; neighbours shouting hello to each other as they went through the morning ritual, climbing into cars and slamming doors; the letter box flapping, a dull thud as the newspapers landed on the hall floor bringing news she was no longer interested in. As a reporter, she always used to scan them. Now they piled up, unread.

She could hear Adam downstairs, making tea she couldn't bring herself to drink. He was trying so hard to be there for her; to reach out and comfort her. Her heart constricted as she recalled how he'd tried to embrace her once the police had left after delivering the news she'd begged them not to tell her. She'd pulled away from him. His arms around her, his palpable grief would have made it real. She didn't want it to be real. Couldn't bear it, had to contain it, the silent scream rising inside her, the terror.

She'd gone upstairs, something driving her, some desperate hope that she would find her son there, lying on his bed, his stuff strewn all over the place, a bemused smile on his face as he wondered what all the fuss was about. He wasn't there. Cassie had whimpered like a wounded animal. She'd heard the sound escaping her mouth as she'd wrapped her arms around herself. She hadn't realised at first that it had come from her.

She'd sensed Adam standing hesitantly behind her as she'd gazed at the newly decorated walls in Josh's room. She couldn't smell him, she'd realised, above the paint fumes. And she'd needed to. Oh God, how she'd needed to. 'It feels as if we painted him out of our lives the day we did this,' she'd whispered.

She'd heard Adam suck in a sharp breath. She hadn't meant to say it. She'd wished dearly she could take it back. She hadn't been thinking of Adam. Of the fact that he'd redecorated the room. She'd just wanted Josh safe back home. She would have given anything, everything – a limb, an eye – for her son to walk through the door. She would have traded her soul to the devil to undo the argument they'd had before he left. To see him smile, listen to his tiresome jokes, pick up his discarded clothes. But he wasn't going to come home. He would never come home again, and all she had left was the guilt and the pain and a room full of nothing. Memories glossed over. His life obliterated.

'He was my son too, Cassie,' Adam had said quietly, after a second. He'd sounded hollow, heartbroken. Still he'd been there for her, catching her as she'd finally crumpled.

Now she turned her face to the pillow, her heart bruising as she felt his crushing hurt all over again. He'd been the best father a man could be, sharing his passions and his hobbies as their boy had grown. He'd been just Josh's age, twenty-four, when he'd come into her life. Josh had immediately taken to him. They never had managed to have a child together. After an awful late miscarriage, quietly grieving the loss of their baby, they'd finally realised her body simply couldn't live up to their dreams. Adam had reassured her it didn't matter, that he was happy as long as they had each other. Had he been? He'd nursed her through surgery after her cancer scare; had always been there. Quietly, though, she'd dreaded that one day he might regret not having a child of his own. And now with Josh gone… He was a handsome man, his dark, rugged looks enhanced rather than marred by the passing of time. Why would he stay with her when he could be with a younger woman, someone who could still help him achieve his dream?

Hearing the bedroom door open behind her, she closed her eyes and pressed the extra pillow closer to her midriff. Adam would want her to get up, try to function, but she couldn't. Not today. She didn't have the energy. She just wanted to lie here reliving each painful memory as every one of Josh's birthdays played through her mind like a slideshow, the reel slowing, melting and snapping as she arrived at the day of his death.

She sensed him come around the bed, place the tea he'd made on the bedside table. Her eyes fluttered open as she felt him sit on the edge of the bed. She watched him run his hands over his face, drape them between his knees.

'Are you okay?' she asked him, pointlessly. She knew he was as lost inside as she was. 'Adam?' She pulled herself up. Moved towards him.

He kneaded his temples. 'Not great,' he said gruffly. 'I have no idea what to do. Where to go. Everything I touch reminds me of him. Apart from the one place that should remind us of him, which I bloody well gutted. *Jesus.*' He sucked in an angry breath, looked heavenwards. 'I'm so sorry about the bedroom, Cas. I never thought... Not in my worst nightmare could I have—'

'Adam, stop!' Cassie shuffled closer and pulled herself to her knees. 'It doesn't matter about the damn bedroom. You were there for him. You were always there for him, the only father he ever knew or wanted.'

'But I wasn't, was I?' Adam's voice was full of remorse. 'Not when he needed me to be.'

Cassie felt her heart turn over. 'Adam, don't.'

'Why didn't I offer to drive into Birmingham for him?' He pressed his thumbs hard against his forehead. 'I knew he'd be home late. Why the hell couldn't I have left the job problems to the site manager and bloody well offered? I could have done *something.*'

'What?' Cassie caught hold of his hand, willed him to look at her.

'Anything,' Adam said gutturally.

'The building site was flooding, Adam. You prioritised because you had to. And now you're blaming yourself. It's *pointless.* Josh wouldn't have wanted you to do that. You know he wouldn't.'

Adam's jaw was taut, his shoulders tense. After a second, he pulled in a breath, blew it out slowly. 'It wasn't suicide, Cassie. He didn't sound down when I last spoke to him. Worried about something, yes. But he wasn't contemplating taking his own life. I know it in my gut. He texted me, for God's sake. Would he have done that if he'd been planning to commit suicide?'

Cassie felt her own breath leave her body. He was finally speaking the words he hadn't dared to say for fear of upsetting her. Even though she knew he was right, she felt as if someone had punched her.

'He might just have fallen,' Adam went on. 'I suppose that's the only other explanation, but I can't help thinking there might have been more to it. One minute he's compos enough to be texting me, then the next… It just doesn't add up. He couldn't have been *that* drunk, could he? So why the bloody hell did he just lie—'

'Adam,' Cassie stopped him, lifting his chin and forcing him to look at her, 'don't do this to yourself, please. You have nothing to blame yourself for. Nothing. Do you hear me?'

He closed his eyes. 'Christ, Cassie, what are we going to do?' he asked throatily.

Cassie hesitated for a second, aware that any intimacy between them had dwindled to none – because of her, because her own guilt wouldn't allow her to seek comfort in his embrace – and then placed her arms around him. Adam reciprocated, and she tensed for a second as he massaged the nape of her neck softly with his thumb. Then she relaxed a little and leant tentatively into him.

Neither of them spoke. They simply stayed like that for a moment, going through the almost impossible task of continuing to breathe, and then Cassie eased away, moving to the middle of the bed, where she reached out for him. Needing no encouragement, Adam followed her. Curving his body around hers, as if that could somehow protect her from all the bad things in the world, he placed an arm gently across her. He was a good man, a strong, caring man. Cassie didn't move to wipe away the tears that slid from her eyes. If only she could protect him, from this and from the bad things that might still come.

She wasn't sure how long they lay there. The doorbell broke the silence.

'Dammit,' Adam cursed when it rang for a second time. 'I'll get it,' he said, pushing himself off the bed.

Cassie got up and went to swill her face, in case it was someone she couldn't avoid, leaving the bathroom door open so she could listen.

'I'm sorry to bother you,' a female voice said. 'I wondered if I could have a quick word. If it's not a good time, I can always come back.'

'No, it's fine,' Adam assured her. 'Is there something I can help you with?'

'I was hoping to speak to both of you,' the woman said – a young woman, Cassie thought. 'Mrs Colby as well, I mean, but if she's not here...'

'She's upstairs,' Adam told the visitor, as Cassie dried her face and headed along the landing, curious. 'Would you like to come in?'

Peering over the stair rail, Cassie watched as Adam stepped out of the front door, puzzled until it became apparent that he was helping their visitor with a pushchair. Planting the chair in the hall, he smiled down at the tiny baby snuggled into it. 'Girl or boy?' he asked.

'A boy, Samuel,' the woman replied, following him into the hall.

Cassie stared at the sweep of flame-red hair. It was her. The girl who had stopped at the church gates and then disappeared so suddenly.

'You have a lovely house. It's very grand,' the girl said, gazing around as Cassie raced through a thousand scenarios as to why she would be here. Was it because it was Josh's birthday? How well had she known him? She'd been wearing his bag, she recalled, a chill of apprehension running through her.

'Thank you,' Adam said. 'Cassie's resting. If you want to wait here, I'll go and fetch her.'

'Oh.' The girl looked flustered. 'No, don't do that. I don't want to disturb her. I can always call—'

'Adam...' Drawing in a fortifying breath, Cassie moved to the top of the stairs. 'Who is it?'

The girl's gaze swivelled in her direction as she made her way down.

'Hello,' Cassie said, smiling uncertainly. 'I saw you at the church gates after the funeral, didn't I?'

Her expression wary, the girl confirmed it with a nod. 'I wanted to speak to you then,' she said, 'but I wasn't sure it was the right place. I was too scared, to be honest.'

'Scared?' Pausing, Cassie exchanged a baffled glance with Adam. 'Why on earth would you be scared?'

'I don't know. I mean, I wasn't sure what to do. The thing is…' Faltering, the girl glanced down and then hesitantly back up before finding her resolve. 'The baby,' she said, as Cassie's heart skidded to a stop in her chest. 'It's Josh's.'

CHAPTER THREE

Cassie felt as if the air had been sucked from her lungs. A whirlpool of emotion churned inside her as she stared at the girl. Shock, disbelief, confusion.

The girl looked at both of them in turn. 'I wasn't sure whether to come,' she said nervously. 'I knew it would be terribly painful for you, but…' She glanced at the baby and then back, 'I thought Josh would have wanted you to know.'

Adam's eyes flicked to Cassie's. He looked as stunned as she felt. 'Come into the lounge,' he said, his voice thick with emotion.

Giving him a small smile, the girl reached for the pushchair.

'How old is he?' Cassie asked, stopping her.

'Ten weeks,' the girl replied. 'Ten weeks, four days and five hours, to be precise.'

Cassie nodded. 'There's someone here in the village who's not long had a baby,' she said, her voice choked despite her best attempts to control her emotions. 'He's just two weeks older. I couldn't help wishing that…' She stopped and breathed. 'Jemma Anderson, do you know her? She's married to Ryan. They were both at the funeral.'

'No. No, I don't,' the girl said. 'I'd never been here before. I wanted to come to the funeral, but as we'd never met…'

Again Cassie nodded, desperately trying to take everything in. Because of the circumstances, she hadn't seen Jemma's baby, but when she'd heard she'd given birth, realised that Josh would never experience all the joy and heartbreak of being a father, the unique moment of holding a precious new life for the first time, it had sharpened the pain of her loss.

'Why didn't you come sooner?' she asked the girl. 'Why wait until—' She stopped, feeling suddenly weak, as if the blood had drained from her body.

'I've got you,' Adam said, threading an arm around her waist and steering her to the lounge. Pushing the door open with his foot, he guided her to the sofa and helped her down onto it. 'Can I get you something?' he asked her, raking a hand shakily through his hair.

'No, I'm fine,' Cassie assured him. 'I haven't eaten, that's all it is.' She turned her attention to the baby, and a deep yearning unfurled inside her. Her gaze travelled over the sleeping child, and any doubt she might have had that he wasn't Josh's evaporated. He was the image of him.

Her heart constricting painfully, she drew her eyes slowly to the girl. Her face was pale, her eyes wide with fear. It *had* been Josh's bag. She'd known it. This girl had been going out with him. They'd created a life together. Hope leapt in her chest. Her son had gone, but might she still have part of him? A living, breathing part?

'Sorry,' Adam said, kneading his forehead as he turned back to the girl. 'Would you like something? Tea? Coffee?'

'Thank you. Water would be nice.' She smiled shyly.

'Would you like to sit down?' Cassie asked as Adam left the room. She looked so nervous and awkward, she couldn't help but feel for her.

The girl glanced at her baby, then to the armchair, and then, offering Cassie a small smile, came to sit on the sofa beside her.

Cassie noted that she was knotting and unknotting her fingers in her lap. Hesitating for a second, she reached to still them. 'It's okay. We don't bite.' She offered her a reassuring smile. 'We should probably introduce ourselves. I'm Cassandra, Cassie for short.'

'Kimberley. Kimberley Summers,' the girl said. 'Most people call me Kim. I really wasn't sure whether I should come, but I thought I should talk to you before…'

Before what? Cassie's heart stalled. 'You don't need to explain, Kim,' she said carefully. 'I'm glad you came. I am shocked, though, I have to admit. Josh never mentioned he was in a serious relationship.'

Kim's eyes flicked down. 'We hadn't been going out for long before the baby… We were a couple, though.' She looked earnestly back at her. 'We did talk about you a little. Josh said that you and he were working through some things, so I wasn't sure whether he'd told you about us or not. He said he was going to, but…'

He didn't feel he could confide in me. Cassie swallowed back the bitter taste of regret as the girl trailed off awkwardly. 'Was he looking forward to becoming a father?' she asked, though it pained her, because she knew the answer. He would have been. Even if she hadn't known about Kim, she knew that much about him.

'Yes.' Kim nodded sadly. 'He was surprised, worried about how to tell you when you've been dealing with so much.' She paused and reached to wipe away a tear that spilled down her cheek. 'But once he got his head around it, he was really pleased. He would have been a brilliant dad.'

Cassie drew in a sharp breath. He'd obviously discussed her illness with Kim then, as well as the fact that they'd fallen out. 'He would have,' she said, her throat catching. 'He loved children.'

'I know.' Kim smiled fondly. 'That was obvious when he talked about the children he taught on his school placement programme. He would have been a brilliant teacher too,' she added, causing Cassie's heart to twist afresh.

'The thing is,' Kim went on, her eyes awash with uncertainty, 'I'm not sure what to do. I mean, if he'd told me he wasn't interested, I wouldn't have gone through with the pregnancy. But when he seemed so genuinely happy at the thought of being a dad, making plans for a future together…' She stopped, glancing away.

'You can talk to me, you know, Kim,' Cassie said kindly, though her stomach was knotting inside her. 'That's why you're here after all, isn't it?'

Kim nodded. 'I'm not sure I'll be able to cope on my own,' she admitted tearfully. 'I don't have anything to offer him. I don't even have a job at the moment. I could end up ruining his life, couldn't I?' She looked at Cassie beseechingly. 'I'm thinking he might have a better future with someone else. Someone who could care for him properly. There are a million people out there who are desperate for a child, aren't there? People much better off than I am.'

Cassie's stomach turned over. She couldn't really be contemplating parting with him? She looked across to the pushchair. He was still sleeping like an angel. Seeing Josh at that age, she stilled an urge to snatch him from his pram and hold him close, breathe in the innocent sweet smell of him and never let him go.

She couldn't allow Kim to do anything rash. Something she would regret. Something that Cassie too would regret for the rest of her life. She took a breath, about to ask her not to make any decisions before they'd all had a chance to talk it through, just as Adam came back into the room.

'It's filtered. We don't have any bottled,' he said, scrutinising Kim carefully as he handed her the glass of water.

'Thanks. That's perfect.' She gave him an appreciative smile.

Adam smiled back, but his expression was guarded. 'What about your parents, Kim? How do they feel about the baby?'

Kim stopped sipping, rested the glass in her lap and lowered her gaze again.

'Are they not willing to help you?' he went on, unaware of Cassie trying to make eye contact with him. Kim's cheeks were flushing furiously; it was clear he was making her feel uncomfortable. 'Assuming they're aware of your circumstances, that is. I would have thought they—'

'They can't.' Kim looked sharply back up. 'I come from a large family. My mum has my three younger brothers at home, as well as me. I have a chance of renting a property, just a small one, but it's not confirmed yet. And then I have to get my benefits sorted out, so I've no choice but to stay at home for now. We live on Tennison Road on the Eastbridge estate.' Her gaze went to Cassie, who understood what she was trying to convey. She'd had one or two assignments on the Eastbridge estate. It consisted largely of rented accommodation and meant the family weren't well off.

'As for my dad... he's due in court next week,' Kim continued, and took a deep breath as if summoning up her courage. 'He assaulted a neighbour. The only blessing was that it wasn't my mum this time. He's not the sort of man you'd want anywhere near a baby.'

Cassie's horrified gaze shot to Adam, who was clearly as shocked as she was.

'Do you mind if I use the loo?' Kim asked, now looking hugely embarrassed.

'No, not at all.' Cassie rose to her feet, trying to get her jumbled thoughts into some sort of order. 'I'll show you where it is.'

Adam waited until Kim had disappeared into the downstairs toilet, then gestured Cassie into the kitchen and reached to push the door shut. 'Do you believe her?' he asked.

Cassie searched his face. 'Yes,' she said, though she was still trying to process the information. 'Why? Don't you?'

'I don't know.' Adam looked troubled. 'It seems a bit odd, that's all. Josh never even mentioned he was seeing anyone.'

'No, but initially he might have been concerned about how we might react to the news of a baby before he'd even completed his teacher training,' Cassie suggested. 'And then, when he left...'

Still Adam looked wary. Cassie understood why he would be, but he must see what was staring him in the face. 'Have you looked at the baby? He's the image of Josh.'

'I know. It's uncanny. It's just…' He stopped and shrugged uncomfortably.

'Just what?' Cassie urged him, glancing worriedly towards the hall. Kim wouldn't be long. She didn't want her thinking they'd retreated to the kitchen to talk about her.

His expression awkward, Adam studied her for a second. 'What if she's just here for money? What if that's all it ever was? She hardly seems Josh's type.'

Cassie was astonished. 'She's not long given birth to a baby, Adam,' she reminded him. 'Our grandchild. And with no one to support her, of course she'll need help. She's on her own. She's come to us. Was that so wrong of her?'

Adam drew in a breath. 'No. I just… Look, Cassie, I know how much this would mean to you. I just don't want you upset if it turns out to be some kind of scam, that's all.'

'*Scam?* She's the mother of Josh's *child*.' Tears stinging her eyes, Cassie stared hard at him. 'How upset do you think I'll be if she decides she has no other choice but to offer the baby up for adoption? She can't afford to keep him, Adam. He could end up anywhere… a million miles away. Do you imagine I could ever forgive myself if that happened?'

Adam ran a hand over his neck. 'No,' he said, expelling a slow breath. 'I don't get why she didn't ask *us* to take him, though. It's the obvious solution if she really believes he would be better off with someone else, isn't it?'

That was precisely what Cassie had thought, but… 'She would hardly have walked through the door and said, "This is your grandson, and oh, by the way, I'm leaving him with you", would she? Not without seeing if we were open to the idea. I don't imagine she actually wants anyone to take him. She's vulnerable. Scared. Yet you're judging her without even knowing her.'

Sweeping a disappointed glance over him, she moved to the door. She was being unfair. She knew Adam wasn't materialistic.

He had a natural work ethic. He'd bought the beautiful Victorian house they lived in and renovated it for her and Josh, his family. He was being protective of her now because he thought *she* was vulnerable, and she was grateful that he cared enough to do that. Her inclination, though, was to feel protective of the child. Her grandchild. How could she not?

'Cassie,' Adam moved towards her, 'wait.'

'We need to talk *to* her, Adam, not about her.' Cassie was resolute. They shouldn't be whispering about the girl behind her back. Pulling the kitchen door open, she stepped into the hall – and stopped dead. The front door was wide open.

She ran to the lounge, her heart dropping like a stone. What had they done? The girl who'd come to them desperate for support had obviously overheard them talking and run.

CHAPTER FOUR

Kimberley

'Where on earth have you been?' her mum asked, almost before Kim was through the front door.

'Just out,' Kim answered shortly. Smelling the oil from the chip pan as she parked the pushchair in the hall, she knew her mum had been slaving in the kitchen. And this was after getting up at the crack of dawn to do her cleaning job and then looking after the kids all day before starting work this evening at the local pub. She'd been waiting for Kim to get back and take over, make sure her youngest brother went to bed at the right time and the other two didn't sit up late watching Netflix. Kim felt bad about snapping at her, but she had her own problems to deal with. Her mum wouldn't be able to rely on her once she'd moved out. Mentally crossing her fingers, she prayed that the guy who she'd learnt through a friend was sub-letting his house got back to her. It was an old property, in need of loads of work, but anything would be better than living here.

'Oi.' Her dad, the reason she was so desperate to get a place of her own, appeared from the lounge as if on cue, his eyes unfocused and a beer can in his hand. Kim couldn't remember a time when she'd seen him without one. He'd probably had his baby formula fed to him in one. 'Show your mother a little respect, you. She's waiting to go out to work.'

Kim almost laughed at that. The only time he'd shown her mother any respect was when he'd accepted she didn't want sex after giving birth to her little brother. Kim had heard it all through the wall. 'No' wouldn't have been an option if he'd decided not to be so gracious. 'Pity you don't do the odd job occasionally, isn't it?' She smiled disdainfully at him. 'Mum wouldn't have to juggle two jobs then, would she?'

'You cheeky little bitch.' Her dad lunged forwards, coming after her with remarkable agility for a man who thought walking to the fridge to fetch his own beer was too much effort.

Kim's heart caught in her chest. She had been about to lift the baby out of the pushchair, but moved away from it, heading swiftly for the kitchen. Her dad was too fast, grabbing hold of her hair and yanking her head back.

'Do not ever bad-mouth me again, or you'll regret the day you were born, do you hear me?' he snarled, his beer breath close to her ear.

'I already do,' Kim assured him, gritting her teeth and trying to twist from his grasp, but he only tugged her hair mercilessly tighter.

'Danny!' Her mum intervened, dropping a pan with a clang, which caused the baby to start in his pram. 'You leave her alone,' she warned him, taking her own life in her hands and squaring up to him.

'Or else?' he growled.

'Or else I'll be late again and I'll get the bloody sack! Then what will you do for your beer money?'

Kim took her chance as he relaxed his grip on her hair. As she darted away, though, the framed photograph she'd taken from Josh's parents' house slipped from where she'd tucked it under her jacket.

Her dad spotted it as she bent to retrieve it. 'Leave it,' he growled. 'I said, leave it.' His boot came down perilously close to her fingers as she scrambled for it anyway.

He wouldn't hesitate to stamp on them. Reluctantly Kim straightened up.

A satisfied smirk on his face, he scooped the photograph up. 'Who's this then?' he asked, his eyes narrowing as he studied it.

'None of your business.' Her gaze flicked back to the pushchair, where the baby had started to whimper.

'Nice frame,' her dad said.

Oh no. It was silver. Worth a fiver down the pub. 'You can have it,' she said, thinking fast and taking a gamble. It might work, depending on how magnanimous he was feeling. 'I only want the photo. It's my friend's brother. He died suddenly. She wants me to do a pencil drawing of it for her.'

Her dad's greedy gaze stayed on the frame as he considered. He knew she loved to draw, that she was good at it. She'd been desperate to do an art degree, but he'd demanded she get a job and contribute to the household.

'She's paying me fifty quid,' she added, a little incentive. That clinched it. She saw the pound signs ping in his eyes.

'Make sure to give your mother something towards the bills,' he said, and immediately set about detaching the back from the frame.

What he really meant was 'Make sure to give your mum some money I can than pilfer from her purse to piss up the wall.' God, he was obnoxious. Her stomach roiling at the proximity of him, Kim said nothing, holding her temper as she waited for him to return the photograph. He would take great pleasure in ripping it up in front of her if she challenged him.

She glanced away as he handed it to her, rather than see the triumphant look on his face, then tucked it back into her jacket and left him to revel in his pathetic little victory while she went to the pushchair to unbuckle Samuel and lift him carefully out.

'Sorry, sweetheart,' her mum said as, the baby in her arms, Kim headed for the stairs.

Kim nodded. She didn't say anything. She wished her mum would bloody well leave him. Even a refuge had to be better than this.

Once upstairs, she elbowed the door of her shoebox of a room open and went inside in hope of some privacy. She needed to think what to do now that Josh's parents had as good as called her a liar. Well, Adam Colby certainly had. Cassandra had tried to defend her, probably because she'd seen the baby as a way of holding onto her son. Perhaps she should try to catch her on her own and talk to her again. Pop a letter through her door maybe and ask to meet up with her.

Placing the baby on the bed, she swallowed her hurt and beamed him a smile. Cooing and soothing him, she set about changing him. 'You're a gorgeous little boy, aren't you, sweetheart? As good as gold.'

Making sure he was dry and comfortable, she lifted him gently into the cot that was squeezed into the corner. 'We'll be out of here soon, darling. Don't you worry, I'll make sure to look after you and keep you safe,' she promised him, tickling his tummy. He offered her a delighted gummy smile, and she sighed, in awe of the perfect wonder of him. He would be hungry soon. She would have to venture back downstairs, she supposed. Her own tummy clenched coldly at the thought of having to encounter her father again, but Samuel was her priority.

Sighing, she pulled Josh's photo from her jacket and studied it. He'd been so good-looking, his eyes the truest sky blue, his lips just full enough to be sensual. She'd fantasised about those eyes holding hers as he made love to her even before she'd spoken to him. She'd fancied him the second she'd seen him on the Worcester to Birmingham train, and had made sure to be on the same one the next morning, in the hope of seeing him again. And then every morning thereafter, though it had cost her all the money from the waitressing job she'd now given up out of necessity. She'd felt a thousand butterflies take off in her tummy the first time he'd smiled at her. She'd loved him completely. Always would. Wiping away the slow tear that slid down her cheek, she swallowed hard.

She would send the letter. Speak to Cassandra, convince her she wasn't the person they'd assumed she was simply because of where she came from. She'd made a promise to Josh at his grave, and she aimed to keep it. She wouldn't let him down as everyone else in his life had.

CHAPTER FIVE

Joshua

December 2018

'Hey, careful.' Josh instinctively grabbed hold of the girl's arms as she bowled into him on the station platform. Steadying her on her feet, he looked her over. The tip of her nose was pink, her cheeks flushed – with a combination of cold and embarrassment, he imagined. Her hair was tucked under a bobble hat with a fur trim, bar a few flame-red tendrils. It was her: the girl he'd sensed watching him every morning on the early train. She averted her gaze whenever he looked up, but he could feel her eyes on him when he went back to his phone. She'd looked startled, like a deer caught in the headlights, when he'd finally decided to break the ice and say good morning to her. She'd mumbled a 'hello' back and then glued her gaze on her book. Josh had smiled quietly when he'd caught it drifting back in his direction minutes later. He'd guessed she must be shy.

Her eyes were green, he noticed, unsurprisingly, given her hair colour and pale complexion. Unusual, though; sage green, but flecked with grey and amber. They were mesmerising.

'Sorry,' she said, her expression flustered. 'New boots.'

'No problem.' He glanced down at her feet, which were adorned with ankle boots with the kind of spiky heels he had no idea how women stood up in, let alone negotiated icy roads in. 'I quite like women throwing themselves at me,' he added, smiling to put her at her ease.

Which he obviously hadn't. Her blush deepening, she dropped her gaze. She probably thought he was hitting on her. He almost suggested she hang onto his arm until the train stopped, but thought that might make her feel even more uncomfortable. 'You probably need to scuff the soles up a bit,' he said instead, and then, smiling again, climbed on board.

Choosing his usual seat at the window, he watched as she passed him by, also taking her usual seat, one up on the opposite side, facing him. She hadn't got him down as someone to be given a wide berth then.

Catching her eye as he dropped his rucksack at his feet, he tried another small smile. At last she smiled back. Josh was relieved. He didn't like the idea that a female travelling companion might have him down as a creep.

She was on the station platform as usual the next morning. 'I scuffed them,' she said as he glanced in her direction. 'My boots,' she clarified, nodding down at her feet.

'Good idea. I think there's snow forecast later,' Josh said.

'Really?' She glanced upwards at the heavy grey skies. 'Do you think that means we might have a white Christmas?'

'It would be nice, wouldn't it? The sun was shining last year. It didn't feel like Christmas at all somehow.'

She smiled at that, and then looked away as the train pulled in. She boarded it ahead of him, this time choosing a seat on the side he usually sat on. He was about to take the one behind her when he realised that might look a bit pointed. Moving on, he nodded at the seat opposite her. 'Okay if I sit here?' he asked.

She looked surprised. 'Of course. I promise not to take up all the leg room.'

Josh doubted she would do that. She was petite, despite the killer heels.

'Likewise.' He smiled. 'I'm Josh, by the way,' he said, extending his hand.

She hesitated, her cheeks flushing. 'Kimberley,' she said. 'Kim for short.'

'So, Kim, do you work in Brum?' he asked after a second.

'Uni,' she answered. 'Fine art course at Birmingham City. You?'

'School experience programme. I have to take a bus out of town once I get off the train. I'd prefer to drive, but I like to think I'm doing my bit and reducing my carbon footprint.'

'Commendable,' Kim said. He didn't think she was being sarcastic. 'So what does the programme entail?'

'Finding out more about the role of a primary school teacher,' Josh replied. 'Also gaining school experience to support my teacher training.'

'Sounds ideal. For someone so patient with children, I mean.' She eyed him thoughtfully. 'I've seen how you interact with them some mornings.'

'I like kids.' He shrugged. 'It would make what I do a bit difficult if I didn't.'

She smiled and continued to study him, making him feel slightly self-conscious.

'What will you do with your degree, do you think?' he asked her.

'Well,' her eyes flickered down and back, 'I was thinking about teaching, actually.'

Josh arched his eyebrows. 'Great minds,' he said approvingly.

'Clearly. It would be weird if I ended up following you around, wouldn't it?'

'As long as you don't keep throwing yourself at me.' Josh risked a joke.

She blushed but was smiling. 'Sorry about that,' she said. 'My reaction, I mean. My former boyfriend was... Well, let's just say it was a relationship I was well out of. He really did think all women were ready to fall at his feet. Full of himself, you know?'

'In which case, I apologise.' Josh felt bad. 'I obviously touched a raw nerve.'

'Not necessary,' she assured him. 'You weren't to know. What about you? Have you managed to patch things up with your girlfriend?'

Josh eyed her, surprised.

'I couldn't help overhearing your phone conversation the other day,' she explained.

Right. Josh guessed she had heard him pleading with his 'girlfriend' to meet up with him. At least talk to him. She'd refused, again. He felt a knot of anger tighten inside him. 'It's… complicated,' he said. It had been complicated from day one. His mother didn't like her the first time he'd gone out with her. They'd been just sixteen then, determined that love would win through. Obviously, it hadn't, for her.

'Ah.' Kim nodded understandingly. 'Not something you want to discuss in public with a near stranger. I get it.'

'No, it's not that. It's just…' Josh hesitated. He would actually very much like to discuss the situation. He was desperate to confide in someone who would give him their take on whether he was being selfish. Adam would be his first choice, but how fair would it be to ask him to keep it from his wife?

'I get it, honestly,' Kim repeated. 'It's none of my business. Don't worry about it.' She turned to look out of the window, leaving Josh feeling uncomfortable. She probably thought from his silence that he was hinting she should butt out.

She was quiet for several minutes, and then, 'I feel the same as you do about the snow,' she said.

Josh looked up from his phone.

'At Christmas,' she went on, her gaze still on the window. 'It makes everything seem… untouched, somehow.'

'Untainted,' Josh agreed.

She nodded, a wistful look in her eyes as she turned to him. 'My sister's desperate for it to snow. She's bought my nephew a sledge. Personally, I think it's her who wants to use it.'

Josh laughed. 'Yup, I understand the attraction of that. Do you see her at Christmas?' He only wondered because being an only child he'd missed having a sister or brother around.

'I see her all the time,' Kim said. 'I live with her up on the new Ravens Wood estate. Do you know it?'

'I do. Nice properties.' Josh was impressed. They were for sale at upwards of three hundred and fifty grand as far as he knew.

'What about you?' Kim asked him. 'Do you see your family at Christmas?'

'I, er…' Josh wasn't sure how to answer that. He opted for 'I'm hoping to.'

Kim looked at him curiously.

'I had an argument with my mother,' Josh admitted, finding her easy to talk to. 'I decided to move out. We didn't part on great terms. I'd hate to turn up and make everyone's Christmas miserable.'

Kim looked astonished. 'I can't imagine you would ever do that,' she said. 'You seem really easy-going.'

Josh smiled reflectively. 'Yeah, maybe too much,' he said with an expansive sigh. It had been a stupid argument, looking back. His mother had accused him of taking her for granted, expecting her to run around cleaning up after him. Josh hadn't realised he was. He'd told her to stop banging on at him, which was pretty juvenile. She had been a bit, but then she hadn't been well, not sleeping due to the steroids she was on. 'I should call her, I suppose,' he added, wondering at his ability to mess up every relationship in his life.

'You should. At least then you'd know where you stand,' Kim said, glancing through the window and then picking up her bag. 'We're here. Will I see you tomorrow?'

'You can count on it,' Josh said, glad that they'd broken the ice. She was nice. He was slightly bemused that he'd opened up to her like that, but he felt better for it. Smiling, he reached to grab his own bag.

When he glimpsed a figure hurrying away from the school as he walked across the playground at the end of the day, Josh wondered if he might be mistaken. He wasn't, though, he was sure of it. There couldn't be many girls her size wearing the exact same blue jacket and fur-trimmed hat. He racked his brains but couldn't remember mentioning which school he was doing his placement at. So what was she doing here?

CHAPTER SIX

Cassandra

Seeing that an envelope had been pushed through her letter box, Cassie bent to scoop it up as she came through the front door. No stamp, she noted, turning it over. It hadn't been there when she'd left at five for her doctor's appointment. Which meant it must have been delivered while she'd been at the surgery.

Curious, she fumbled the envelope open and drew the letter out, and her heart fluttered with nervous apprehension as she glimpsed the signature at the bottom. Quickly, she read it:

Dear Mrs Colby,

Please accept my apologies for leaving so abruptly. I heard you and Mr Colby arguing and I gathered you didn't trust me. I just wanted you to know I understand. It must have been difficult for you to believe Josh had fallen in love with someone who's so obviously not of his social background.

Please accept my deepest condolences on your loss. Josh spoke kindly about you. He was right. You seem really nice. I wish we could have got along better for Samuel's sake.

I thought you should know that I've made my decision about his future, so you won't hear from me again.

I wish you both well.

Yours truly,
Kim

God, no. Cassie's blood froze. She couldn't let her do this. The girl didn't want to go down this route, clearly. Why else would she have come to see them? Digging in her handbag, she pulled out her mobile. Kim had included her telephone number in her letter, thank God. She'd mentioned which street she lived on, but not the house number. Cassie had already made up her mind to drive over there, knock on every door until she found her. She felt like going straight there now, but she couldn't do that without speaking to her first. Hopefully Kim would be amenable to meeting up this evening. She had to talk to her, apologise to her and convince her she had other options.

Keying in the number, she waited, fearing the call might go to voicemail. Relief flooded through her when it was answered.

'Hello?' Kim said warily.

'Kim, hi. It's Cassandra. Cassie Colby. I hope you don't mind me calling. I got your letter and I had to talk to you.'

'Oh. No…' Kim said, sounding uncertain. 'I mean, it's fine. It's just…'

Cassie's heart skipped a beat. Please God she wouldn't say she wanted nothing to do with her.

'It's not easy to talk,' Kim went on, lowering her voice. 'My dad…'

Cassie felt a rush of relief. She didn't want to talk because he was there. A violent man. The sort of man you wouldn't want anywhere near a baby. She remembered every word Kim had said before she'd left. 'Could you come to me?' she suggested. 'Or perhaps we could meet somewhere.'

'I can't. I have to look after my little brother while Mum's at work,' Kim whispered hurriedly.

'Could your father not look after him for a while?' Cassie knew it was a long shot, but she desperately needed to talk to her.

Kim said nothing, which gave her the answer. Clearly her father wasn't the sort of man you would trust with an older child either. What kind of existence did she have? What kind of existence would that tiny baby have? This had been Kim's thinking, why she'd come to them in the first place. She was trying to find a way out of her appalling situation, looking at renting somewhere, a place of safety for her and her baby. She'd struggled through the birth and the first months of his life on her own. She'd needed sympathy and under-standing, financial help – obviously she would need that – which they could afford. And instead, all she'd met with was suspicion.

Adam pushed his key into the lock and came through the door as she tried to think what to do. Cassie acknowledged him with a small smile and continued her conversation. 'I could come over there,' she suggested hopefully. 'We could perhaps go for a coffee or something.'

'Maybe.' Still Kim was hesitant. Then, 'You'd have to give me an hour,' she said. 'I have to change Samuel and get Jack into bed. Don't knock on the door when you arrive, though. I'll keep an eye out for you.'

Cassie released a breath she hadn't realised she'd been holding. 'I'll be outside in an hour,' she promised, ending the call and turning back to Adam.

'Outside where in an hour?' he asked, frowning curiously.

'Kim's house. She contacted me. We need to talk to her, Adam. We have to. We can't let her just disappear from our lives. She came here for our help and we as good as turned her away. I think she's decided to put the baby up for adoption. I can't let her go through with it just because she feels she has no choice. We're talking about Josh's child. Surely you must know how much this means to me?'

'Of course I do.' Adam sighed but looked reticent. 'I'm just…'

'What?' Squeezing back tears, Cassie scanned his face, bewildered. She didn't understand. This wasn't like Adam. He'd loved Josh unreservedly. Surely this baby meant as much to him as it did to her? Unless… He'd been through so much, her illness, losing Josh, giving up the option of having children of his own to be with her. Was it that he didn't want to commit to such a huge responsibility because he might no longer want to be committed to her? God, Cassie hoped that wasn't it. She couldn't bear to lose him too. 'The baby's our grandson, Adam,' she appealed to him, her heart faltering uncertainly. 'Why are you so reluctant? I don't—'

'Because I'm scared!' Adam raised his voice, causing her to jolt. 'I'm scared, Cas,' he repeated, more quietly. 'What if it's not Josh's baby? What if it is and she's already looking at some illegal private adoption arrangement? There are millions of people out there ready to pay vast sums of money for a child. What do we do if she's already put the wheels in motion?'

Cassie wasn't sure what to say. She'd hated herself for thinking it, but after Adam's initial reaction, the thought had occurred to her that Kim might be after a one-off payment. That she would relinquish the baby's care to them only if she was sufficiently remunerated. But what if, even after they'd paid her, she wouldn't allow them to take the baby? What then? Cassie had no idea where they would stand legally. And the absolute last thing she would want would be to have the police involved, digging into Josh's history.

'Aren't you wondering about her story?' Adam asked. 'Why would Josh have been out getting drunk, possibly feeling suicidal, according to the police, when he apparently had everything to look forward to? Where was she when all this was going on?'

Cassie was floored by that. 'I don't know. I… Perhaps they'd had an argument. They're both so young, after all. Were…' She stopped, a wave of grief crashing so forcefully through her it took her breath away.

'Why didn't he call me?' Adam said suddenly, his eyes haunted as he locked them on hers. 'He texted me to say he would. I tried to call him back but he was on the phone. To *her*? Did they argue then? Might that have been why he wasn't concentrating?' He searched her face, his expression anguished. 'Christ, why didn't he just *call*?' Swallowing slowly, he stopped and glanced away.

'I... don't know, Adam,' Cassie said, feeling wretched for him. He was still blaming himself. It was eating away at him. Was that the basis of his reluctance to accept Kim as genuine? Was he scared of investing emotionally in Josh's child, only to have him cruelly snatched away too? The hard lump in her chest expanding, she went to him. 'There was nothing you could have done,' she said softly. 'Nothing. Please believe that Josh wouldn't want you to live the rest of your life in purgatory because you couldn't do the impossible.'

With a shuddery breath, Adam closed his eyes.

Cassie leant into him, kissing him softly, the salty tears on her lips mingling with his. Easing away from him, she scanned his eyes, which were now shot through with heart-wrenching sadness. 'We have to do this,' she whispered. 'We have to talk to her, despite our uncertainties, try to convince her not to do anything she'll regret later; be there for her. That's what Josh would have wanted. Could we really live with ourselves if we didn't?'

Adam didn't speak. Taking another deep breath, he nodded slowly, and then pressed his forehead lightly to hers.

CHAPTER SEVEN

Kimberley

Keeping a watch from the kitchen window an hour later, Kim saw the car pull up, a metallic blue BMW Z4. Adam Colby's car, she assumed. Cassie drove a white Mini convertible. Kim couldn't help but feel upset at the way they'd treated her. Would they have made the same assumptions if they weren't well off? She hadn't gone to see them demanding anything. She'd gone there scared, vulnerable.

Praying they'd had a change of heart, she headed quickly for the hall, catching a glimpse of the lounge as she passed. Her dad was in his usual chair, glued to the telly with a beer in his hand. She knew that if he got the slightest whiff of money, he would be out after her like a shot, pretending concern, which was absolute bullshit. She could have died at birth and he wouldn't even have noticed, but for the fact he wouldn't have had an excuse to wet the baby's head until he was too paralytic to remember he had one.

Unhitching her jacket, which she'd hung ready on the stair rail, she pulled it on, slipped out of the front door and headed up the path, skirting around the rusty carcass of an ancient Ford Focus that her dad was 'doing up'. He'd been doing it up since Jack was born, seven years ago. It wasn't going to go very far without the wheels he'd flogged to some bloke for spare parts, as her mum had pointed out.

Adam, who'd obviously been a good father to Josh despite the awful things he'd said about her, didn't seem to think much of his efforts. She noticed him eyeing the car through the BMW's window. Cassie was looking over the front of the house. With a smashed window boarded up upstairs – they were still waiting for the housing association to fix it; her dad was as likely to do it as he was to get a job – and yellowing net at the rest of the windows, it looked exactly like what it was. A sad, neglected property, starved of love inside and out. It was embarrassing, but at least it would convey why she'd been desperate enough to swallow her pride and go to the Colbys.

Cassie climbed out of their car as Kim reached the pavement. 'Where's Samuel?' she asked, glancing anxiously past her.

'With my friend. Don't worry, he's fine. She has a little boy of her own.'

Cassie nodded, but looked troubled. It wasn't surprising, now she'd seen the circumstances Kim lived in.

'Would you like to go and find somewhere to have a coffee?' She smiled kindly. 'Or we could just sit in the car, if you like.'

'Do you mind if we drive around?' Kim glanced nervously behind her. 'It's just I haven't got much time and I'd rather not have my dad interfering.' It might actually be no bad thing if he did come out. They would at least see what an aggressive Neanderthal he was, but they'd stand little chance of having a conversation.

'No problem.' Adam offered her a small smile as she glanced tentatively at him.

Feeling her cheeks burning, Kim dropped her gaze and cursed her pale complexion. She was always nervous under scrutiny, feeling as if she were being judged. She didn't doubt that that was what was happening here.

'I'll sit in the back with you,' Cassie offered. Kim noticed to her huge relief that her expression was sympathetic.

'Thanks.' She gave a grateful smile as Cassie opened the passenger door for her and slid in after her.

'How's your little brother?'

Kim sensed she was trying to relate to her, which was a good sign. 'Good,' she said. 'He's gone to bed with his new football tucked under his duvet. Mum bought it for him for his birthday.'

'He's obviously attached to it.' Cassie smiled, fastening her seat belt as Adam started the car and pulled off.

'I think he's trying to make sure Dad doesn't break it,' Kim explained with a sigh. 'He burst his last one when Jack kept banging it against the fence, so he's not letting this one out of his sight.'

Cassie's face fell, her gaze flicking towards Adam, who glanced in the rear-view mirror. Kim saw him draw in a breath.

'I owe you an apology, Kim,' he said. 'For the things you must have heard me say the other day. I was concerned about Josh, his state of mind… I don't know you, though, what you two had together, and… Well, I'm sorry.'

Kim breathed a quiet sigh of relief. She hadn't been sure whether to believe everything Josh had told her about his stepfather, but he was obviously man enough to admit it when he thought he was wrong. 'But you did say those things,' she pointed out, her voice full of hurt. 'You obviously think I'm dishonest. That I'm not good enough for Josh to have had a relationship with.'

Dragging a hand over his neck, Adam sighed heavily. 'I can't take the words back, Kim. I can only hope that you'll accept my apology and allow me… Cassie and me… to try to make amends.'

Kim nodded thoughtfully and turned to look out of the window.

Cassie reached to place a hand over hers. 'We were wrong to make assumptions about you, Kim. Adam didn't mean the things he said. He was scared, that was all, for me. He couldn't bear the thought of me finding hope only to have it snatched away. We were both upset the day you came. It was Josh's birthday, and…' She stopped, her voice catching.

'I know.' Kim looked sadly back at her. 'That's why I decided to come. I thought that... I don't know. I suppose I thought you'd be pleased; that you would want Samuel to be part of your life.'

'We do,' Cassie said emphatically. 'You have no idea how much. We were shocked when you arrived on our doorstep, naturally. And mortified when we realised we'd driven you away. We're desperate to try to... Look, can we pull over?' She glanced at Adam. 'I know you haven't got long, Kim, but if we could just have five minutes. I don't want you to do anything because of your circumstances that you'll regret.'

Kim considered. 'Okay,' she said, at length. Did the woman realise that she was also being judged? she wondered.

'Do you mind if we walk?' Cassie asked, as Adam drew up at the kerb.

He certainly was trying to make amends, around to her door to open it before she'd unfastened her belt, offering her a hand to assist her out.

'You said you were considering putting Samuel up for adoption,' said Cassie. 'Are you still of the same mind?'

'I wouldn't be considering it if I didn't think it would be the best option for him,' Kim pointed out, still obviously upset. 'It's Samuel I'm thinking of, not me.'

'Yes. Yes, of course you are. I just...' Cassie stopped, sounding flustered. 'You said you have a chance of a property of your own. Is that certain yet, or...'

'It is,' Kim confirmed, relieved that the guy who was letting it had rung her back. 'It's mine if I want it. It's not Buckingham Palace, but it's in a decent area. Even then, though, he won't have much of a future, will he? Without a job I won't be able to provide him with all the things children need, the things other kids have. Not just material things, but a stable family environment, a support network and a chance in life.'

Cassie stopped walking and turned to face her. 'You could always come and stay with us,' she suggested. 'We have plenty of room, and I can't think of a better use for it now than to make sure this baby has the best start in life he possibly can. It would give you a chance to have a life too. You might even consider us as adoptive parents for Samuel if…'

'If what?' Kim narrowed her eyes as Cassie trailed off. 'I'm not trying to palm him off, Cassandra,' she said firmly. 'I wasn't thinking about adoption because I don't want the bother of looking after my own baby. It would crucify me to part with him. He's my life. I love him with every fibre of my being.'

Cassie looked flustered. 'I know, I just…' She faltered, clearly at a loss how to respond.

Kim's eyes filled up. 'Is that really what you think? That it's your money I'm after? That I'm trying to scam you, pleading poverty to get you to offer me payment to adopt him?' She felt her cheeks flush furiously.

'No!' Cassie exclaimed. 'I just thought that if you genuinely felt you couldn't cope…' She stopped, close to tears herself. 'He's my grandson, Kim. You must know that I would be desperate to keep him in my life. I was trying to offer you alternatives, that's all. I'm sorry, I didn't mean to imply…'

Kim nodded slowly, accepting the apology. 'Thank you for the offer to stay with you,' she said, with a small smile. 'It's lovely of you, but if I'm going to be bringing up my son, with or without the support of his family, I need to establish a home, a space for myself and Samuel.'

Cassie almost wilted with relief. 'You're not going ahead with adoption then?'

Kim shook her head. 'He'll be better off with me,' she said determinedly. 'A mother's love is the best thing he can have in life, after all. I couldn't live with myself knowing he would think I'd turned my back on him.'

'No.' Cassie swallowed visibly and dropped her gaze.

'Who chose the name Samuel?' Adam enquired. He was looking at her curiously when Kim turned to him, but there was no suspicion there, she noted. He was probably trying to imagine how Josh had felt, how involved he'd been, whether he'd been excited at the prospect of fatherhood. Josh had been right about him. Despite their bumpy start, Kim could see he was a caring man.

'I did,' she told him proudly. 'Josh and I thought of a few. We liked Zach and Ethan. But I thought Samuel suited him more. I wanted him to have a strong name, like Josh's. I always thought his name reflected his character.'

'It's perfect,' Cassie murmured. Her expression a combination of sadness and longing, she glanced at Adam and then back at Kim. 'I understand what you mean about wanting your own space, Kim. And what you said about wanting him to have a stable family environment. We could be that family… if you wanted us to be. We could make sure that Samuel has all he deserves in life – computers and bicycles and trainers; everything a little boy might need as he grows. A father figure in his life, too. I'm sure Adam would want to be that, for now, at least.'

She looked at Adam. Kim could feel her willing him to agree.

Adam's forehead creased briefly into a frown as he considered, and then, 'I think that's what Josh would have wanted,' he said, smiling.

'Kim?' Cassie looked at her hopefully.

Kim felt her heart leap. This was perfect. Now she could make plans. She should have spent the rest of her life with Josh. Instead, she would spend it fulfilling the promise she'd made him. 'I'm not sure what to say.' She emitted a tearful laugh.

'Say yes,' Cassie urged her. 'We'll help you move, get you set up with everything you might need. And if the property you're moving into needs any renovation or redecoration, Adam's your man. Right, Adam?'

'It doesn't look like I have any choice.' Adam sighed expansively, and then gave Kim a reassuring wink.

'In that case – yes!' Kim agreed excitedly, and then, hesitating for only a second, she reached to give Cassie a hug.

CHAPTER EIGHT

Joshua

December 2018

He wasn't sure Kim would be there the next morning. It was possible he was mistaken, but he'd been sure it was her he'd seen hurrying away from his school, and he was perplexed. She might have had a perfectly valid reason for being there that was nothing to do with him – they were just passing acquaintances, commuters on the same train, after all – but still, it seemed odd. Checking his watch, he kept an eye out for her. The train was coming into the station when she flew down the steps and along the platform.

'Hey,' he said, opening the carriage door as she reached him and allowing her to climb aboard before him. 'I see you ditched the killer heels.' He couldn't help noticing as he followed her to their usual spot. It possibly hadn't been a good idea to comment, though, noting the curious look she threw him as she sat down.

'They were watermarked,' she said, giving him a timid smile.

Josh returned the smile, reminding himself to engage his brain before opening his mouth. She was nice, naturally pretty, and she did have great legs. In other circumstances… He sighed inwardly. He'd told her his situation was complicated. She probably wasn't interested anyway, and bearing in mind what she'd said about her own relationship history, he didn't want to cross any lines.

Wondering whether any of his many texts or calls to the woman he'd thought he had a future with had been returned, he pulled out his phone and checked. There was nothing, communicating her message loud and clear. She didn't want him. He should just forget her, but it wasn't going to be easy.

'They obviously weren't suitable for wearing in mud and slush,' Kim went on, jarring him from his thoughts.

Josh glanced back at her, confused, and then remembered they'd been talking about her boots. 'Kind of makes you wonder what the point of them is then,' he said, amused.

'Going out in, getting dressed up,' she said, mock-po-faced. 'Not that I go out very much since splitting with my ex.'

Josh felt uncomfortable at the mention of her ex. He needed to stay away from relationship territory if he wasn't going to put his foot in it, something he seemed adept at. 'So, how are you doing?' he asked, changing the subject.

'Good,' she said, smiling. 'I'm looking into teacher training courses actually. I thought I'd get on with it after our discussion yesterday.'

'Ah, that would explain it. I wondered why you were loitering outside my school,' Josh joked.

'Loitering?' A frown crossed her face. 'Outside *where*?'

He noted her bemused expression. She didn't look as if she had a clue what he was talking about. 'My school,' he said, now definitely feeling uncomfortable.

'Your...?' Shaking her head, she squinted at him. 'Why on earth would I have been there?'

Shit! He had been mistaken. But he could have sworn... 'I, er, don't know. I just thought...' Shrugging awkwardly, he trailed off.

She laughed, incredulous. 'Wow, you really are full of yourself, aren't you?' she said, surveying him with obvious disillusionment. 'Did you think I was stalking you, is that it?'

'No,' Josh said quickly. 'I just... I saw someone remarkably like you, that was all. Same jacket, same hat.' Without the flame-red tendrils of hair escaping from it, though, he now realised, his heart sinking. 'I was obviously—'

'I'm not that desperate, Josh,' she cut in tearfully. 'Despite what I said about my not getting out a lot, and you being so drop-dead gorgeous no woman could resist falling at your feet, *obviously*, I don't have to resort to following men around. For your information, the jacket and hat I'm wearing are everywhere at the moment. Thanks for the company.' She snatched up her bag and jumped to her feet.

'Kim…' His heart flipping over, Josh grabbed his rucksack and followed. He really was good at messing things up, wasn't he? Anyone would think he worked at it. 'I'm sorry,' he said, almost falling into her as the train lurched to a stop. 'It was a genuine mistake.'

Ignoring him, she hit the doors open button and stepped down onto the platform.

Josh followed, feeling worse by the second. Had he really upset her that much? 'Kim,' he called, almost at a run to keep up with her as she neared the steps to street level. 'I was mistaken. Please don't go off upset. I didn't mean—'

'Let go of my arm, please,' she cut in, her cheeks blazing.

'What?' Josh followed her gaze down. 'Right, sorry.' He hadn't even realised he was holding onto it.

'Thank you,' she said curtly. 'Now, do you think *you* could stop following *me*?'

He stared at her, thunderstruck. 'I'm not…' Christ, what was she talking about? This was his station. He wasn't *following* her. 'Look, I've said I'm sorry. I'm going now, okay.' Holding his hands up, he stepped away from her.

'Good,' she said, tears springing to her eyes. 'You know, I can't believe I was so wrong about you. That I actually thought you were *nice*.'

Watching her whirl around and fly up the steps, he shook his head in bewilderment, then turned away.

He was a yard along the platform, trying to work out what the hell had just happened, when a sharp scream stopped him in his tracks.

Spinning back, he saw her tumbling down the steps and instinctively ran.

'Shit,' he muttered, dropping to his knees at her side. 'Kim?' he said, fear gripping him as she lay motionless, swiftly followed by immeasurable relief when she stirred. *Thank God.* 'Don't move,' he urged her, thinking she might have injuries that weren't obvious.

'What happened?' she mumbled, clearly disorientated.

Josh shuffled around to support her shoulders as she insisted on trying to raise herself. 'You fell,' he told her. 'You lost consciousness. It's probably better if you stay still. You might have broken something.' He prayed that she hadn't. God forbid she'd damaged her neck or her spine. He would never forgive himself if she had.

He searched her eyes. They were flecked with confusion. 'Does it hurt anywhere?' he asked gently.

Blinking, she attempted to move, and then winced. 'My ankle,' she said, squeezing her eyes closed.

'I've called an ambulance,' a guy in the gathering crowd said. 'Here, would she like my coat?' he asked, halfway out of it.

'No. I'm all right.' Kim pulled herself to a sitting position, despite Josh advising her not to. 'It's only my ankle. If I could just get to a taxi.'

'The ambulance is already on its way,' the guy told her. 'If I were you, I'd stay put. It'll be a hell of an effort getting up those stairs. You could take the lift, but then you have to get out of the station to the taxi rank.'

'He's right,' Josh agreed. 'I could help you if you really want to get a taxi, but it's probably better not to put any weight on that ankle, just in case.'

As she scanned his face, fresh tears in her eyes, Josh felt incredibly guilty. He wasn't sure how this whole thing had started, but he could definitely have handled it better. 'I could wait with you,' he offered. 'Come with you to the hospital if you like.'

She dropped her gaze. 'I'd like that,' she said quietly.

Once the crowd had started to disperse, she looked back at him, her expression full of remorse. 'I'm sorry, Josh. I overreacted. It was childish. It's not you…' she faltered. 'My ex accused me of all sorts of things. He said I was stalking him, when it was the other way around. He told my friends I was obsessed with him, when all I wanted was him out of my life. He was so convincing…' She stopped, looking desperate.

'Hey, it's okay,' Josh tried to reassure her, his heart wrenching as a sob escaped her.

'None of the things he said were true,' Kim went on, looking at him beseechingly, as if she needed him to believe her. 'Even when I first went out with him, he tried to make me think everything was my fault, that I deserved all I got, and now…'

All she got? Which was what, precisely? Josh felt his gut twist. 'There's no harm done, I promise you,' he said, supporting her with one arm and reaching with his other hand to wipe a tear gently away from her cheek with his thumb. 'Apart from that ankle.'

She sniffed. 'You were right,' she said with a tremulous smile. 'Looks like I was determined to throw myself at you.'

'Pretty spectacularly, as it happens.' Josh smiled back. He didn't know how he'd managed to get himself into this, but there was no way he could leave her now.

CHAPTER NINE

'Is it okay if I go in?' Pocketing his mobile after ringing the school to explain his absence, Josh nodded towards the cubicle curtain.

'And you are…?' asked the harassed-looking doctor exiting it.

'My boyfriend.' Kim's voice came from behind the curtain. 'He can come in.'

Josh arched an eyebrow. He'd obviously gone up in her estimation, considering she'd all but called him a total shit only hours earlier.

The doctor smiled. 'That's fine,' she said. 'I've asked a porter to bring a wheelchair. Do you think you could help Kim through to reception when he does? We need the cubicles, I'm afraid.'

'Will do.' Josh nodded, then slipped through the curtain. 'How are you doing?' he asked.

'Okay.' Kim managed a smile. 'It's not too badly swollen. They think it might be sprained, but they're giving me an X-ray just in case. Sorry about pretending you were my boyfriend, by the way. I didn't think they'd let you in with me in a state of undress. I hope you don't mind me flashing my ankles.'

'Not at all.' Josh smiled back at her, though in truth he was feeling a bit awkward. He'd wanted to make sure she really was okay, and to patch things up between them – he could never be comfortable knowing he'd upset someone, however inadvertently – but still, he was concerned about sending out the wrong signals. If things had been different, maybe they could have got together, assuming it was something she wanted. He liked her, her smile, her enthusiasm, her quirkiness – or he had until things had got surreal between them that morning. In his current situation, though, a relationship with anyone wasn't something he would be considering for the foreseeable future.

'Thanks for coming with me,' she said. 'Being here. I hate hospitals. I seemed to spend my life in A&E when I was with…' An alarmed look crossed her face, as if she were about to divulge something she shouldn't, and she trailed off and glanced hurriedly down.

'When you were with…?' Josh urged her. He had a feeling in his gut he knew what she'd been about to say. 'Kim?' He stepped closer.

She glanced up at him. He noted the fearful apprehension in her eyes, the fingers she was knotting and unknotting in her lap. 'My ex…' she said eventually, leaving him to draw his own conclusions.

Josh's anger mounted. Her gaze was fixed on her lap again, as if she was ashamed of what had gone on in her previous relationship. He recalled what she'd said at the station. *None of the things he said were true… he tried to make me think everything was my fault, that I deserved all I got…* Her eyes had been filled with guilt. Now it made sense, her defensiveness, though he hadn't really accused her of anything. He dearly wished he could get hold of the bloke who'd done this to her and give him a taste of what it felt like to be on the end of bullying, abusive behaviour.

'He really was a piece of work, wasn't he?' he growled, his throat tight.

She nodded, a visible shudder running through her.

Bastard. Josh cursed silently, hesitated, then carefully reached to take hold of her hand. 'We're not all like that, Kim,' he said softly. 'I promise you.'

Swallowing, she wiped her other hand across her eyes and then looked back at him. 'I know.' She attempted a brave smile. 'You're clearly not. I'm really sorry I was so horrible to you.'

'You've already apologised,' he reminded her. 'And it wasn't necessary that time either.'

'Er…' She closed one eye and laughed. 'A bit, possibly.'

Thinking it prudent to say nothing, Josh smiled instead.

'Did you ring the school?' she asked, her eyes growing wide, as if she'd just remembered there was somewhere else he should be. The guilt was back, he noticed despairingly.

'I did. They're okay about it. No problem.'

'Good.' She breathed out a sigh of relief. 'Even so, you should probably go,' she said. 'I'll be fine now. I'm really grateful for your support, Josh. Thanks again.'

'Right,' he said. 'And you propose getting home how, exactly?'

'Um…' She furrowed her brow. 'I have no idea. The train, I suppose, if I ever get out of here. They seem to be taking ages to organise the X-ray.'

'Backed up probably. The waiting room's packed,' Josh said. 'Don't worry about how you'll get back. I'll pay for a taxi. I rang my stepdad hoping he might be able to fetch us, but he's out on site, so a taxi's the only other viable option.'

Kim looked at him aghast. 'I can't let you do that. It will cost an absolute fortune.'

'It's not open for debate,' Josh said firmly. 'It's the least I can do. There's no way I'm going to let you hop about on public transport. I don't know whether you've noticed, but I suspect you might be just the tiniest bit accident-prone.'

He winced inwardly as soon as the words were out of his mouth. He'd be willing to bet that was how she would have explained away her injuries on her many previous hospital visits.

Thankfully she didn't seem to pick up on it. 'Damn, I'm found out.' She sighed dramatically. 'It's a ploy,' she said, 'to win men over in the hope I'll find my white knight.'

Josh smiled, but he felt his heart drop. He couldn't be her white knight. He was feeling more like the villain lately, rather than a hero. She had won him over, though. Who wouldn't feel protective of a woman who'd fallen victim to some coward's manipulation and abuse?

As he tried to think of a suitable response, the porter bustled in with a wheelchair. 'Your chariot, ma'am,' he said. 'If your boyfriend would like to be a gentleman and assist you down, we'll be on our way to the executive waiting area in no time.'

Kim laughed as they helped her into the chair. 'Do I get to sip champagne while I wait?'

'Er, no, sorry. Vending machine's out of order,' the porter replied with a despairing roll of his eyes.

'Honestly, you wonder why you bother to book first class, don't you?' Kim played along as he wheeled her to the corridor. 'Oh, Josh,' she called back, 'could you grab my phone from the locker, please?'

Two hours later, the taxi pulled up outside Kim's sister's house on the Ravens Wood estate.

Josh opened his door and climbed out to help her, though Kim protested she'd be fine. 'Uh-uh,' he said. 'I've come this far. I'm not going anywhere until you're safely at your front door.'

'A white knight, definitely.' She gave him an amused smile.

'I try,' Josh said, and went around to open her door for her.

Making sure she was stable on her crutches, he glanced at the driver. 'Two minutes,' he said, turning to walk her up the path.

'Josh,' Kim laughed, 'I'll be fine from here. You've already run up a fortune on the meter, and the driver probably has another fare waiting. Be gone.'

'You're sure?' he asked.

'It's five yards. I'm sure.'

Reluctantly he climbed back into the taxi, waiting nevertheless until she'd reached the front door and given him a wave before instructing the driver to drive on. She'd said she'd obviously have to take few days off. He'd said he would see her at the station soon. He hadn't dared say more. He'd seen a flicker of disappointment in her eyes, though. She'd clearly expected him to.

He was walking through his own front door, tugging off his coat and wondering what inedible cuisine his housemate, who fancied himself as a chef, was cooking, when he felt something inside one of the pockets clunk against the hall wall.

Shit! Kim's phone. He groaned as he pulled it out. He'd forgotten to give it back. 'Damn.' He sighed wearily. He was knackered, but he could hardly leave her without her phone. Pulling his coat back on, he about-faced, checking his other pocket for his car keys as he headed back out.

A short while later, he was standing on the doorstep of the house the taxi had dropped Kim off at, wondering if he was going slightly mad.

'And you don't know her surname?' The guy who'd answered the door squinted at him, puzzled.

'No,' Josh confessed, confused. 'I don't really know her that well. We shared a taxi home.' Thinking the whole story would sound too complicated, he gave him a shortened version. 'I was positive it dropped her off here.'

'Sorry, mate.' The guy shrugged apologetically. 'No one here by that name. I've never heard of her. We haven't long moved in, though. You could try the neighbouring houses.'

Josh did as he suggested, his confusion growing as they didn't yield anyone by the name of Kim either, which meant he was either mistaken – the houses did all look pretty similar and he hadn't noted the number – or he really was going mad. Or else she was lying. But why would she do that?

CHAPTER TEN

Cassandra

Cassie was rushing downstairs, pushing an earring into her ear lobe, when Adam came through the front door. He'd been working from home lately. Keeping an eye on her, Cassie suspected, though he denied that. He'd been called out unexpectedly to look at snagging problems on a new-build site, and then had to call into his office for various bits of paperwork. Cassie still couldn't bear to be alone for too long in the house – its walls were steeped in memories of Josh – but she wished Adam would realise it was safe to leave her for short periods, that she wasn't going to cocoon herself under her duvet and sink into depression, as she had in the weeks after Josh had gone. Or worse.

He arched an eyebrow and looked her over as she passed him in the hall. Approvingly, Cassie hoped, now she'd finally put some make-up on and made herself presentable. 'Are we supposed to be doing something this evening?' he asked her as she flew onwards to the kitchen.

'No,' Cassie called back. 'I have something on.'

'Oh, right.' Adam sounded perplexed, unsurprisingly. She'd had no interest in going out since the funeral, other than for basic food shopping.

Glancing around the kitchen, she knitted her brow as she checked in all the usual places: the hooks on the utility room door, the work surfaces, the fruit bowl on the kitchen island. Giving up, she headed back to the hall, plucked her bag from where she'd hung it on the stair rail and rummaged in it. 'Haven't seen my car keys, have you?' she asked, feeling not quite the woman-in-control she was trying to be.

Adam stepped back and picked them up from the hall table, where they'd been sitting obviously behind him. 'Care to share?' He smiled, handing them to her.

Cassie rolled her eyes in despair at herself. 'I had a call from the local newspaper,' she explained, passing him her bag to hold and grabbing her jacket from the peg. 'They need someone to cover a story,' she went on, slipping her arms into it. 'They have an interview scheduled with a woman who lost her son to suicide.' She spilled it out quickly but didn't miss Adam flinching as she spoke. 'The reporter who organised it is off sick, apparently, so as it's in my area, they offered it to me.'

Pausing, she glanced at him, guessing his first reaction would be to feel as if someone had punched him, as she had when she'd heard what the interview was about. 'And are you okay with it?' he asked her, obvious concern in his eyes.

He was worried she might not be emotionally strong enough to cover this particular story. Cassie was glad that he cared enough to worry, but she wanted to see the smile back in his eyes, for him to think of her as someone he could smile with again, rather than someone he had to constantly fret about.

Taking a breath, she nodded. 'I wasn't sure I was, but… Things have changed, haven't they? With Kim's situation, I mean.' She searched his eyes, hoping he would get that she needed to do this, painful though it might be. 'I want to be there for her and Samuel. She needs someone who cares in her life. I'd like to be that someone, but I need to be fully functioning, capable of making decisions and supporting her, not drifting around with no sense of purpose. Do you understand?'

Adam nodded, and there it was, a hint of a smile, thank goodness. Cassie's ghosts would never go away, but she hoped that one day Adam might not feel so haunted by Josh's death. He didn't deserve to carry his misplaced guilt for the rest of his life. 'I do,' he assured her, his mouth curving up at the corners. 'And I'm proud of you.'

His gaze was definitely approving as he leant in to kiss her cheek.

Cassie felt buoyed by that. She couldn't turn back the ravages of time, but she could make a bit of an effort with what she'd got, which wasn't too abysmal considering all her body had been through. The intimacy between them had dwindled to almost non-existent. Her fault, not his. Her emotions had shut down the day Josh had died. She had to reach out to him now. A relationship without physical contact wasn't sustainable. Adam was solid, dependable, caring, but he wasn't a saint. He needed the comfort closeness brought. Comfort she'd wanted to offer him but hadn't felt able to, leaving him to cope alone with his grief.

She gave him a bright smile – which was a start. At least she might look approachable, rather than miserable. Skirting around him to the front door, she reached absent-mindedly to straighten the Japanese statue on the hall table, which wasn't quite in its correct position, then snatched her hand away. She was obsessing, something she was trying very hard to stop doing, since it had caused the rift with Josh that had never been fixed. She had to get a grip. Constantly fussing would send out a clear signal to Adam that she wasn't coping.

Determinedly she opened the door. 'Good luck. Drive carefully,' Adam called after her as she dashed to her car.

'Thanks. I will.' Cassie waved behind her.

She was in reasonable spirits as she drove. Now that little Samuel had come into her life, she had a purpose. Josh had given her that purpose once. She would never stop feeling guilty for what had happened between them, all because of her ridiculous tendency to be too house-proud. Her anxiety about her illness, the prognosis, the medication, the insomnia… she'd been exhausted. And then she'd exhausted herself more by fixating on every little thing that needed doing in the house, things she didn't have the energy to do. Josh had suffered the brunt of her frustration.

She couldn't make it up to him, would never forgive herself for the part she'd played in the events that had led up to his death. If only he'd been living at home…

Breathing deeply, she curtailed her thoughts. She would drive herself mad constantly thinking about the ifs and buts. Josh had been her reason for living. Now his son had given her a reason to keep living. For her own son's sake, she would be there for him. A normal, balanced, smiling nana, not the neurotic woman of before. She wouldn't let Samuel down. She would make sure he had everything he should have in life, in the absence of a father.

Arriving with time to spare, she pulled out her phone, deciding to cancel the counselling session she had booked. She'd tried to talk through her grief, but she simply couldn't. There was little point going when she couldn't reveal all of herself: her anxieties, her long-ago secret that she'd felt unable to share even with Adam, although she bitterly wished she had. It might have been better to have lost him earlier, rather than now, when she couldn't bear the thought of a future without him.

Once the appointment was cancelled, she used the time she had left before the interview to scroll to the groups she regularly checked on Facebook. She was familiar with them all. She'd joined some of them as part of her research for an article on drug-dependent parents and the effect on their children. The broadsheet she'd been writing the article for had paid well, promising a future regular spot, otherwise she might have turned it down. As it was, it had been useful research, should she ever need it. Her heart had stopped beating when she'd discovered a video posted on one of the sites by the woman she'd kept tabs on for years.

Bracing herself, she flicked to the woman's profile page, as she regularly did. She was clean now. Cassie had been surprised when she'd learnt that. She'd been so dependent when she knew her, she hadn't been capable of caring for anyone – not herself, not her children. Cassie's heart had broken for them, for the innocence that had been stolen living with a mother whose drug addiction would have dictated her every mood. She'd obviously turned her life around.

Realising the time, she exited the site and was about to climb out of the car when she received a text. Pausing, she checked it. The message was short. Blood-freezing. *I know all about you*, it read.

CHAPTER ELEVEN

'I think I have everything I need.' Cassie smiled at the grieving mother she'd come to talk to, while praying that she really had got everything. She'd run through the interview with her mind frantically racing, wondering who the text was from. It had been sent anonymously, the caller ID blocked, making it more ominous. The message had been a warning, quite obviously, but what did it mean? For it to be the woman whose profile she'd been studying at that moment, someone she'd hoped never to encounter again, would be incredible. Cassie could only think it *was* her, though, hinting that she intended to go to the papers. In which case, everything she'd worked so hard to keep hidden would come out.

A chill ran through her as she imagined Adam's reaction. Her marriage, the foundations of which she feared were already shaking, would crumble. Her career would be over. She would lose everything. She would lose Samuel before she had even got to know him. All this despite the fact that her intention, though also self-serving, had been to keep safe someone who was so very vulnerable.

What if it wasn't her? Her heart banging against her chest, Cassie scrambled to think who else it could be. What if the threat was nothing to do with her distant past, but what was happening in her life now?

Swallowing back icy fear, she switched off her voice recorder, picked up her phone and notepad and got to her feet. Already standing, the woman smiled tremulously, but her face was etched with grief. Her eyes wore the same haunted look Cassie caught whenever she glanced into a mirror. She was still plagued by what Josh had gone through, her mind relentlessly conjuring up images of her son's last moments. Adam would hold her when she woke sobbing, try to reassure her. This grieving mother had no one. A single mother, her only son had struggled with his mental health and committed suicide after being discharged by the psychiatric treatment team. He'd attempted to take his own life twice before, yet had been abandoned. His mother blamed herself, inevitably. Cassie's heart bled for her.

Overwhelmed suddenly by images of Josh growing up, smiling, laughing, crying, she caught a breath in her throat and moved towards the lounge door before the walls rushed in and suffocated her.

Following her to the front door, the woman extended her hand. 'People need to know,' she said, as Cassie took it. 'Callum was vulnerable and scared,' she went on, a flash of determination in her eyes. 'He was in need of help and the people who should have offered that help let him down.'

This was this woman's reason for continuing to live when her life must seem empty and pointless. She needed to stay strong to get justice. Her focus was on highlighting the flaws in the system and trying to prevent the tragic death of another vulnerable young person.

Cassie wished her well, hoping that her article – which she had to get right, no matter what was going on in her own life – might help. 'We'll make sure this gets front page,' she promised, and then, sensing the woman's need, she reached out to hug her. 'Stay strong,' she murmured. 'You'll get through this.'

Once in her car, Cassie swiped the tears from her face, gripped the steering wheel and took several slow breaths as images of Josh once again flooded her mind. She pictured him as a toddler, when his love for her was unquestioning. Her love for him had been all-consuming, from the second she'd first held him to the second she lost him. She'd known when that second was. She was sure she'd felt some primal pull on her heartstrings. Only a mother could ever feel that. No matter what happened, no one could ever take that pure love away from her.

Feeling more composed after a minute, she started the car. She was heading for home when she realised she was approaching the park she'd visited so often with Josh. It was like a magnet.

She could hear the thwack of tennis balls as she walked past the courts where she'd spent hours on Sundays teaching Josh how to play. There was no one on the courts now; only the ghost of him. No children on the roundabout or the swings as they creaked in the wind, but still she could hear the melodic sound of laughter. She was glad when a young man playing fetch with his dog hurried on. She'd probably scared him off. She must look pretty pathetic, a grown woman sitting on a swing weeping.

'I'm sorry, Josh,' she whispered. *Please forgive me.*

She sat for a while, careless of the rain that had started. What did the person who'd texted her want? After Josh had gone, she'd thought there was nothing left that anyone could take from her. But there was. This person might take everything she'd realised was worth living for.

She glanced at the heavens. Droplets of rain falling like saltless tears on her cheeks, she prayed silently for God to give her strength to fight whatever battle might come, and then reached for her phone.

What do you know? she typed.

You know as well as I do, came the reply. *How do you sleep at night?*

CHAPTER TWELVE

Kimberley

Kim's heart sank when she saw the guy she was renting the house from. He was a younger version of her dad, stinking of body odour, a beer bottle in his hand. She didn't dare look at Cassie and Adam behind her. Hopefully they would be more impressed with the house. One of a small row of houses on a quiet lane just outside Hibbleton, it had a cottagey feel. Despite it being old, it didn't look in that bad a bad state of repair from the outside, which had been Adam's concern, and had two bedrooms and a box room inside, as well as a small kitchen and dining room, a living room, and a conservatory on the back. It probably needed a lick of paint inside, the man had said.

Noting his gaze straying warily from her to Adam, who was considerably taller than he was, and also muscular, Kim thought she'd better introduce them. She wanted this little house. It was part of her plan for the future. She had a feeling her 'landlord' might back out if he thought there was a chance anyone would find out about him sub-letting the property, which was something she hadn't mentioned to Adam or Cassie. 'This is Adam,' she said, giving the man a smile. 'My dead fiancé's father.' Her eyes filling up, as they were bound to when she thought about Josh, she glanced sadly down at Samuel in the pushchair. 'He's going to help me redecorate.'

Seeming somewhat placated, the guy nodded.

'And this is Cassie, his mum. She's been helping me with little Samuel since his dad died,' Kim went on, knowing she was playing the sympathy card but suspecting Cassie wouldn't mind, given her reasons.

'We've been offering each other emotional support,' Cassie picked up, extending her hand. The man looked surprised. He'd probably never had a classy-looking woman wanting to shake his hand before. 'Pleased to meet you…?'

'Jonnie,' he supplied, swapping his beer to his left hand before offering the right.

'I'm going to help Kim with the furnishings for the nursery.' Cassie smiled. 'I hope you don't mind me having a quick look?'

The man shrugged. 'Knock yourself out,' he said, tipping the dregs of his beer back and then turning to park the bottle to the side of the front door. 'Slam the door on the way out, yeah. I'm off down the pub for a pint.'

Standing aside to let him by, Adam raised an eyebrow. 'Trusting sort, isn't he?' he said, his expression curious as he watched him saunter off.

'I've already paid him half of the deposit,' Kim said, tipping the pushchair back and wheeling it through the front door, which led straight to the lounge. She supposed that made her the trusting one in Adam's eyes.

She stopped and gazed around the small room. The wallpaper wasn't too bad, old coffee-coloured Anaglypta. The paintwork was awful, though, a mucky chocolate brown, and the furniture was ugly: a tatty old two-seater sofa and chair standing on a threadbare red and brown floral rug. The floorboards, also painted brown, added to the depressing ambience.

'Oh,' said Cassie.

Kim smiled weakly. 'It's not too bad,' she said, aware that she didn't sound very convincing. 'Maybe I could get some cheerful scatter cushions and pictures off eBay to brighten it up.'

'We'll refurnish it,' Adam said decisively. 'If Jonnie boy has any objections to us getting rid of this stuff, we'll put it in storage.'

Kim looked at him agog. 'I can't let you do that, Adam. I do need your support, I won't lie, but I'm not looking for handouts.'

'It's not a handout,' Adam assured her. 'I have contacts who will let me have stuff at cost price. And the storage won't be a problem if we need it. I have a couple of units for house clearance purposes. Don't worry about it.'

Cassie smiled kindly as Kim glanced uncertainly at her. 'It's fine, Kim. We guessed it might need some furnishings, and there's no way I would rest knowing you were stuck here on your own with a new baby. It's far too depressing like this.' Giving her shoulders a quick squeeze, she headed off towards the room adjoining the lounge.

Kim glanced gratefully at Adam. 'Thanks,' she said, giving him an appreciative smile.

'Not a problem.' Adam smiled warmly back. 'Shall we?' He nodded after Cassie.

They found her eyeing the conservatory backing onto the tiny dining room, the walls of which were also a dirty brown. 'I think we might need a bit of TLC in here too,' she said, smiling knowingly at Adam. 'And the conservatory looks a bit dilapidated.'

Adam checked the windows and seals. 'It's mendable,' he said. 'I could probably do something with it.'

The kitchen wasn't too dreadful, thank God. Kim had been expecting it to be cold and damp, with cupboard doors hanging off. The cupboards looked sound, though, confirmed by Adam. And the work surfaces were light, a white and grey marble effect.

'Thick with grime, unfortunately,' Cassie said, trailing a finger along one of them. 'Nothing a bit of elbow grease won't fix, though. I'll get some cloths and antibacterial spray in,' she added, giving Kim an optimistic smile and then plucking some wet wipes from her bag and cleaning her hands.

Kim checked the oven, which would need a thorough clean, and then sighed. 'Thanks, Cassie,' she said, straightening up. 'I'm not sure I could do all this without you.'

'No problem.' Cassie echoed what Adam had said, leaving Kim wondering how she and Josh had fallen out so badly.

'Shall I unbuckle Samuel,' she asked, 'so we can take a look upstairs?'

Kim nodded. It was obvious that Cassie couldn't wait to pick him up and cuddle him. Very obvious. She watched as she undid his straps, lifting him gently out of the pushchair and holding him close, then pressing her face to his soft downy head, breathing in the freshly shampooed smell of him. Kim felt for her. She must badly regret falling out with Josh and all that had followed.

Cassie made her way to the stairs leading off the dining room, Samuel nestled against her shoulder. Adam was watching her, a look of deep longing in his eyes. Kim felt even more for him. He must feel so adrift without Josh in his life, and with no children of his own.

'So, Kim…' he turned to her as Cassie climbed the stairs, as if sensing her gaze on him, 'were you and Josh living together?'

Caught unawares, Kim felt slightly off kilter. 'No.' She sighed regretfully. 'He wanted us to, but I didn't fancy sharing with his housemate. We were looking at properties, but we were still trying to work out dates. You know, for the wedding?'

'Really?' Adam's look was a combination of surprise and hurt.

Kim glanced down and back. 'I'm sure he was going to tell you,' she said hesitantly. 'As soon as we'd made a decision.'

Adam nodded slowly, his expression reflective.

'He wanted to get married straight away,' Kim hurried on, 'but I thought we should take our time, get a house lined up first. And to be quite honest, I wasn't too keen on walking down the aisle pregnant.'

Adam smiled understandingly. 'So where were you thinking of living?'

God, what was this, the third degree? 'Birmingham,' Kim replied. 'We looked at a lovely ground-floor apartment on the waterfront.'

Adam arched an eyebrow. 'Birmingham?'

'Possibly,' Kim amended, seeing a flicker of incredulity cross his face. 'He thought it might be a good idea if he was closer to his school.'

'Ah, I see,' Adam said.

Kim noted the dubious edge to his voice. 'You seem surprised.'

'I am a bit,' Adam admitted, his brow furrowed. 'He was coming up to the end of his placement, wasn't he?'

'Yes.' Kim smiled uncertainly, wondering at all the sudden questions. 'But they said there was a chance of a job there, so he thought, under the circumstances...'

'Right. Of course.' Adam nodded. 'He was always an outdoor sort, that's all. He'd said he was hoping to teach more locally, but... Clearly his circumstances had changed. Sorry, I...' Dragging a hand over his neck, he took a breath. 'How did he seem, Kim?' he asked, his voice tight. 'Before he... Had he been depressed at all?'

Not sure what to say, Kim glanced away.

'I'm just trying to put the pieces together. Pointless, probably...' Trailing off, Adam sighed heavily.

Kim noted the look in his eyes, and realised he was torturing himself. He would undoubtedly have a thousand unanswered questions in his mind, some of which he was hoping she might supply the answers to. 'His mood was generally okay, but...' she faltered, studying him carefully, 'I thought he might have been a bit down the previous evening.'

Adam eyed her questioningly.

'We were at his house and I heard him on the phone in the kitchen. I thought he was finally talking to Cassie. He looked upset when he came back into the lounge. I asked him about it, but he said it was just stuff, and that it would sort itself out.'

Adam looked winded at that, as if she'd punched him.

Kim pressed a hand to his arm, looking concerned. 'I was obviously mistaken, though, as Cassie and you didn't know anything about me.'

'What made you think it was—' Adam started, and then stopped when Cassie called from the landing.

'Are you two coming? We're getting lonely up here.'

Wanting time to put her thoughts in some sort of order, Kim left Adam to go up and went outside to the car for Samuel's baby bag. As she was coming up the stairs, she heard Adam talking to Cassie about the phone call, and paused apprehensively.

'So you didn't speak to him at all?' Adam was asking.

'No. God knows I wish I had.' Cassie sounded tearful. 'I left him a message a few days before, but… I'll regret not trying harder to get hold of him for the rest of my life. I should have rung the school. Driven over there. Made more of an effort. He might still…' She broke off with a sob.

Approaching the door of the bedroom they were in, Kim saw Adam place his arm gently around Cassie, draw her to him. Their backs were towards her as they looked out of the window. 'You sound like me,' he said softly. 'I think we both need to stop blaming ourselves, Cas. You're right, Josh wouldn't have wanted us tearing ourselves apart.'

Cassie moved closer, slid her arm around his waist. Kim couldn't help thinking she should be counting her blessings, having a steadfast man like Adam to lean on. She was about to go in when any sympathy she might have had for Cassie vanished.

'Do you think that man we saw really does own the property?' she asked Adam. 'I have a feeling he might be sub-letting.'

'Very likely,' Adam answered with a sigh.

'We really should insist on Kim coming to stay with us, you know,' Cassie said, glancing tentatively up at him. 'I know this place can be improved – it would have huge potential if it were legally rented – but I'm worried that Kim might not be able to cope with it all.'

'She wants her independence, Cas,' Adam pointed out. 'We have to respect that.'

'I suppose,' Cassie agreed half-heartedly.

Thinking she should make her presence known, Kim took another step towards them, and then froze as the woman went on. 'Do you think we should look at our options anyway regarding adoption? Find out what our legal rights are, I mean, just in case?'

CHAPTER THIRTEEN

Cassandra

Seeing a familiar shock of red hair through the glass in the front door, Cassie guessed it was Kim back from her doctor's appointment. Cassie had wanted to go with her, particularly as Samuel was having his second round of injections, but she hadn't pushed it when Kim had said she was calling at a friend's house on the way. She was desperate to spend more time with her grandson, but also keen not to appear to be constantly hovering.

Smiling in anticipation of their shopping trip to buy furniture for the nursery, she opened the door, and froze.

'Everything's fine,' Kim gushed. 'They've checked his weight and length, and he's had his vaccines as good as gold, haven't you, darling?' she went on, looking not the least bit troubled, which only added to Cassie's horror and confusion.

'Kim, what in God's name happened?' she asked, looking her over aghast as she helped her manoeuvre the pram in.

'Sorry. I got delayed,' Kim said, seemingly oblivious to Cassie's stunned expression – and her own condition. 'There was an emergency at the surgery. We had to wait for over forty minutes. Luckily Samuel had had his feed. I tried to ring you, but your phone went to voicemail, so I thought I would just come straight here.'

'No...' Cassie shook her head, confounded. 'I meant your face.' Was she not aware of how dreadful she looked? 'Have you had some kind of accident?'

'Oh.' Kim dropped her gaze, her hand going tentatively to the livid blue-black bruising on her cheek. She had a cut on her forehead too. Cassie's stomach turned over. If that animal posing as a father had hurt her, she swore she wouldn't be responsible for her actions. Hurriedly, she ushered her in and closed the door.

'Tell me what happened, Kim,' she begged, concerned too for Samuel. She glanced quickly down at him. He looked a little tired and fractious. Had he been caught up in the middle of something? *Dear God.* Noting Adam coming downstairs, she looked worriedly up at him.

'What the...?' He ground to a halt halfway down, his shocked gaze pivoting from Kim to Cassie and back. 'What happened, Kim?' he asked her, slowly descending the rest of the stairs. The tight tone of his voice told Cassie that his thinking was on a par with hers.

'I tripped and fell,' Kim said quickly, her eyes filled with guilt as they flicked back to Cassie's. She was lying. Cassie noticed the flush to her cheeks and knew she was covering for someone. She felt a hard knot of anger tighten inside her.

'Against what?' Adam asked, an agitated tic playing at his cheek, which was a sure sign of his mounting anger.

Kim didn't answer. Her head bowed, she fiddled nervously with the zip of her jacket.

'Kim?' Adam urged her.

'I wasn't looking where I was going,' she mumbled. 'Jack left his trainers in the kitchen. I tripped over them and fell against the cupboard.' She glanced at him anxiously.

'Right.' Adam narrowed his eyes. 'That bastard's fist, you mean,' he growled furiously, striding past her to the front door.

'No!' Kim followed him. 'It wasn't him. I swear it wasn't. Adam, *please*,' she beseeched as he snatched up his car keys. 'You'll only make it worse.'

'Adam, *wait*.' Cassie stepped towards him, torn between lifting Samuel out of his pushchair and bodily barring Adam from leaving. 'Where are you going?'

Raking a hand through his hair, Adam stopped. 'Where the hell do you think I'm going?' he retorted. 'To give that piece of cowardly scum a taste of his own medicine.'

'Please don't.' Kim swiped at a tear rolling down her cheek. 'He'll only take it out on my mum or my little brother. I couldn't bear it if he did that. I'm moving out soon. *Please*, Adam.'

Hearing her choked sob behind him, Adam wavered.

'Tell him not to go, Cassie,' Kim pleaded. 'My dad will do something awful, I know he will.' With another wretched sob, she launched herself towards her and wrapped her arms tightly around her, taking Cassie by surprise.

She wasn't sure what to do as the girl cried on her shoulder. She'd been a hair's breadth from storming around there herself. But now she realised it would serve no purpose other than to rile a man who was obviously some kind of monster. Who knew where that might lead? 'Don't go, Adam,' she appealed to him, rocking a distraught Kim in her arms.

Adam appeared to debate with himself; then, sucking in a breath and blowing it out slowly, he turned to face them. 'He needs to be told, Cassie,' he seethed, visibly trying to control his temper. 'If I get hold of him, I swear to God I'll break the bastard's neck.'

Kim cried harder at that. Samuel sobbed heart-wrenchingly along with her.

Cassie glanced between them, her own blood boiling. Adam was right. The man needed to be taught a lesson. She doubted whether the police would be able to do much unless Kim pressed charges. Judging by what she'd just said about not wanting to create a backlash for her family, Cassie doubted she would do that. Adam was tall and strong, thanks to his many years of manual work. If anyone could scare the bastard, he could. But this wasn't the way.

'Leave it, Adam, for now. At least until we decide what to do,' she said, her gaze flicking meaningfully towards Kim. 'Violence will only incite more violence, and Kim and Samuel will be in the thick of it.'

'Christ.' Glancing upwards, Adam tugged in another sharp breath, and then bent to gather Samuel from his pushchair, pressing the baby protectively to his shoulder.

Cassie breathed a sigh of relief. 'It's all right, Kim,' she said, giving her a reassuring squeeze. 'He's not going to go.'

The tension leaving her body, Kim answered with a small nod.

'Have you decided on a moving date yet?' Cassie asked her, guessing that Adam was as determined as she was to get her away from her father rather than risk this sort of thing happening again. Or worse. Nausea knotted her stomach as she imagined what might happen to a tiny vulnerable baby in the middle of all this.

'Next week,' Kim sniffed. 'I have a friend who's going to help me, but she can't do it until then. I don't have much, but…'

'You're moving today,' Adam said determinedly.

'I *can't*.' Kim spun away from Cassie to face him. 'I have to pay a month in advance, as well as the rest of the deposit. Then there are Samuel's things. I have to get those organised. I—'

'How soon can you be organised once the monies are paid?' Adam cut in, handing Samuel to Cassie, the baby's bewildered whimpers somewhat placated.

'Any time. Tomorrow,' said Kim. 'But my friend's at work. She works in a pub. She won't be able to help me until—'

'Tomorrow then,' Adam stated firmly. 'I'll pay whatever's needed and we'll move you. And if your father has any objections, he'll have me to answer to.'

Kim's gaze travelled between them. Her expression was a mixture of bewilderment and fear. Cassie's heart went out to her. 'It's fine, Kim. You need to get out of there, for Samuel's sake as well as your own.' She smiled encouragingly. 'Was your doctor's appointment after this happened?' she asked, still concerned that Samuel had been caught up in it. That he might even have sustained an injury.

Kim nodded. 'Samuel's fine,' she said, clearly getting the gist of what Cassie was asking. 'The doctor checked him all over. She said he was a handsome little boy, just like his father. Josh used to come with me to my…' She faltered. 'Oh God, I miss him so much.'

Adam moved quickly towards her, easing her into his arms as a fresh sob shook through her. 'It's okay,' he said throatily. 'You'll get through this. We all will.'

Watching Kim bury her face in his shoulder, Cassie felt a ripple of apprehension. Her heart squeezing, she pressed Samuel closer. Adam had given up the chance of having children of his own to be with her. He was still with her, even after all the upset and the heartbreak, the lack of closeness between them. Did he want to be? she asked herself. He had always been a caring man; it was simply the way he was, tactile and affectionate. But, as much as she told herself she was being ridiculous and neurotic, she couldn't help wondering: had Josh been the glue that had held them together?

CHAPTER FOURTEEN

Kimberley

Her dad was still stuck in front of the telly while her mum was out working her fingers to the bone. Bypassing the lounge door from the kitchen, Kim curled a lip in disgust as he took a swig from his beer and flicked through the TV channels. He obviously wasn't about to move any time soon. She headed upstairs to her bedroom to finish packing her clothes, Samuel safe out of harm's way – at her friend's, she'd assured Cassie. Adam had picked up the cot and the baby's few things, which she'd left outside early that morning while her dad was sleeping off last night's skinful and her mum was out cleaning. She didn't have much else, she'd told them, and Adam had immediately started ringing around for furniture while Cassie went online for bed linen and things for the nursery, making it clear to Kim how much she wanted her grandson in her life.

Noting the time on the landing clock, she tried to quell her nerves. Adam had been at the house in Hibbleton earlier. He'd already purchased and organised the delivery of a washing machine and a fridge/freezer for her. He was a good man. He clearly had loved Josh as his own. Kim hadn't been sure what to think of him when she'd first met him, but now she was getting to know him, she realised she liked him.

He and Cassie had agreed to pick her up and were due any moment. Going into her bedroom, she was alarmed to see Jack standing in his PJs staring down at her overnight bag and the clothes strewn on her bed. 'Jack, did you have a bad dream?' She looked him over, concerned.

Her little brother turned to face her, his eyes full of bewilderment. 'Are you going to live in your new house tonight?' he whispered.

Kim went across to him. 'Yes, but it's not far away. I'll still be taking you to school and picking you up. And you'll be visiting me lots. We talked about it, remember?' Crouching down in front of him, she noted his fearful expression and her heart dropped. As far as Jack was concerned, she'd been his mummy, the person whose bed he crawled into whenever he had nightmares or when their dad was raving drunk. She got him up for school while their mum was at work, made sure he had breakfast and socks on his feet. It was Kim who tucked him up at night and read him his bedtime stories so he could escape his harsh reality and live in a glorious fantasy world where all men were heroes.

'When can I come?' he asked, making a brave attempt to stem his tears.

Kim made sure to look into his eyes. 'Soon,' she assured him. 'You can stay with me at weekends. Would you like that?'

Jack nodded fervently, his gaze flitting to the door behind her. He was worried their father might overhear something that would set him off. It wasn't difficult. A simple hello when he was drunk, or in one of his foul morning-after moods, was enough to do it.

'I've written my number down for you,' Kim said, giving him a reassuring smile and getting to her feet to grab the note with her mobile number on, should there be an emergency. 'You're to call me if you need me. Any time, Jack. If you're frightened or worried about anything, ring and I'll come.'

'Promise?' he asked, his hazel eyes wide.

'Promise,' she assured him, taking hold of his hand to lead him back to his room.

He was scrambling into bed when her phone signalled an incoming text from Cassie. *Hope everything's OK. We're not far from you. Are you good to go?*

Kim keyed in a short reply. *Ten minutes. I just have to tuck Jack into bed and grab my things. See you outside.* Taking a breath, she went to give Jack a firm hug.

'Mum will be home soon,' she assured him, her heart aching for her little brother, who would be lost without her. She didn't want to leave him, but what choice did she have? 'Close your eyes and dream about superheroes and magical things,' she said, reaching to turn on the fairy lights she'd taken from her own room and strung around his headboard. 'I'll see you very soon, okay?'

Jack nodded, but didn't close his eyes. Swallowing back a lump of emotion in her throat, Kim ruffled his fringe and then hurried back to her bedroom. Quickly she stuffed the last of her things in her bag, did a final sweep of the place she couldn't wait to see the back of, then tiptoed along the landing. Part way down the stairs she stopped, her heart skidding against her ribcage as she heard the downstairs loo flush. There was a loud belch as her dad emerged to head across the hall to the lounge. She gave him a minute before continuing down.

The front door squeaked as she opened it. Adrenalin pumping, she waited a minute, heart sinking as he reappeared. 'Oi, where do you think you're going without a sodding word?' he demanded in his usual polite tones. 'You're supposed to be looking after your brother.'

'To get some milk,' Kim informed him. 'For Mum's tea when she gets back. I've just tucked Jack in.'

'Don't be long,' he muttered grudgingly, 'or the bolt will be on.'

'I won't. Course you could always go and get it yourself, couldn't you, assuming you could walk in a straight line.' Kim glanced back over her shoulder. That had pissed him off. She noted the deep crease forming in his forehead. She didn't actually care, not now that she was getting out. She couldn't have risked Samuel being dragged into anything yesterday, but she would have loved to have seen Adam cut the obnoxious slob down to size. Samuel wasn't here now, though, was he? Her dad might just be in for the biggest surprise of his life if he came out after her, which he undoubtedly would, and which, also undoubtedly, would cement her in Adam's mind as a vulnerable person in need of support.

Stepping out, she scanned the road. He wasn't here yet. A knot of apprehension tightened inside her, until she saw the car approaching and breathed out a sigh of relief.

She waved and hurried towards it as Adam slowed, headlights sweeping the road as he reversed into a side road to turn around. She was poised on the kerb, ready to climb in, when she heard her dad's slurred voice behind her.

'Oi!' he shouted. 'Get back in 'ere now, you cheeky little cow!'

Kim didn't answer. She wanted to – wanted very much to give her loving father a mouthful – but knowing that that wouldn't paint her in a very good light, she decided that keeping quiet was her best option.

'Don't you fucking well ignore me!' he seethed, lumbering towards her and grabbing her jacket.

'Let me *go*.' As Kim struggled, Adam screeched to a halt and leapt out of the car.

Her dad froze. So did Kim, apart from her heart, which was fluttering like a terrified bird in her chest.

Adam looked her dad over, clearly assessing him. 'I think you should back off, mate, don't you?' he suggested, his expression stony, his tone quiet. Dangerously quiet. Kim could feel his anger. It was emanating palpably from him. Her awe-filled gaze went to his eyes, which were hard-edged and flinty under the glow of the street lamp, the eyes of a man who wasn't about to take no for an answer.

'Mate?' Her dad laughed. 'I'm her father,' he sneered, and yanked her proprietorially towards him. 'Who the fuck are you when you're around?'

Adam surveyed him unflinchingly for a second longer. 'I'm the guy who's about to do you a serious injury if you don't heed my advice,' he informed him evenly, a small tic playing at his cheek.

Kim's gaze shot to her dad, who gawked at Adam and then narrowed his eyes. 'Piss off,' he muttered. 'And take whoever that silly cow is with you.' He nodded past him to where Cassie had climbed out of the passenger side of the car.

'I've called the police,' she warned him, unperturbed. 'I'd let her go if I were you.'

'Yeah, right,' her dad jeered. 'She's my daughter, luv. She does what *I* say while she's under my roof. Now why don't you piss off an' all? Coming round here in your swanky car, thinking you can tell decent, law-abiding people what to do. Get inside, you.' He attempted to tug Kim in the direction of the house.

Lunging forwards, Adam grabbed hold of her dad's shirt, bunching it tight to his throat with both hands. 'I have a suggestion,' he growled, lifting him almost off the ground. 'Why don't you let her go before I kill you where you stand?'

Kim noticed the lump sliding down her dad's throat. He was bricking himself. *Good.* Not so big and brave now, was he? 'Get off, you mad bastard,' he rasped, letting go of Kim and attempting to prise Adam's hands away. 'You're strangling me.'

'I know,' Adam assured him, his face an inch away from her dad's. 'And trust me, if I see you anywhere near her ever again, I'll finish the job.' With a hard stare, he held him a fraction longer before dropping him and stepping back.

Gasping for breath, her dad staggered, but didn't go down. More was the pity. Kim would have very much liked to leave him on his knees.

'Go to Cassie, Kim,' Adam said, his gaze locked meaningfully on her father, warning him not to follow her.

Seeing her dad's stupefied expression, his hands pressed to his throat, Kim's mouth curved into a satisfied smile. If ever she'd wanted revenge on him – and she had, many times – this was it, and it tasted so very sweet. He would never have imagined that people like Adam and Cassie, driving an expensive car and clearly well off, would have anything to do with the likes of her. How wrong he was. Despite their rocky start, they were growing fond of her, as evidenced by them coming to her rescue. *Perfect.* It was all going exactly as she'd hoped it might. She felt bad that Adam, who'd shot up several notches in her estimation, was caught up in the middle of all this, but needs must. She'd made a promise to Josh. In living up to that promise, she'd guessed there might be casualties along the way. Shooting her dad a triumphant glare, she lifted her chin and turned towards Cassie.

An hour later, though, she'd begun to wonder about Cassie's fondness. Coming back from the car with one of the boxes of pretty ornaments and bright pictures the woman had thoughtfully bought for the cottage – she heard Adam and Cassie talking. They were in the conservatory, looking out over the garden. Cassie's arms were folded, her body language tense. 'I just can't help thinking it's terribly risky,' she was saying, attempting to keep her voice low. 'If that animal has access to her, God only knows what might happen.'

Adam ran a hand across his neck. 'She said she hasn't given him the address,' he pointed out. 'I doubt she's likely to, don't you?'

'There are ways and means of finding people, Adam, especially in this day and age. Have you any idea about how much we give away about ourselves on social media?' Cassie asked. 'How many people post pictures of themselves right outside their house? With their geographical location right there on their profile? It doesn't take a genius to work out where they live.'

'I suppose,' Adam agreed.

'I would be happier if we had a contingency plan in place, that's all, for Samuel's sake,' Cassie went on, causing Kim's heart to stall in her chest. 'At least then we would know where we stand.'

Yes, and now Kim knew where she stood too, with Cassandra at least.

CHAPTER FIFTEEN

Cassandra

Cassie eyed the grey skies as she waited outside the Parkside Café. She and Kim had decided they would treat themselves to a calorific coffee and cake before going to the shop on the trading estate where you could buy ex-season top brands for surprisingly low prices. They were supposed to be going to Boots afterwards to stock up on essentials for Samuel, but with rain threatening, Cassie was wondering whether it might be better to do it the other way around.

Assuming Kim had been delayed, she fished her phone from her shoulder bag and was about to call her when it rang. The girl was obviously psychic. 'Hi, Cassie, I'm so sorry but I'm not going to be able to make it,' she said apologetically. 'It's nothing to worry about, but Samuel has a bit of a sniffle.'

'Oh no.' Cassie's pulse quickened. 'Bless his heart. Is he all right? He doesn't have a temperature, does he?'

'No, I've taken it,' Kim assured her. 'He's just a bit miserable, poor thing. I thought with rain forecast, though, it might be better to keep him tucked up indoors.'

'Of course,' Cassie agreed. She had been so looking forward to seeing him, but Kim was doing the right thing. She'd probably been unfair in her estimation of Kim's ability to cope with a small baby, but she couldn't help but be concerned after the appalling episode with her father. She felt a shudder run through her at the thought of the man being anywhere near her grandchild. 'I'm here in town anyway. Is there anything you need me to grab from Boots?' she offered. 'I could pop round on my way home.'

'Nappies,' Kim said. 'I'm running low on those. And would you mind getting some baby wipes while you're at it? I'm not fussed which ones as long as they're fragrance-free.'

Cassie swallowed back a lump of guilt. She had definitely judged the girl too harshly. She was obviously extremely conscientious. She had managed up until now without anyone's help, after all. 'Will do,' she said. 'And I'll bring you some cake from the café as well, since you're missing out. You'll need it for energy.'

'Ooh, I'd die for a slice of chocolate gateau.' Kim sighed longingly.

'Josh's favourite,' Cassie replied, her voice tinged with sadness.

'I know.' Kim laughed fondly. 'He would eat the whole cake if you let him.'

'Washed down with vanilla milkshake,' Cassie added.

'And half of mine,' Kim said, and sniffled.

Cassie waited a beat while her heart stilled. 'I'll be there with supplies as soon as I can,' she said, drawing in a breath.

'Thanks, Cassie,' Kim murmured, making an obvious effort not to cry.

'My pleasure,' Cassie said, her heart palpitating as she ended the call.

Her thoughts were elsewhere as she made her selections in the café and stowed the cake in her shoulder bag. Her mind was on her beautiful boy and his reaction the first time he'd eaten chocolate.

She was coming out of the café when her phone beeped. Wondering whether it might be Kim remembering something else she needed, she paused and fumbled it from her pocket, then froze, panic knotting her stomach.

The text was from the same anonymous caller as before – the woman, she assumed, who'd emerged from her past. Why? After all these years? Goose bumps prickling her skin, she opened it. *You took everything that was worth anything away from me*, it read. *Now you need to pay.*

Cassie didn't reply. Her fingers trembling with a combination of fear and anger, she swallowed back the apprehension rising inside her, switched the phone to silent and dropped it back in her pocket. What did the woman want? Money, clearly. But what if it didn't stop her?

CHAPTER SIXTEEN

Distracted, her mind still on the frightening text she'd received, Cassie had got as far as the checkout in Boots when she realised she'd forgotten the bottle warmer she would need for when Samuel stayed with them. Kim had seemed reticent when she'd mentioned it. Cassie realised it would be difficult for her to trust anyone else with her baby when up to now she'd been his sole carer, but she would want a break, some kind of social life, she'd pointed out. And now she could have one, safe in the knowledge that Samuel would be well cared for.

Checking her basket as she walked back to the baby aisle, she found she'd picked up fragranced baby wipes by mistake. Sighing at her incompetence, she swapped the wipes then headed for the bottle warmers. Scanning the shelves, her shoulders sank. She should have researched them online; she was hopelessly out of date. There were different brands, travel varieties, a vast disparity in prices. Staring at them in confusion, she picked one up, attempting to read the bumf, but was still struggling to concentrate. People jostling by every time she tried to crouch down and have a closer look didn't help.

She would have to leave it. There was no point wasting time here achieving nothing. She was about to go back to the checkout when she spotted a shop assistant flying by the end of the aisle. She left her basket and bag where they were and gave chase.

'Excuse me,' she called. 'Excuse me?'

The assistant turned around. 'Sorry,' she smiled and pointed over her shoulder, 'I'm just with a customer. I'll be with you shortly.'

Burying a disappointed sigh, Cassie went to collect up her things. Back at the tills, her mind still elsewhere, she queued again and eventually paid for the items.

Glad to be out of the shop, which was becoming claustrophobic, she was halfway across the precinct when a man called out behind her. 'Excuse me, madam.'

Not sure whether he was speaking to her, Cassie stopped and turned around, and was perplexed to see the security guard she'd passed at the door hurrying towards her.

'I have reason to believe you have an item in your bag that hasn't been paid for,' he said bluntly.

Cassie reeled inwardly. 'What?' She laughed, shocked.

'Do you have a receipt for the items you've purchased, madam?' he asked, stopping in front of her.

Bewildered, Cassie scanned his face. His eyes were steely, hard and unflinching. 'Of course I do.' Her throat suddenly parched, she dropped her gaze and searched hurriedly in her carrier bag, only to find no receipt.

'I paid for everything. I'm sure I did. I had to go to the checkout twice. I picked up the wrong item and… Hold on.' She rummaged through her pockets. 'It's here somewhere,' she assured him, growing more and more flustered at the curious glances of passers-by. 'There.' She practically thrust the receipt at him, relief flooding through her, then waited, a hot flush of humiliation heating her cheeks, as he perused it agonisingly slowly.

Finally he looked back at her, his expression inscrutable. 'I have to ask you to walk with me back to the store, madam,' he said dispassionately. 'We need to check the contents of your bag.'

Cassie's heart turned over. 'But… there are only the items I paid for in there,' she stammered. 'There must be some mistake.'

The man said nothing, glancing pointedly instead at her shoulder bag.

'This is ridiculous,' Cassie muttered, a hard lump climbing her throat. She pulled the bag from her shoulder and yanked it open, and her blood froze. 'Those aren't mine,' she said, sweat dampening her forehead as she stared horrified at the hair straighteners in her bag.

'If you'd like to come back with me to the store,' he repeated.

Cassie stared at him, uncomprehending for a second, and then panic clutched at her chest as she realised the police could be involved. Would it be on her record, the last time she'd inadvertently left a store with an item she hadn't paid for? They'd cautioned her, that was all, taken into account her diagnosis, which she'd had that very morning. She hadn't even known why she'd gone shopping. She'd never breathed a word to Adam. Why, she didn't know, except she'd been so embarrassed. Nausea engulfed her as she recalled them saying it would stay on her record for six years. What would happen now? She hadn't taken anything. Why wouldn't he believe her? She *hadn't*.

'I don't need bloody hair straighteners!' she shouted tearfully. 'I have short hair!'

He looked from her face to the hair she'd cropped short when she'd realised the medication she was on was causing it to fall out. She'd been so pleased she'd managed to grow it back a little and could now style it into a pixie cut, but anyone could see she had no need for hair straighteners.

A flicker of uncertainty crossed his face, but he remained resolute. 'Under section 24A of the Police and Criminal Evidence Act 1984, I have the power to make a citizen's arrest,' he informed her authoritatively. 'Or you could just walk back with me while we clear this up.'

Disorientated, Cassie blinked hard. She didn't even remember picking the straighteners up. Unless… She'd been so preoccupied.

Might she have done it without realising? Or had someone put them in her bag? But who? Why would they have done that? Were they here in the precinct, enjoying her humiliation?

They were. Cassie could feel it, eyes watching her closely, malice in the air, as, with no other choice, she allowed the man to lead her back to the store.

CHAPTER SEVENTEEN

Still in a state of complete shock, Cassie glanced past the female officer who was standing at the door of the interview room, guarding her as if she were a common criminal. Through the partially open door she could see Adam in the corridor deep in conversation with the solicitor he'd managed to get to the station within half an hour of her being brought into custody. Cassie's cheeks burned with deep shame as she recalled his stunned response when she'd called him, the incredulity in his voice when he'd repeated, '*Shoplifting?*' What must he think of her?

Her gaze travelled to the solicitor, a crisp-suited, competent woman in her mid-thirties. Her hair was a lustrous rich brown flecked with subtle auburn highlights. It was shoulder length, the same length Cassie's own hair had been before she'd decided on her radical cut. It was hard to imagine that she herself had once been that in-control woman. She didn't know who she was any more. Bit by bit she seemed to have lost little pieces of herself. What made it more frightening was that Adam had looked at her so guardedly. Of all the consequences of this new nightmare, the worst would be for the chasm she'd sensed between them to widen. He'd always been her rock, and she couldn't bear the idea that he might wake up one day and realise he didn't want to be there for her any more.

She glanced back at him. He still wore that deep furrow she'd noticed when he'd walked in, looking as shell-shocked as she felt. 'So what now?' she heard him ask the solicitor, his voice strained.

The woman offered him a smile, one of condolence, Cassie suspected. 'Well, she obviously didn't do it for the purpose of acquiring the item,' she said, her gaze going to her notes.

Cassie's hand strayed self-consciously to the bare nape of her neck. It was small consolation that at least one person had realised she had no need of hair straighteners, unless it was to sell them on eBay.

'Obviously.' Adam sighed, glancing from the solicitor to Cassie. He managed a small smile, but that was little consolation. Even from here, she could still see the bewildered disbelief in his eyes. He'd been through so much with her, because of her. Too much.

'They don't have adequate CCTV footage,' the woman went on. 'That's key, but—'

'Assuming she did take the item,' Adam cut in, his agitation made obvious by the hand he was dragging across the back of his neck.

'Quite,' the woman said, her smile short and professional. 'Nevertheless, it is a plus. Taking into account the information you supplied regarding the recent tragic loss of your son, she'll probably get no more than a fixed penalty fine despite the previous incident.'

'Right.' Sucking in a breath, Adam glanced upwards. 'And will this also form part of a criminal record?' he asked, causing Cassie's heart to sink to the pit of her stomach. She was a common criminal. She would never be able to go into that shop again. Never be able to hold her head up. God knew, she'd struggled to do that anyway after what had happened with Josh, the guilt she carried like a stone in her chest, but now… People who might judge her kindly would imagine she'd been driven mad by grief. Had she? The whole episode was still foggy in her mind, her recollection of her time in the shop fractured and incomplete. It was as if she were floating through another nightmare, unable to grasp onto anything tangible.

'I'll be pushing the extenuating circumstances,' the solicitor answered with an uncertain shrug. 'At least she's not looking at a prison sentence.'

Cassie felt nausea swill inside her. She almost wished she could hide away in prison, where she wouldn't see fingers pointing, the disillusionment that was bound to be in Adam's eyes.

'I'll go and check the paperwork is under way,' the woman said, pressing a hand lightly to Adam's arm. Even that simple gesture of reassurance sent a ripple of jealousy through Cassie. If she'd thought she might lose him before, she was growing certain of it now.

'You'll probably need to wait in reception, but it shouldn't be too long and then you can get Mrs Colby back home.' The solicitor nodded towards what Cassie assumed was the desk area. She'd been so dazed when they'd brought her here, she hadn't noticed her surroundings. She was still utterly disorientated, as if her life were disjointed, coming apart at the seams. How had this happened?

Closing her eyes, she wiped a hand over her wet cheeks and then looked back to Adam. What was he thinking? she wondered as he finally fixed his gaze in her direction. Imagining what was going through his mind, Cassie felt a cold chill prickle her skin. And then a brief moment of relief when his face relaxed into a small smile. 'Hang in there,' he said, giving her a determined nod before turning to go after the solicitor.

They didn't chat much while the police were going through the formalities of her release. Cassie guessed Adam didn't know what to say to her. She wished he would make proper eye contact. His gaze had skimmed her a few times, but she couldn't read what was there.

They were driving away from the station when he spoke. 'Okay?' he asked, glancing in her direction. His voice was still choked, his hands gripping the steering wheel.

Cassie nodded. She couldn't trust herself to speak.

'I'll run you a hot bath when we get home,' he offered. He was trying to make her feel better, to fix things. He was a fixer by nature. It should be *her* fixing things, not him, but she didn't know how, when their lives were so broken. When she obviously was.

'Do you remember taking them, Cassie?' he asked, after an interminably long minute.

'*No.*' Twisting to look at him, Cassie repeated what she'd insisted since the security guard had appeared to blow what was left of her world apart. 'I've already said, someone must have put them…' She stopped, her throat thick with emotion.

Had she taken the straighteners? Inadvertently dropped them into her bag? Fear twisting inside her, she tried hard to think back. She'd been so distracted, as she had been the last time. She'd been shopping for Josh then, for his birthday, needing to distract herself. She'd walked out with one of the leather bags on her arm with her own. She could see how she'd done that. But this? She still couldn't imagine taking the straighteners, even unconsciously.

Adam didn't mention it, the 'previous incident', as the solicitor had referred to it, falling silent instead.

'I didn't realise you'd changed your name,' he said eventually. 'The maiden name on the paperwork, it wasn't Tyler.'

Cassie's stomach lurched. 'No.' She thought fast. 'I wanted something zappier. Professionally, I mean. Smith was hardly that, so I changed it to Tyler.'

Adam drew in a breath, nodded tersely.

'And then you came along and saved me. Cassie Colby is certainly zappy, you have to admit.' She laughed, a strangled, desperate sound.

Adam said nothing. Kept his gaze fixed forward.

Cassie looked at him. He would have cracked a joke once, said *At your service* or something. But his shoulders were stiff, his jaw taut. He wouldn't save her now. He didn't believe her.

She watched him take a hand from the wheel and knead his forehead, heard his sigh. He would be wondering who could have put the stolen item into her bag. Why anyone would want to. And Cassie had no answer to give him. It could only have been the woman who was texting her, but to tell him that, she would have to tell him everything. And she couldn't bear to imagine what she would see in his eyes then.

CHAPTER EIGHTEEN

Kimberley

'Hi.' Kim smiled tentatively when Adam pulled his front door open. Looking him over, she was shocked. He looked dreadful, as if he was carrying the weight of the world on his shoulders. He probably felt that he was. Kim's heart went out to him. He'd done nothing to deserve any of the awful things that were happening in his life. The poor man must wonder what had hit him.

'I've been shopping,' she said, realising it was probably best not to probe. He didn't know her that well, after all, and men didn't easily share what was troubling them. Her mind went back to Josh, his evasive answers when she'd asked him what was wrong. She'd known he was hurting because of other people. He and Adam might not have been blood relations, but they were so similar in nature, easy-going and caring, they could have been father and son.

'I thought I'd pop by and show you,' she went on as he gazed at her distractedly.

Adam took a second to answer. Then, 'Sorry, Kim.' He shook his head and mustered up a smile. 'Miles away.'

'I gathered. Anything I can help with?' Kim asked as he stepped out to help her with the pushchair.

'Not really. A few problems, that's all. I'm sure it will all sort itself out.'

Kim nodded, though she doubted it would without a little intervention. In her experience, if you wanted a problem solved, then you had to be proactive, as she was. 'I've probably splurged a bit more than I should,' she chatted on as he closed the door behind her. 'I couldn't resist, though. You'll see why when I show you.'

'Weren't you meeting up with Cassie today?' Adam asked, his brow creasing into a frown as he helped her unhook her bags from the handles of the pushchair.

'I was,' Kim said, 'but Samuel had a touch of the sniffles, so I rang her and postponed. The nurse said it was nothing to worry about when I popped into the surgery, though, so I went on to the shops afterwards.'

'Ah.' Adam nodded. 'And is he all right now?' He looked concerned for the baby. He really was a caring man.

'Bright as a button, as you can see,' Kim assured him as, after glancing at her to check it was okay, he bent to lift Samuel out. Handling him carefully, he nestled him in the crook of his arm, a smile lighting his eyes as he gazed down at him. Kim reflected again on what a good father he would have been and how much he must have given up for Cassie's sake. She wondered whether Cassie appreciated it. Appreciated him. Because looking at him now, seeing the quiet longing in his eyes, it was obvious he had wanted children of his own, dearly. He was possibly still mourning the baby he'd lost, as well as Josh.

'Hey, little guy, have you been worrying your mum, hey?' he asked, crooking a finger to stroke Samuel's peachy cheek. Samuel jiggled his arms and chuckled delightedly. From the mouths of babes, as they said. Plainly Samuel rated Adam too.

'I can't wait to show Cassie the things I've bought.' Kim glanced expectantly past him towards the kitchen.

Adam's face clouded over. 'Ah, sorry. She's not feeling too well. She's taken a sleeping pill and gone to bed early. She'll be sad she's missed you, but it's probably best not to wake her.'

'Oh no.' Kim looked at him, alarmed. 'Is she okay? She's not poorly, is she?'

Adam shook his head. 'No. She hasn't been sleeping much, that's all. I'm sure the rest will do her good.'

Kim nodded slowly. 'Right, well…' She glanced at him uncertainly. 'I'll call back then, shall I?'

'You could. I think she's home all day tomorrow. Since you're here, though, you might want to show me,' he suggested. 'I'm possibly not the authority on baby clothes that Cassie is, but I'd love to see them.'

Kim hesitated. She didn't want to appear blasé about the fact that Cassie had taken to her bed.

'I was just about to put the kettle on,' Adam added. 'And I believe we have chocolate cake, if you fancy a slice.'

Kim eyed him. 'You're not trying to tempt me by any chance, are you?'

'Absolutely,' Adam assured her, his mouth curving into a smile as he nodded towards the kitchen.

Laughing, Kim followed him. 'I'll do it,' she offered, heading for the kettle. 'You're going to struggle with your arms full of baby.'

'I think your mother might be doubting my multi-tasking skills, Samuel, but we'll let her off, shall we?' Adam's amused gaze was on the baby, who was searching his face and babbling excitedly. Kim watched in awe as Samuel stretched out a hand, which Adam caught, lowering his head to press a soft kiss to it.

'He looks a lot like Josh, doesn't he?' she ventured, as Adam studied him with the same sense of wonder he always did.

His expression darkening, he took a second to answer. 'Very much,' he said hoarsely.

Kim's heart ached for him. She wanted to go to him, to comfort him, but sensed that wouldn't be a good move when he was clearly working to control his emotions. Emotions that would be in turmoil with everything coming at him. 'Are you okay, Adam?' she asked gently.

He attempted to compose himself, smiling for Samuel's benefit. 'Fine,' he answered, his voice tight.

'Are you sure?' Kim pressed. He was visibly upset. She hadn't come here with the intention of upsetting him further.

'Positive.' Adam looked up at her, and Kim felt her heart constrict. He had tears in his eyes. She'd never seen a grown man cry before. 'I, er…'

His voice cracked as he trailed off, and she went to him. How could she not? 'It's okay, Adam,' she said, sliding a comforting arm around his shoulders.

'*Damn.* Sorry. Do you think you could…?' Heaving in a breath, Adam nodded down at Samuel.

Understanding, Kim eased the baby from his arms. 'You can talk to me, you know, Adam,' she assured him. 'I'm a good listener. And I promise you I'm the soul of discretion.'

Adam pressed his thumb and forefinger against his eyes and took another long breath. 'It's Cassie,' he said at last, glancing at the ceiling. 'She's been accused of shoplifting. Charged, to be precise.'

'Oh my God.' Holding Samuel closer to her, Kim stared at him.

'She says she didn't…' He faltered, his expression cautious as he scanned her face. 'She hasn't been well, as you know. And then, with what happened to Josh… She's been distracted, depressed, I think. Not sleeping. She might have put something in her bag without realising. I probably shouldn't have told you, but…'

'You didn't want me to hear it from anyone else,' Kim finished sympathetically. 'What was it?' she asked him. 'The item she…'

'Hair straighteners.' Adam laughed wryly.

Kim widened her eyes. 'But that's bonkers. She doesn't need… Unless she wanted to straighten her fringe maybe?' she pondered out loud.

'I've no idea.' Adam sighed heavily. 'I'd appreciate it if you didn't mention it, Kim,' he said, now looking guilty.

'I wouldn't dream of it,' Kim promised. 'And if Cassie says anything, she can count on me for support. I get why she would have been distracted, trust me.'

Adam's smile was one of immense relief. 'Thanks,' he said throatily. 'I should probably go up and check on—'

They both glanced upwards as a floorboard creaked overhead.

Kim's gaze slid back to him. 'It might be better for me to pop back tomorrow after she's had a good sleep,' she suggested. 'She might want an ear, you never know.'

'Thanks. I'm not sure she knows how to talk to me. Or whether she wants to, to be honest.'

'Not a problem,' Kim assured him. 'I suppose she won't be able to apply to adopt Samuel now, will she?' she asked carefully. 'Not that I was thinking she would want to, when we're all getting along so well,' she added. 'It's just that I overheard you talking.'

A troubled frown crossed Adam's face. 'I don't think she could have…' He stopped, glancing awkwardly at her. 'I doubt she was serious, Kim. She was just worried, for Samuel's sake. She knows you're doing a fabulous job with him. We both do.'

'Thank you. And don't worry, I'm not judging her. She has a lot on her mind.' Kim paused. 'I'd better get off.'

Turning, she collected up her bags, cursing as the handle of the large carrier she'd stuffed other purchases into gave way. She froze as she noticed that one of the items was in full view on the floor. Adam had clearly also noticed it. She watched him bend to scoop it up, her heart almost stopping dead as he squinted quizzically at the Boots own-brand nappies and then at her.

'You were in Boots?' he asked her.

Kim panicked for a second, and then realised there was actually no reason she shouldn't have been. 'Yes,' she said, arranging her face into an innocent smile. 'Cassie said she would grab some things for me, but as I was out…'

CHAPTER NINETEEN

Joshua

January 2019

Josh watched Kim carefully as she came down the station steps. He couldn't see any sign of a limp. He'd wondered whether she would show up again, whether she might have been taking a later train, thus avoiding him. It was no skin off his nose if she was, but he would quite like to establish why she'd lied to him about where she lived. He'd gone back to the estate a couple of times, made a nuisance of himself knocking on doors. No one had even heard of anyone fitting her description. It shouldn't bother him, but it did, and not because he'd shelled out a fortune on the cab fare, but because of the things she'd said before she'd stormed off up the steps at the station. She'd asked him to stop following her – and this was after he'd seen *her* at his school. He'd believed her when she'd denied she was there, convinced himself he must have been mistaken. Now, he wasn't so sure. He really couldn't get his head around any of it. Either she had a serious problem, or she thought *he* did, and that was why she'd given him a false address. And that did bother him.

Walking along the platform, she faltered as she saw him. Then, taking a visible breath, she continued on, stopping a foot or so away to search his face nervously. Why the hell would she be nervous of him?

'I have your phone,' he said coolly. Drawing it from his pocket, he handed it to her, holding eye contact as he did; trying to read what was going on in her mind.

Accepting it, she glanced down. 'I owe you an apology,' she said, appearing to brace herself as she looked back at him.

Josh waited. He didn't want an apology. An explanation might be nice, though.

'You probably think I'm mad.'

Correct, Josh didn't say.

'Do you mind if we…' She indicated the far end of the platform, where there were fewer people.

Josh glanced over his shoulder and then looked back at her. She wanted to speak in private, he guessed. He was tempted to walk away, but there was something in her eyes. Desperation, almost. Also, Adam had always told him that walking away from a problem rarely solved it.

Giving Kim a short nod, he led the way along the platform. He hoped it was good, this explanation, because he couldn't think of any plausible reason for her lie.

He stopped and turned to face her. 'How's the ankle?' Had she lied about that too? he pondered, and then pulled himself up. He was getting paranoid. She obviously did have problems. He just wished to God he hadn't invited them into his life.

'It's fine. As good as new now,' she said awkwardly. 'Look, Josh, I just want to tell you I'm sorry. I like you. I like you a lot. You're obviously a nice guy, and I didn't mean—'

'Right.' Josh laughed cynically. 'Not a nutter you need to avoid then.'

'*No*,' she said forcefully. 'I don't think that, I promise you. I don't know why I…' Stopping, she glanced skywards, pulling in a long breath before looking back at him. 'My ex-boyfriend, I think I mentioned he was a stalker. He was also abusive, in ways it's hard to imagine if you're not on the receiving end. He wouldn't leave me alone, no matter how hard I tried to tell him it was over.'

Josh shook his head. Was he really supposed to buy this? Whatever her ex was – and he was starting to think he should take everything with a pinch of salt – it wasn't what *he* was. Nor was he even her boyfriend, for Christ's sake.

'I know you have your reasons to doubt me, Josh, but I swear to God it's the truth. He followed me everywhere: to work, when I went out. He would follow me home. Every single night I would look out of my bedroom window and he would just be standing there, gazing up at me. He would put notes through my door, ring me at all hours, I stopped answering my landline in the end. He even broke into my house… while I was in *bed.* Have you any idea how that feels? Realising that someone who means you harm has been watching you while you're sleeping?'

Josh narrowed his eyes. *Was* this bullshit? He'd been sceptical, with good reason, but seeing the fear in her eyes, he was thinking she might be telling the truth. 'Did you report him?' he asked. 'Surely the police could have done something?'

'Three times. And three times they let him go "under investigation". And every time they did, he came back more aggressive than the last time. He meant to get me. He was biding his time. Getting a kick out of the fact that I knew that.'

Josh's gut tightened. 'And the police did *nothing?*'

'Not until he attacked me so violently he knocked me unconscious, no,' she said, her voice quavering.

Josh's heart jolted. 'Unconscious?'

She paused, looking away. 'He raped me,' she whispered, her cheeks blazing with humiliation.

Josh stared hard at her, shocked to the core. 'Jesus Christ,' he muttered, swallowing back a sick taste in his throat. Unsure what to do, he watched helplessly as a slow tear slid down her face.

'I swore I would never, *ever* give my address to a man I went out with again,' she said, fixing her gaze back on him. Josh could see the determination in her eyes, as if she'd resolved not to let what that bastard had done to her defeat her. 'As it happens, I'm obviously so vile – as my ex frequently pointed out – that you had no inclination of asking me out anyway. But I just wanted to say I'm sorry,' she repeated shakily. 'You didn't deserve that. I was just… scared of letting my guard down, I suppose.'

Josh didn't know what to say. He felt so *fucking* angry. Anger he had no idea what to do with. He wanted to reach out and hold her. Comfort her in some way. But how could he, without invading her space when she would undoubtedly be feeling vulnerable? 'You're not vile, Kim,' he assured her. 'You're pretty, intelligent, funny. Don't give him the satisfaction of feeling bad about yourself. I didn't understand – obviously I couldn't have – but I promise you there's nothing you have to apologise for.'

Her expression uncertain, she scrutinised him thoughtfully. 'Did I mention you're a nice person, Josh Colby?' she said, her mouth curving into a small smile.

'Yeah.' Running a hand over his neck, Josh smiled ruefully. He only wished the woman he'd given his heart and bared his soul to thought that. 'So where *do* you live then – without giving me exact details.'

'With a friend,' Kim said. 'Just for a while. I'm hoping to get my own place soon. I shouldn't have lied, but… I panicked. It's not easy to explain, and I prefer not to if I don't have to.'

'I get it, Kim,' Josh assured her. 'We're all good, honestly.'

She nodded with a smile of relief. Josh hoped she realised there were people she could confide in. She shouldn't keep all this bottled up. 'And your sister?' he asked.

'She's in Wales. She moved there to be with the man of her dreams,' Kim said with a wistful sigh. 'They're living happily ever after shearing sheep together.'

Conjuring up an image of the happy couple gazing doe-eyed at each other over their flock, Josh smiled. 'Might have been a bit expensive in a taxi,' he joked.

A flicker of guilt crossed her face. Then, seeing his expression, she laughed. A laugh that turned into a sob that caught in her throat. And then another, which shook through her body. What was he going to do, stand by and watch while her heart broke?

The train came into the station as he held her. She made no attempt to move away. Saying nothing, guessing it might be therapeutic for her to cry her tears out, he waited until her sobs slowed. 'About that date I didn't ask you on,' he said softly. 'It's not that I wouldn't have liked to. I was trying to do the right thing, that was all.'

She looked up at him, her wide green eyes awash with tears. 'Because you didn't think you were ready for another relationship?'

'That's right.' Josh nodded, now feeling incredibly guilty. He'd led her on, given her reason to think this might be going somewhere. He wasn't sure he was doing the right thing, but… Would it change anything? If he denied himself the company of other women, would it make the one he'd imagined he might have a future with see him in a different light? At least have some contact with him? Josh had hoped, but now he very much doubted it.

'I didn't, but…' He hesitated, and prayed she wouldn't think he was doing this out of pity. 'I would hate it if you thought I was asking for any other reason than that I like you, but… would you do me the honour of going out with me? For a meal? Or to see a film maybe?'

She searched his eyes. 'Such a gentleman,' she said, a smile lighting her own. 'I'd like that.' She nestled back into him. 'Very much.'

CHAPTER TWENTY

Cassandra

Cassie stepped out of the bedroom as Adam reached the top of the stairs, causing him to jump. 'I thought I heard Kim downstairs,' she said, studying him apprehensively.

'Christ, you nearly gave me a heart attack.' Adam gathered himself. 'I thought you'd taken a sleeping tablet?'

'I decided against. They only make me feel worse in the morning. I did doze for a while, though.' Cassie gave him a small smile. '*Was* it Kim I heard?'

'I, er…' Adam's gaze flicked towards her, and then away again. 'Yes,' he said eventually. 'She'd been out shopping. She came to show us some baby clothes she'd bought.'

Cassie squinted at him. 'What, today?'

Adam nodded, his gaze troubled. 'She said she called you about meeting up. That Samuel seemed a bit off colour.'

'She did.' Cassie knitted her brow. 'But… why would she have done that and then gone to the shops anyway?'

'She went to the doctor's surgery apparently. The nurse she saw confirmed Samuel was fine, so as she was out…' He stopped, studying her carefully.

Cassie nodded. She hated this wariness between them. They'd never been like this before. They'd had arguments – what married couple didn't? – real humdingers occasionally, but they'd never done this, stood on opposite sides of some invisible fence, avoiding the elephant in the room.

It made sense that Kim would go to the shops if she was already out, she supposed. She might have needed the nappies urgently, and the shops were only a stone's throw from the surgery. 'Did you not think to come and get me?' she asked him.

'No. I thought you were fast asleep. I didn't want to disturb you.'

'I see.'

'Would you like some tea? Something stronger?' He seemed not to know what to say, and Cassie felt an uneasiness spread through her. Why? Was she imagining it? Being neurotic, insecure? Having heard him confiding in Kim when she'd come out onto the landing after hearing voices downstairs, she couldn't help feeling that the divide between them had widened another inch, that he'd slipped further away from her – and that Kim had moved closer.

Thinking she was losing her grip, imagining people conspiring against her, she pulled herself up. Adam didn't have a disloyal bone in his body. If she pushed it, she would only appear suspicious.

'No thanks. I'm actually quite sleepy, despite everything. I think I'll just go back to bed.'

'Right.' Adam smiled, still looking uncomfortable. 'I'll just sort out a few outstanding invoices and then I'll join you.'

Aware of the empty space in the bed, the time on her alarm clock slipping through one hour and then two, Cassie listened to the silence downstairs. Had he fallen asleep? she wondered. He was obviously reluctant to come up. Her heart, which had been sinking since she'd seen the bewilderment in his eyes at the police station, settled like ice in her chest. She hadn't realised she'd drifted off until she was jolted awake by the raucous squeal of brakes, metal grinding mercilessly against metal. Her son's petrified cry dying in his throat, as if he were right here in the room. Sweat pooling in the hollow of her neck, her chest pelting, she pulled herself up, squinting in the semi-dark. Adam still wasn't here, and she needed him to be, holding her, drawing her close, spooning her with his firm body.

It was after three o'clock when he eventually did come, squeaking the bedroom door quietly open. Hearing him carefully undressing, Cassie kept her eyes closed, feigning sleep. She knew he would be as confused emotionally as she was, worried about what had gone on today, about her. Still, she didn't think she could bear it if he knew she was awake and he couldn't bring himself to reach out to her.

CHAPTER TWENTY-ONE

Joshua

January 2019

'Whoops, careful.' Josh steadied Kim as they exited the Italian restaurant. They'd shared a bottle of wine with their meal and had a liqueur coffee afterwards. She was definitely a bit tipsy.

'It's the shoes,' she said, turning towards him with a mischievous smile.

Josh sighed in mock despair. 'I suppose that means you'll be throwing yourself at my feet again then?'

'Like you don't regularly have women throwing themselves at your feet,' she teased, surprising him and sliding her hand around his waist as they walked.

'Obviously. But I only pick the pretty ones up,' Josh quipped. He hesitated, and then circled his arm around her too as they neared the bridge over the River Severn, heading for the high street to get a taxi.

'Flatterer.' She laughed.

'It's one of my better qualities,' Josh assured her. He was glad she was smiling more easily.

She'd been nervous the first time they'd gone out. He hadn't realised how nervous until he'd attempted to kiss her goodnight. He'd been feeling guilty, his mind still on the first woman he'd ever made meaningful love with. Kim had flinched, and then blushed furiously. 'It's not you, Josh. It's me,' she'd said quickly, as he'd mumbled an apology. 'I haven't been out with anyone since... You know.' It was obviously too much too soon. He'd been relieved to a degree. It was probably better for both of them to take things slowly rather than rush into a physical relationship, which Kim clearly wasn't ready for.

'So what will you do with your weekend?' she asked him now.

'Not much on Saturday,' he said. 'I'm canoeing on Sunday with my stepdad.'

Kim squeezed her arm tighter around his waist. 'He sounds really nice. You must get on well.'

'He is, and we do,' Josh said. 'Adam's a good bloke. Caring, you know? Genuinely, I mean. He'd do anything for anybody if he thought they were worth the effort. There was this one time when we walked past a homeless woman in the street and he saw she hadn't got much to keep her warm, so he went into the twenty-four-hour supermarket and bought her a sleeping bag.'

Kim looked impressed. 'What a lovely thing to do. Not many people would go to that effort, even if they could afford it. He sounds like my kind of guy.'

'Yeah. That's just the way he is.' Selfless, his mother had once called him, saying that was why she loved him. 'He always looked out for me. Still does, really.'

'Did they not have children together, your mum and Adam?' Kim asked. 'He's clearly been such a great dad to you.'

'No.' Josh sighed, wishing that they had. At least then he wouldn't have been his mother's centre of attention. She'd told him often as a kid that he was her whole world. It was just what mothers did, he guessed, but it was a lot to live up to. 'They tried. Adam would have loved to have kids of his own, and I know Mum wanted another baby, but... she miscarried. It broke their hearts. I guess they accepted it wasn't going to happen after a while.'

'Oh God, that's awful,' Kim commiserated, slowing her pace as they walked across the bridge. 'For your mum and for Adam. He must really be a special kind of guy.'

'Yeah. He is. Mum's been unwell recently and he's been there for her. I suppose I should go and see her,' he added, feeling guilty. At least now he no longer lived there, she wouldn't be able to bang on at him about clearing up after himself. He sighed. He still wasn't sure how the argument had escalated so quickly. She'd seemed furious with him, and he just didn't get why. The medication, he supposed, looking back.

'I could come with you if you like,' Kim offered. 'If you want some company, I mean.'

Josh glanced at her. 'Maybe.' He smiled. He wasn't sure he was ready to take a girl home to meet his mother. He wasn't even sure he and Kim were leading anywhere. 'Like I say, she hasn't been well. Things weren't great between us when I left. I should probably meet up with her on my own, see how the land lies.'

'Can you not just pop round?' Kim asked, eyeing him curiously.

'I could,' Josh considered, and then decided against it. 'It might be better to meet on neutral territory, though.'

'Oh dear. It sounds as if things really are bad,' Kim said sympathetically.

'No.' Josh shook his head. 'Not really. I just don't want to do anything to make the situation worse. She, er, gets a bit neurotic about mess in the house. Or she did. It was probably due to her illness, but…'

'It caused a rift between you,' Kim surmised.

'And some,' Josh sighed. 'We'll work it out.' They might, if he acted like an adult and made an effort to get in touch.

'You will. You love her.' Kim gave his waist another squeeze.

'She's my mother.' Josh smiled.

As they neared the middle of the bridge, Kim turned to look over the river. 'Love's a powerful thing,' she said. 'It can inspire us, drive us to create great works of art. It can also drive us to acts of despair when it's the wrong kind. You know, obsessive love, or unrequited love.'

Josh arched an eyebrow, impressed. 'Very poetic.'

Kim smiled. Holding her gaze, he saw the blush that came whenever she felt embarrassed. She was very pretty, particularly when she smiled. She seemed more relaxed, less... brittle. He wasn't sure why that word sprang to mind; perhaps it was that she was someone who had to be handled carefully. He reprimanded himself. Of course she was. And he knew why.

'It's true, though,' she went on, turning back to the water. 'How many murders are committed by some spurned lover driven mad by despair? It happens, as I well know. I shudder to think how close I came to being a statistic.'

Anger tightened Josh's chest. 'He's out of your life now,' he said softly, reaching an arm around her shoulders and easing her closer. He would never get how some twisted individuals could do what that bastard had done to her.

Kim rested her head on his shoulder as they looked out across the water. The tide was high. The river was close to flooding, but it was beautiful, the lights from the buildings on the bank dancing on the water.

'Romantic, isn't it?' she murmured.

'Definitely.'

'Can I ask you something?'

'Anything,' Josh assured her. He wasn't sure, though, how truthfully he could answer if she wanted to know more about his former relationships.

She hesitated and then turned to face him. 'Make love with me,' she whispered, her mesmerising green eyes luminous in the light from the lantern above and filled with trepidation.

Josh's heart missed a beat. He wasn't sure whether it was with anticipation or panic. Both, he suspected. 'Are you sure?' he asked after a stunned second. He'd resigned himself to the fact that it wasn't going to happen, at least not for a while. He wasn't sure he even wanted it to – for her sake, given that his heart wasn't fully invested. How could she not end up getting hurt? He liked her, but he didn't love her. And he wasn't that much of a saint that he would turn her down. But she wanted more than a casual relationship, he was sure. He needed to move on emotionally, he knew that, but could he deliver?

A whisper away from him, Kim scanned his eyes and then leant towards him, closing her mouth over his. And Josh was lost. Tentatively he kissed her back, gently at first, and then more boldly as her tongue found his, inviting him into her mouth. He wanted her, and she clearly felt the same way. Her kiss grew more urgent, her hands finding bare flesh under his shirt.

Josh eased away a fraction. 'I think my housemate's out,' he said, his throat hoarse.

Hands all over each other, he was surprised they made it to the bedroom. Once inside, it took her a second to pull her dress up over her head. Josh emitted a throaty moan as she unhooked her bra, revealing firm milk-white breasts. He wanted to do this, he very much wanted to, but there was a warning voice in his head. What would happen afterwards? What if he couldn't commit to a relationship?

Smiling, she walked across to him, not the least bit embarrassed. With a surge of pure lust, Josh ran appreciative eyes over her. She was beautiful. 'Lie down,' she urged, the look in her eyes confident where before it had been unsure.

'You're at my mercy now,' she said, her mouth curving into a teasing smile as she lay next to him. Lapping his cheek with the length of her tongue, she reached to unfasten his jeans. When she took him into her mouth, Josh was surprised. *Jesus.* She'd obviously decided that she would be in control of the situation. He had no objections. On the contrary. It just wasn't what he'd expected.

Watching as she straddled him, impish eyes locked on his, her glorious red hair hanging loose and wild as she guided him inside her, Josh lay back and went with it. He didn't really have a lot of choice. Slowly rotating her hips, she was dictating the pace. And he was happy to let her. Catching hold of her, he gave up agonising about the rights and wrongs and drove himself deep inside her.

She was also into spooning, it seemed. A smile curving his mouth, Josh was happy to oblige there too. He wasn't exactly a virgin, but he'd never experienced anything quite like the mind-blowing orgasm she'd just given him. 'Okay?' he asked, wrapping an arm around her as she nestled in close to him.

'Perfect,' she murmured.

Josh's eyelids were growing heavy when she next spoke. 'Do you want children, Josh?' she asked him, trailing her fingernails through the hairs on his forearm.

Josh's eyes sprang open. 'Some day,' he said awkwardly. 'You?'

She nodded. 'Definitely. But it would have to be with the right man. Someone caring, like you or your stepdad.'

Josh smiled. 'You're not fussy about age then?'

'Not really, as long as he was kind and respectful of women,' Kim said. She changed the subject. 'Tell me about your previous girlfriend. Why didn't your mother like her?'

Josh hesitated. 'It's complicated,' he answered evasively. 'It's over, obviously, or I wouldn't be lying here with you.' He gave her a reassuring squeeze.

He was drifting off again when the alarm bells ringing in his head jarred him awake. He couldn't recall ever having mentioned that his mother hadn't liked her.

CHAPTER TWENTY-TWO

Cassandra

Cassie had been surprised when Kim had called her. Chatting as if everything were perfectly normal, she'd invited her over, suggesting they take a walk along the canal bank, since it was such a beautiful day. She'd apologised for cancelling their shopping trip, mentioning that she'd gone into town anyway and was sorry she'd missed her. She hadn't said anything about the shoplifting, but then Cassie knew Adam had asked her not to. She guessed she would have to mention it, rather than ignore it, but not over the phone.

Twenty minutes early when she approached Kim's cottage, she parked a short distance away and decided to apply a little make-up. She needed to hang on to what little pride she had left, to pull herself together for her grandson's sake, for Kim's. For Adam, who'd at least looked at her this morning with a semblance of a smile in his eyes.

She was part way through her mascara when she noticed a car that had been parked just past Kim's cottage approaching. She realised she recognised the silver-grey VW Polo, also the driver at the wheel. Jemma Anderson? What on earth was she doing here? Kim had said she didn't know her when Cassie had asked her.

She watched, confused, as Jemma drove distractedly past, her attention more on the dashboard than the road. Had they become friends since Kim had moved here? she wondered. If so, why hadn't Kim mentioned it? But then there was no reason why she should.

Quickly finishing off her mascara, she climbed out of her car and walked to the cottage, where she rang the doorbell and waited.

Eventually Kim threw the bedroom window open. 'Sorry,' she called. 'I was in the bathroom. Won't be a sec.'

The front door of the neighbouring house inched open as Cassie stood on the doorstep, and the wizened face of an old lady peered out. 'Are you the mother?' the woman asked.

Realising she could never again claim that title now that her child no longer walked the earth, Cassie felt a crushing wave of grief. 'Mother-in-law,' she provided, with a tolerant smile. 'In a manner of speaking.'

The woman looked her over through narrowed eyes. 'So is she married or not?' she asked bluntly, inclining her head towards Kim's door. 'It's just that I do like to know who's coming and going, since she lives right the other side of my living room wall. There's been delivery vans blocking the road, that wretched man hammering and drilling and no doubt carrying on with her—'

'That would be my husband,' Cassie cut in curtly, aware that Adam had had to make some plumbing adjustments to house the washing machine.

The woman raised her eyebrows at that. 'Oh,' she said. 'Not *her* husband then?'

Cassie's tolerance evaporated. What on earth was the old fool talking about?

'Then there's that woman parking her car outside my house,' she prattled on. 'I'm not one to cause trouble, and I've no objection to babies – Lord knows I've had enough of my own – but I'm wondering whether the housing association knows about her running—'

'You're a nosy old cow,' Kim cut in, having swung her own front door open. 'Go back inside and mind your own business, why don't you?' she added rudely. Stepping back, she rolled her eyes skywards and gestured Cassie inside.

'Ignore her,' she said, as Cassie pulled her gaze away from the shocked woman and stepped in. 'She's the mind-everybody-else's-business sort and obviously gaga.'

'I gathered,' Cassie said, feeling immensely irritated herself. Nosy neighbours had been the bane of her existence as a child. The whispered gossip after her father's affair with a sixteen-year-old pupil at the school he taught at had ruined her mother's life. She had never lived down the shame, retreating into herself, turning to religion, endlessly going on about how cleanliness was next to godliness. It had ruined Cassie's life, too. She'd lived in fear of being struck down if she were ever to be slovenly.

'She accused me of blaring my records the other day,' Kim went on tetchily. 'I could have clocked her one, I swear. I'd just got Samuel to sleep, so I was hardly likely to be blaring music, was I?'

'Oh dear. You'll have to turn a deaf ear, I suspect.' Cassie smiled sympathetically and followed Kim through to the kitchen.

'I'm trying.' Kim sighed. 'She's hard work, though.'

'You don't get to choose your neighbours, unfortunately,' Cassie said.

'No. More's the pity. Tea?'

'That would be lovely.' Cassie smiled. 'I had to go into Worcester this morning for a meeting with some colleagues regarding future articles. It went on for ages. I'm absolutely parched.'

Glancing around the kitchen, which really could do with more of a clean than the lick Kim had given it, she seated herself at the table. 'I ran into Jemma on the way here. She asked after you,' she twisted the truth a little, making sure to sound casual. 'I hadn't realised you two had got to know each other.'

'Who?' Kim said, her back to Cassie as she poured hot water into mugs.

'Jemma Anderson. I mentioned that she and her husband were at Josh's funeral. I thought you might have met her at the doctor's surgery.'

Kim glanced back at her, her forehead creased as if trying to recall. 'Yeah,' she said vaguely. 'I don't really remember.'

Cassie tugged in a tight breath. Held it.

'To be honest, I try to avoid getting too heavily into conversation with other mums. I find it difficult explaining about Josh and what happened to him, as I'm sure you understand.' Walking across with the tea, Kim looked into Cassie's eyes, her own tearful.

'I do. Completely,' Cassie said, her heart pumping as she lowered her gaze.

'I'll just go and fetch Samuel.' Placing a mug in front of Cassie, Kim turned away from the table. 'He fell asleep after his feed, bless him, so I thought I'd leave him a while. There's bickies in the barrel if you fancy one.' Nodding over her shoulder to the work surface, she headed through the dining room to the stairs, leaving Cassie bewildered.

Kim was telling lies. Why would she? Her stomach knotting, she got to her feet, instinctively fishing the dishcloth from the sink to wipe up the puddle of tea Kim had left on the work surface. Running some water into the bowl, she fetched the antibacterial spray she'd bought from under the sink and channelled her energies into wiping the cooker top while she tried to think. It was possible that Jemma had been lost and had just paused in the lane. She'd seemed to be fiddling with her sat nav when she'd driven past.

Possible, but not likely. Trying to still the panic in her chest, Cassie glanced around. The skirting boards were filthy. Crouching down, she applied herself to the task of cleaning those too. Her efforts would barely scratch the surface without scouring cream, though – after years' worth of dirt collecting on them, the grime was ingrained – but at least they would be free of dust, which might be bad for the baby's health.

She was applying herself to a particularly stubborn section when she heard Kim return with Samuel. Straightening up, Cassie smiled as her eyes lighted on him. He was such a little angel. Just like his father. Her heart hitched painfully.

'Cassie... you don't have to do that.'

'Oh, I don't mind.' Cassie went across to wash her hands at the sink. 'I thought I'd make myself useful while I was here, and it keeps me out of mischief,' she said, grabbing some paper towels to dry them as she walked across to her grandson. 'Doesn't it, my gorgeous little one? Do you want to come for a walk with Nana and Mummy, darling?' she asked him. 'See all the colourful boats bobbing on the water?'

Kim passed him across to her, and she nestled him in her arms, kissing his forehead softly and breathing in the special baby smell of him. Immediately she was transported back to this time with Josh, when she'd promised to love and protect him. She'd let him down. *I won't let your son down, Josh*, she told him now.

'Actually, I was wondering...' Kim looked at her hesitantly. 'Do you mind if we postpone?'

Glancing back at her, Cassie noticed that she looked pale. 'No, no problem. Are you all right? You're not poorly, are you?'

'I'm fine.' Kim assured her. 'Just a bit tired,' she added, stifling a yawn. 'I was up a lot with Samuel last night.'

Cassie nodded understandingly. 'You're bound to be. I was looking forward to taking him out, but of course we can postpone if you're not up to it.'

'Thanks, Cassie.' Kim smiled. 'I knew you'd understand. I thought we could have a bit of a chat instead and then maybe visit the cemetery later.' She glanced down, fresh tears brimming in her eyes. 'I don't know why, but I'm really missing him today.'

'I'd like that,' Cassie said, smiling back at her. In reality, it would crucify her. She hadn't been able to bring herself to go there since the funeral. But going with Kim might be a good thing, therapeutic for both of them. It would also give her the opportunity to dig a little deeper regarding her relationship with Jemma.

Kim was watching her. 'You know, Cassie, if there's ever anything you want to confide in me about, you'll find I'm a good listener,' she said, with a look of earnest sympathy. 'And I promise you I'm the soul of discretion.'

Cassie looked at her slightly disbelievingly. Hadn't she said these exact same words to Adam?

CHAPTER TWENTY-THREE

Jemma

'He's sleeping like a baby,' Ryan joked, coming into the kitchen having performed a small miracle upstairs.

Or rather, like babies were supposed to sleep. Jemma sighed inwardly, despairing of her own inability to work the magic Ryan did and lull their baby into slumber. Smiling her appreciation at his parenting skills, she straightened up from the dishwasher and rolled her shoulders. She loved her job as a teaching assistant, but it had been a full-on day at school, followed by a full-on evening with Liam. Nothing she could do seemed to settle him. 'Thank you,' she said. 'I have no idea how you do it, but I'm so glad that you do.'

Ryan walked across to her. 'It's easier to be less stressed when you don't have the brunt of the parenting duties.' Easing her unruly tangle of hair aside, he kissed the nape of her neck, and then placed his hands on her shoulders and massaged her knotted muscles with his thumbs. 'Sorry I was late back. I had to wait until the engineers were finished. Why don't you grab yourself a glass of wine and have a soak in a hot bath.'

Jemma understood why his job as chief railway technician meant unpredictable hours, but the long days, rotational night shifts and frequent call-outs left her with most of the responsibility for Liam. That she was consumed with guilt at having to leave her baby all day while she worked didn't help her stress levels when

Liam was fractious and reluctant to feed. She felt neglectful, incompetent. He was so small and vulnerable. Her heart wrenched when he cried, and yet she – his own mother – couldn't seem to soothe him. Surely there must be something wrong with her. The midwife had assured her that the maternal bond wasn't always there instantaneously, that sometimes it took a little longer for the special connection between mother and baby to form, especially after a difficult birth. It was perfectly normal, she'd said encouragingly. It would happen, and then she would wonder why she'd worried so much.

It would, Jemma tried to reassure herself as Ryan's gentle ministrations eased the tension in her shoulders. Liam was a beautiful baby, smiley and content in his father's company. She hadn't planned him, any more than she'd planned her last pregnancy, but she loved him so fiercely she knew she would die to protect him.

A crushing sense of sadness washed through her as she thought about the child she'd lost. She'd wanted that baby. Wanted him so much after feeling that first flutter like butterflies in her tummy. She'd vowed she would do a better job of parenting than her own workaholic mother had. Jemma knew she had never really been wanted. In her more charitable moments, she'd thought that perhaps her mother hadn't realised the full impact a child would have on her busy life. She vowed to make time for her own children, to be everything a child needed in a mother. To love them unconditionally.

And she'd loved Noah. Some people didn't understand why she'd insisted on naming him; why she grieved so deeply over a baby so small she could cradle him in the palm of her hand. Her own mother included. When Jemma had tried to talk to her about how she felt – desolate and empty, filled with feelings of hopelessness – she'd thoughtlessly pointed out that the pregnancy hadn't gone full-term. Her face had been perplexed, as if she genuinely couldn't comprehend that Jemma's body had gone through all the changes of pregnancy, that hormones had flooded her body, regardless of the outcome. After talking to her doctor, Jemma eventually understood that she was suffering from post-natal depression.

Some of those feelings had crept back since she'd had Liam. They weren't as severe, but they were there. The feelings of not being able to cope were the worst. But she had to, even when she felt as if she didn't have the energy. She couldn't put Ryan through all that again. She hadn't realised how much he was hurting, how much he was grieving, until she'd visited the cemetery to find him weeping at the spot that marked their baby's grave. Having been brought up in care, he'd only ever wanted to be part of a family, a home to call his own. Despite his upbringing, possibly because he'd been starved of parental affection, he was so caring and kind…

'Better?' he asked her softly.

'Much,' she said, turning to rest her head on his shoulder. She really did love him, couldn't imagine being without him. She wouldn't ever lose sight of what mattered again.

CHAPTER TWENTY-FOUR

Joshua

February 2019

Josh parked in the secluded lane just outside the village, and waited, as instructed, though not very patiently. Checking the clock on his dash, he realised it had stopped working again. He sighed and checked the time on his phone instead. Maybe it should be no big surprise that she didn't want any kind of future with him, a bloke who drove around in an ancient PT Cruiser and lived in rented accommodation. Adam had offered to help him get a more reliable car, but Josh didn't feel comfortable taking money from him. He had to learn to stand on his own two feet. He'd been determined to, in fact, particularly after his mother had said she doubted he would cope without someone to cook for him and clean up after him. It was said in the heat of the moment, but even so, it had hurt. He'd tried to help out after her operation, which was when her obsession with having the house clean had seemed to kick in, but she had just been way too fastidious. He was coping, he'd told Adam. Privately, though, he didn't actually feel he was. His personal life was a disaster and he had no idea what to do about any of it, other than what his conscience told him.

Would she come? Nervous as well as agitated, he wiped the condensation from his windscreen and squinted through it for any sign of her. He almost had minor heart failure as his headlights caught something or someone shrinking back into the woodland beside the lane. A fox, probably. He was getting jumpy, imagining he was being followed. It was no wonder, he supposed, when he was sneaking about like a thief in the night, meeting up with her in the middle of nowhere.

Concerned for her safety, nevertheless, he decided to walk down the lane to meet her. It wasn't far from her new house, so she'd said she would be coming on foot. The area was dark and remote, the nearest properties the Plough and Dog pub and then nothing but a deserted farm. Whatever was happening between them, he didn't like to think of her walking around here on her own. He couldn't be a hundred per cent sure it was a fox slinking about in the woods.

He'd only gone a few yards when he saw her hurrying around the bend towards him. She hesitated when she spotted him, hugged her coat tight around her, then glanced over her shoulder and walked on, not over-enthusiastically.

'That keen to see me then?' he joked when she reached him. It was met with a scathing glance.

'What are you doing, Josh?' Jemma demanded, her violet eyes peering out through her tangle of blonde hair like those of a hostile animal. Josh guessed that pretty much indicated how she felt about him. Whatever happened to the open-faced girl who was beautiful without seeming to know it? he wondered. She was still beautiful, undeniably, but now she seemed hard-edged and cynical. Had that always been there and he'd just been too blind to see it?

'You weren't on your way to my house, were you?' she asked. 'Because if you were—'

'No!' Josh failed to curtail his anger. 'I got the message, Jemma. Loud and clear.' He looked her over, guessing there wasn't much affection in his own eyes. Right now, he was close to hating her, yet at the same time, he'd never stopped loving her, ever since he'd fallen for her in their first year of college. Even when she'd dumped him, going out with Ryan instead, because he was working and renting his own place, he'd kept on loving her. Why? 'I was looking out for you, that's all.' He shrugged disconsolately. 'It's an isolated area and...' He stopped. Why was he bothering to offer explanations? 'I won't come to your house, Jemma. I said I wouldn't, and I won't.'

She looked him over suspiciously, and then nodded.

He'd done some small thing right in her eyes at last. He didn't want to keep arguing. He just wanted to find a way forward that didn't include him disappearing off the face of the earth, which was what she appeared to want him to do. 'Do you want to talk in the car?' he asked, nodding towards it.

She shook her head hard, and Josh sighed heavily. She didn't want to be reminded of the time they'd made love in it, he supposed. At least that was what he'd thought they were doing.

'So?' He looked at her curiously, wondering what she'd come to say. Something, presumably, since she'd finally agreed to meet with him.

Still gauging him warily, she didn't answer for a second. Then, 'What do you want, Josh?' she asked.

Josh stared at her, incredulous. 'What do I *want*?' he repeated, his anger almost off the scale despite his best efforts to stay calm. 'You really did think I was going to just walk away, didn't you? Why did you tell me?' he went on, before she could answer. 'What was it *you* wanted, Jemma? Because I'm buggered if I know.'

'I...' Jemma looked away. 'I don't know. I wasn't sure what I was going to do. And then—'

'Right,' Josh cut in abruptly. 'So when you'd made up your mind, presumably having first decided to keep your options open, you told me to piss off. Does that sound right to you, Jemma? In any sense of the word, does it sound fair?'

'No. I...' Jemma's gaze flicked back to him, and then quickly away again. 'I hoped you would walk away, I suppose. For Ryan's sake.'

Josh stared hard at her. She was looking uncomfortable, and no wonder. Aside from the fact that this was basically emotional blackmail, did she not realise that he would never be able to look Ryan in the eye again? That twisted his gut, the fact that he'd betrayed his friend, even if Jemma had told him her marriage was over, that they couldn't get past losing their first child. It might not have been a conscious lie – she and Ryan *were* separated – but she'd used Josh, and he still struggled to understand why. She'd needed some company, a shoulder to cry on after all that she'd gone through, he got that, but did she have to bloody well choose his? Christ, he'd been an idiot.

'Why did you do it, Jem?' he asked her, his voice choked. He guessed he didn't need to clarify what he meant.

'I don't know,' she repeated forlornly. 'I was confused, grieving. I didn't mean—'

'Not half as confused as I am,' Josh grated.

'I'm *sorry*,' Jemma blurted tearfully. 'I was depressed, Josh. I'd lost a child. I was drinking too much, trying to *feel* something other than totally bereft. I didn't mean for any of this to happen; to hurt you. Please try to understand. If you insist on being involved, it will only end up hurting everyone.'

Being involved? Josh laughed scornfully. He couldn't *be* more involved, for Christ's sake. She was having his *baby*. 'I can't do it, Jemma,' he said, his eyes not leaving hers, making sure that she knew he meant it. 'I can't just turn my back.' No way, he thought determinedly. He'd always sworn he would never cause any child of his the pain his father had caused him, making it obvious by his complete absence from his life that he was an insignificant nothing to him. 'I want to be part of my child's life. I have a right to be.'

Jemma's expression was intense, a mixture of anger and frustration. Clearly she had been banking on him shirking his responsibility. Did he really come across as the kind of person who would do that? He had no clue any more how the bloody hell he came across. He thought he was doing everything right by Jemma. He'd evidently got it all wrong. He thought he'd behaved reasonably with Kim. He hadn't said he loved her, because he didn't. In truth, he'd felt manipulated into sleeping with her, which sounded ridiculous. She'd told him she loved him, though, after their steamy sex, and had obviously been upset when he hadn't responded. He was beginning to think he needed relationship counselling – as in how to have a relationship without majorly pissing women off.

'You'll ruin my life!' Jemma shouted, causing a bird in the trees above them to take flight. 'You'll ruin *Ryan's* life. Can you imagine what it will do to him if he finds out? Do you even care?' Swiping a tear from her cheek, she glared hard at him.

His anger now very close to boiling over, Josh cautioned himself not to lose it. 'I care, Jemma, more than you give me credit for,' he said tersely. *Though it's pretty clear that you don't give a damn about what all of this is doing to me*, he didn't bother to add. 'I'm sorry.' He steeled his resolve. 'I'm not prepared to walk away. I can't. What kind of person would that make me?'

'A selfish one!' Jemma cried.

'Right.' Josh smiled cynically, and turned his gaze to the sky. There were no stars out. Everything looked pretty shitty black from where he was standing.

'Will you tell him?' Jemma asked shakily.

Tugging in a ragged breath, Josh looked back at her. 'He's going to find out eventually,' he said quietly. 'He can't fail to.'

Jemma didn't speak for what seemed like an eternity. Then, 'I wish I was dead,' she said wretchedly.

Josh's heart dropped. 'Jemma…' He moved towards her. 'Please don't talk like—'

She whirled around. 'I wish *you* were!' she seethed, scrambling to get away from him. 'God help you if Ryan does find out. You'd better make yourself scarce, Josh. I would if I were you.'

CHAPTER TWENTY-FIVE

Cassandra

Something wasn't right. Cassie couldn't shake the feeling that her life was unravelling, that events seemed to be conspiring against her, pushing her already fragile emotions right to the edge. The texts and the shoplifting incident – assuming she hadn't had a mental aberration and truly stolen the straighteners – coming at the very time she was trying to hold on by her fingernails, for the sake of her grandson, as well as her sanity, had to have been prompted by Josh's death. The woman was clearly after recompense, money she should have had had Cassie been in a position to pay what she'd promised. What she would have paid had the local tabloid she'd had several articles lined up with not folded.

She hadn't answered the last text, but she couldn't hide away from the fact that her past, no matter how hard she had tried to erase it, might catch up with her. The only way to make it go away was to face it full on. But how could she do that when she couldn't be sure who was texting? She had to talk to her, but first she had to establish where she was, and whether she was still clean. If she wasn't, she might need money fast, in which case Cassie might not have much time before the woman made good on her obvious threat to sell her story.

Taking a calming breath, she debated, and then rang an old colleague, who now wrote a regular financial advice column and who wouldn't mind doing her a favour, especially knowing her circumstances. She hated asking her on that basis, but she had to do something – prepare herself at least for whatever this woman might want.

'Michelle Rearden.' Her colleague answered her phone straight away, sounding as sharp and efficient as ever. Cassie, by contrast, felt dulled, her mind careering from frantic suspicion of Adam, searching for signs he might leave her, to stultified fear and confusion. She had to pull herself together if she wanted to stop her marriage from crumbling. Move on, impossible though it felt, from the tragedy that had caused it to fracture. She couldn't do that with this cloud hanging over her.

'Hi, Shell, it's Cassie,' she said, trying to inject some brightness into her voice.

'Cas!' Shell exclaimed delightedly. Then, 'Oh God, Cas, I'm so sorry about Josh. You must be absolutely devastated.'

'Thanks, Shell. I am,' Cassie admitted, tears welling.

Michelle's voice was full of sympathy. 'Do you want to meet up, lovely? Have a good chat over a bottle of wine?'

'I'd love to,' Cassie said, thinking it might be therapeutic to catch up. 'I confess I called for a small favour, though. I hope you don't think I'm taking liberties. I'm trying to get back to work and… well, I hoped you wouldn't mind.'

'Of course I don't,' Michelle assured her. 'You dug me out of enough holes in the past. Shoot.'

Cassie braced herself. 'There's this woman I'm trying to get background on. I wondered if you could run a financial check on her. I'm not sure whether it's going anywhere yet, but it would be useful information.'

'Consider it done,' Michelle said confidently. 'Give me twenty minutes and I'll call you back.'

After relaying details from the woman's online profile, Cassie waited, her heart thrumming in her chest. Fifteen minutes later,

Michelle called. 'She scores badly,' she said. 'Several debts and two county court judgements.'

'Thought as much. That's really useful. Thanks, Shell. I owe you,' Cassie replied calmly, though with her fears confirmed, her heart was now banging. Whether or not the woman was using drugs, she was evidently in desperate need of money. It *had* to be her who'd been texting. Cassie couldn't imagine it being anyone else.

'You can get the first round in,' Michelle said. 'It all sounds very intriguing. You'll have to fill me in when we meet.'

'Will do,' Cassie promised. 'I'll give you a call and we'll arrange something. I'm just off to meet Adam.'

'Bless him. Give him my love and a huge hug for me.'

'He could probably use one,' Cassie said, feeling very much in need of one herself.

Signing off, she sat frozen in her car, trying to work out her next move. She had to talk to the woman. Undoubtedly she would have to pay her off. Was she likely to just go away, though, even if Cassie did give her what she wanted? If she was still dependent on drugs, wasn't she more likely to come back for more, until Cassie had nothing left to give?

Her home might end up being at risk, hers and Adam's, as well as her job. Her marriage was already at risk. If this all came out, it would be over. Why had she done it? She'd wanted to turn back, so many times she'd wanted to tell the truth, but the more lies she'd told, the more tangled the web became, until she didn't know how to extract herself.

She'd only ever wanted to protect those she loved. No, she hadn't. Shame washed through her as she caught herself in another lie. She'd wanted to protect herself – from the anger and the hurt she would see in their eyes when they learnt of her lies. From the pain of losing what mattered most in the world to her. They could never have forgiven her. And now, that was exactly what she was suffering.

She couldn't bear this. She wasn't strong enough. But she had to be. She couldn't lose Samuel. Had to try to hold onto Adam. She had to meet this woman face to face. And if the woman threatened what she most feared, then she would meet those threats with whatever she had to.

That decision made, she breathed deeply and braced herself to make her next call. Shakily she selected Jemma's number. She wasn't sure why Kim had lied to her, but her instinct told her she had. She had no doubt that Samuel was Josh's child. He really was the living, breathing image of him. The rest, she just wasn't sure. And she was scared.

CHAPTER TWENTY-SIX

Kimberley

Kim was growing worried. Going into the kitchen, she found Cassie cleaning the kitchen cupboards. Every nook and cranny of them. She'd also cleaned the conservatory windows, which Kim was happy to let her do if she really felt compelled to. She'd been a bit perturbed when she'd found her balancing on Adam's ladder, spraying Cif onto the high mid beam running across the roof. It was yellow with tobacco stains, she'd told her, straining to reach to wipe them. It hadn't even occurred to Kim to notice, but Cassie obviously had. She was like a woman on a mission.

She'd been the same the last time she was here. Kim couldn't help but notice how she'd collected up the plates when they'd barely finished the cake she'd brought with her. She'd then run a bowlful of water to wash them, where Kim would have just swilled them off, and proceeded to spray antibacterial spray on the work surfaces before wiping those vigorously down. It was obviously her way of channelling her emotions. Kim supposed the shoplifting arrest had kicked off her manic behaviour. Her nerves must be shot to shreds. She'd been shaking when she'd confided in Kim, convinced that she would be worried about the consequences for Samuel, that it would impact on Cassie's relationship with him.

'What consequences?' Kim had blinked at her, mystified. 'It will be some time before he can spell the word shoplifting, let alone understand what it means,' she'd told her reassuringly, adding that she doubted anyone would be taking him aside when he was ten and informing him that his nana had a criminal record. Cassie hadn't looked very reassured, even when Kim had added that the gossip would soon die down in favour of the next neighbourhood scandal. Kim guessed she would also be worrying about the impact on her relationship with Adam, who'd clearly been knocked sideways by the whole distasteful event.

'Would you like some tea, Cassie?' she ventured, as the woman paused, wiping a rubber-gloved hand across her forehead and eyeing up the front of the cooker. God, surely she wasn't going to start on that?

Cassie eyed her distractedly, then, 'No thanks, Kim. I'm fine,' she said with a wan smile, 'but you have one. I'm all finished over there.' She nodded towards the kettle, which had a polished sheen.

'I'm good. I'll make one later.' Cassie would be bound to wipe up after her, she thought. She was only here while Adam finished off the fitted wardrobe he was installing in the bedroom, so she wouldn't be wielding her cloth much longer, thank goodness. 'Oh, I've asked Adam if you wouldn't mind dropping me off at the doctor's surgery on your way home,' she said, making sure Cassie knew she hadn't got time to start on the oven. 'Hope that's okay.'

'Of course.' Cassie looked slightly alarmed. 'I could come in with you if you like.'

Kim sighed inside. Obviously she assumed it was an appointment for Samuel. 'That's really kind of you, Cassie.' She smiled, though she had to force it a bit. She was, she had to admit, beginning to feel just the tiniest bit claustrophobic. 'It's a personal appointment, though.'

'Oh.' Cassie nodded thoughtfully. 'Well, I could still come, if you fancy some company. We could take Samuel to the park afterwards. And then get some—'

'No,' Kim said, more stridently than she'd intended, and then, noting the other woman's hurt expression, tempered her tone. 'Thanks, Cassie, but I'm meeting a friend afterwards.'

'Ah, I see. Jemma?' she enquired, clearly trying to sound casual. Now Kim was really worried. Why was Cassie so fixated on Jemma Anderson?

CHAPTER TWENTY-SEVEN

Did Adam realise how oddly Cassie was behaving? Kim wondered. It had to be affecting him too. Going into the bedroom with the coffee she'd decided to brave the kitchen for, she wondered whether it might be time to alert him. Noting that he'd taken his shirt off and was working in his T-shirt, she felt a bit guilty. She'd turned the heating up after Cassie had opened windows downstairs.

'Are you too hot?' she asked him.

'Sorry, what?' Caught unawares, Adam turned around to face her.

'The heating. Would you like me to turn it down? Cassie had the windows open, so I turned it up. It's probably way too warm for you working up here, though.'

'Ah right.' Adam nodded as if he wasn't surprised. He did know his wife was becoming neurotic about cleanliness then. Mind you, there'd been so much grease on Kim's mum's kitchen floor, the soles of her shoes had squelched. Kim supposed she might not be qualified to judge the difference between diligent and obsessive cleaning.

'I'm good.' Wiping his forearm across his forehead, Adam smiled. 'You can always throw a bucket of water over me if I pass out. Thanks for the coffee.'

'No problem.' Kim smiled back. As long as he didn't ask Cassie to throw a bucket of water over him. It would probably be ninety-nine per cent bleach. 'So are you doing anything over the weekend?' she asked him as he went back to work on the wardrobe.

'Nothing much,' Adam said, reaching to push a screw into the sliding mechanism at the top.

Kim couldn't help but notice his muscular arms as he did. He was extremely handsome. He had that hair-greying-at-the-sides thing going on, soft crinkles at the corners of his eyes and a twinkle when he smiled. It was now clear that he absolutely was the caring man that Josh had told her he was. He was a good man, the type of man a woman could depend on. They were few and far between, in Kim's mind. She had to wonder why he would stick with a woman who didn't seem to care for him. Cassie was clearly oblivious to the impact her behaviour might be having on him. Kim was surprised he hadn't already given up in despair.

Was Cassie aware that there were many women out there who would snap him up in an instant? She didn't seem to care how she looked either. She could easily make more of herself, wear a bit more make-up. Some colour on her cheeks definitely wouldn't go amiss. And she should make a hairdresser's appointment. Kim had first thought her short style suited her; it defined her cheekbones. She'd looked like a woman in control. Now, though, she was becoming pale and drawn, and acting like a woman *out* of control. Some auburn highlights would look great against the dark brown. Or blonde, possibly, which would lift her face. She was pretty, Kim considered, but she could be really attractive if she put some effort into it, which didn't seem to occur to her. She really should channel her energies into herself, rather than worrying about a bit of muck and dust here and there, which was hardly going to kill anybody. But then it suited Kim's purposes that Cassie was so distracted. She'd be superglued to her side otherwise.

'I was going to come over here and finish the wardrobe,' Adam went on, 'assuming you were okay with it. But then I remembered it was Cassie's birthday. I suppose I should try and organise something.'

'Oh my God, you should! Take her away for the weekend, why don't you? That would be dead romantic.' Kim sighed wistfully, though she was actually thinking that this was the perfect opportunity for her to grab a little space back.

Adam furrowed his brow as he thought about it. 'Nice idea,' he said, crouching to check the runner at the bottom. 'Bit short notice, though.'

'No it isn't,' Kim insisted. 'The whole thing is about the element of surprise, and there are loads of cosy country hotels quite close to here, so you wouldn't have to go far.'

Adam got to his feet and nodded thoughtfully. He was going for it.

'I reckon Cassie deserves to be pampered a bit after all she's been through,' Kim said, giving him a little more incentive.

'The Boots thing, you mean?' His eyes narrowed as he turned to look at her.

Kim glanced down. 'That, yes,' she said, nodding sadly. 'It must have really shaken her. I was thinking more of Josh, though, which was obviously what sparked the whole awful incident off. You should book a spa weekend,' she hurried on. 'Tell you what, I'll google some hotels and you could book it now. I bet Cassie will be thrilled. I know I would.'

'But what about you?' Adam asked worriedly.

He really was a sweetie. 'Well, it's lovely of you to ask, but don't you think three might be a crowd?' Kim teased. Noting his awkward expression, she backtracked. 'I was joking, Adam. I'll be fine. My dad doesn't know where I am, I promise.' Guessing that was what he was concerned about, she stepped towards him and gave his arm a reassuring squeeze. 'My sister's invited me to stay with her at their cottage in Wales, in any case. I was going to take Jack with me for company, but then I wasn't sure whether to go, because I didn't want Cassie to worry.' She paused, and went on hesitantly, 'Don't get me wrong, Cassie's lovely, really kind and attentive, but...'

'But?' Adam eyed her curiously.

'To be honest, I would really appreciate a bit of space. She's, um,' Kim took a breath and then took the bull by the horns, 'a bit house proud, isn't she?'

Adam looked taken aback for a second. Then, 'It's just because she cares,' he said with a small smile.

'I'm not complaining. I understand why she would be,' Kim said quickly.

'Don't worry, I get it,' Adam assured her. 'She's been worse than ever since…'

Seeing his eyes darken, the way they did whenever he talked about Josh, Kim felt her heart squeeze for him. 'All the more reason to take her away,' she urged him.

'Are you sure you and Samuel will be okay, though?' Adam searched her eyes. His really were striking – kind, steel blue and full of concern.

'I'm a big girl, Adam,' she assured him. 'We'll both be fine. I'll call you if I need to.' Debating, she hesitated for a second, and then reached to give him a firm hug. 'Thank you,' she murmured, appreciating him even if no one else seemed to, 'for everything. I'd be lost without you.'

Adam smiled awkwardly. 'No problem,' he said, and then, '*Shit*,' he muttered, his gaze shooting towards the door

Cassie coughed pointedly. 'Your son was crying,' she said, as Adam stepped smartly back and Kim turned apprehensively to face her. 'I thought you might have heard him.' Her gaze ice cool, she looked between the two of them. 'But you were obviously otherwise occupied.'

CHAPTER TWENTY-EIGHT

Cassandra

'You've booked it? Without asking me?' Cassie stared at Adam in astonishment. She couldn't believe that he'd gone ahead and made arrangements without discussing it with her first.

'I thought you'd be pleased.' Adam's look was somewhere between crestfallen and frustrated. 'You need a break, Cas. It's a spa weekend. It will do you good. Do us both—'

'But there's no way I can go away for a whole weekend and leave Kim on her own,' Cassie pointed out, feeling confused and panicky as she went to turn off the oven timer, which was pinging manically and driving her to distraction.

'Why?' Adam asked shortly.

'Because…' Cassie wasn't sure why. Why the hard knot of fear that was constantly lodged in her chest kept tightening. She felt as if she were waiting for a guillotine to drop, that she needed to be constantly on alert. 'I know she's doing her best,' she went on, sounding as flustered as she felt, 'but you must see she's not that competent yet. She left him crying, for goodness' sake.'

'Babies cry, Cassie,' Adam said tiredly.

Cassie's heart sank. He obviously thought she was overreacting, that she was being overbearing and overemotional. Kim clearly did too, since they'd apparently organised this together, thinking she was in need of a break after the shoplifting incident – which in their minds she was guilty of. 'He was due his feed,' she said, sure that she wasn't being any of those things. Her only concern was for Samuel. 'He needed changing. I can't go, Adam. I'm sorry, I just wouldn't rest.'

Adam plunged his hands in his pockets and eyed the ceiling. 'It's in Malvern, Cassie. It's half an hour's drive away. It was supposed to be a surprise for your birthday.'

'And what if something happens while I'm lounging around in a bathrobe?' she asked him. 'If there's some kind of emergency?'

'You get dressed?' Adam suggested, with a half-hearted smile.

Cassie's heart sank another inch. She was disappointing him again. She wanted to go to the spa. There was nothing more she wanted than to be able to just sit back and relax, but with everything that had happened lately… 'What if there's an accident?' she asked him. 'Or Samuel gets sick and she can't get hold of us?'

'We'll have our mobiles,' Adam reminded her, his frustration growing, as indicated by the hand going through his hair. 'We can always call her, and we can leave a message with reception if it's a low signal area.'

'A low signal area?' Cassie felt the blood drain from her body. She'd been desperately trying to get hold of Jemma, who hadn't returned her calls. She was already worried to death about the ominous text messages and the catastrophic consequences there might be, without having to worry about Kim having some kind of crisis.

'Which is highly unlikely,' Adam added, sounding now utterly exasperated.

'I can't go, Adam.' Cassie turned to the oven to retrieve the chicken Kiev before it was burned.

'Right.' Adam sighed again, heavily. 'Well that was a waste of time, wasn't it?'

Lowering the oven pan onto the cooker hob, making herself ignore the spitting fat, Cassie turned around to find Adam looking extremely dejected, and felt awful. He'd done this for her, and she was acting like an ungrateful cow. She couldn't go, though. It was more than concern for Samuel. She didn't know what, but she just couldn't escape the cold feeling in the pit of her stomach that some disaster was looming.

'I'm sorry,' she said, wishing she had a way to explain that wouldn't make her sound as emotionally unstable as he plainly thought she was. 'It was a sweet gesture, Adam, and I really appreciate it, but I would only worry.'

Adam nodded slowly. 'Cassie, I understand why you would, really I do,' he said kindly, 'but nothing's going to happen. And if it does, Kim's a grown woman. She's already told me she's going away herself this week. She's promised to call us, so there really is no reason you can't spend a little time looking after yourself.'

Going away? Taken aback, Cassie stared at him. Kim had mentioned this to Adam and not her? The hairs rose over her skin. Try as she might to dismiss it, the intimate exchange between them in the bedroom came jarringly back to mind. They'd been having an in-depth discussion about her, she realised, an excruciating stab of jealousy piercing her heart. 'Going away where?' she asked, breathing deeply, trying to stop the tears from spilling over. 'Kim didn't say anything to me. Neither of you did.'

Adam scanned her eyes, his own wary. 'To her sister's. In Wales.'

'Her *sister's*?' But Kim had never said she had a sister. 'She can't go,' she said emphatically. 'All the way to Wales on her own? On public transport? It's too risky.'

'All the way…?' Adam looked at her askance. 'Cassie, you're—'

'I need to speak to her.' Cassie fetched her car keys from their hook on the utility room door and flew past him to the hall.

Adam followed her. 'Cassie, stop,' he said quietly as she reached for her coat.

She couldn't stop. She had to see her. She had no idea what was going on here, but one thing she did know was that however hard she tried, for some reason it appeared she was in the wrong.

'Cassie…' Adam tried again as she turned to the door. 'Christ almighty!' he shouted. 'Are you trying to drive her away as well!'

Cassie froze, her insides turning over.

'Jesus. I shouldn't have said that.' He came towards her. 'I'm sorry. I didn't mean…'

'Yes you did.' Wrapping her arms about herself, Cassie swallowed back a sharp lump in her throat.

'You're pushing people away, Cassie,' Adam said, his voice gruff. 'I understand why, but you're being possessive, obsessive. Don't do this, storm around there and try to dictate what she can and can't do. You'll lose her.'

You'll lose me. Cassie heard another dire warning, and her heart twisted with terror at the thought of losing the man she loved, had always loved. They would both leave her. A cold sense of foreboding shivered through her.

CHAPTER TWENTY-NINE

With its humid air and soothing aromas that claimed to ease tension in the body, the steam chamber at the spa had lived up to its promise. Despite her worries, Cassie was actually relaxing, feeling more like her old self, before all the bad things had started happening. Listening to Adam across the room pouring them both a glass of chilled wine, she kept her eyes closed, enjoying the stillness, the luxury of having absolutely nothing to do.

She heard him walk across to her, sensed him setting the wine down on the bedside table, and then felt the bed dip as he sat on the side of it next to her. 'How are you doing?' he asked her.

Her eyelids fluttering open, Cassie smiled up at him. Noting that his eyes weren't full of the pain she'd seen there almost permanently since they'd lost Josh, she felt a huge sense of relief. He'd been devastated by Josh's death, tried so hard to pick up the pieces and carry on when she'd been falling apart, and then he'd been devastated all over again by her odd behaviour and the ridiculous notion that she'd turned into a kleptomaniac. She'd tried to explain on the drive here about the first shoplifting incident, how distracted she'd been, her mind on her diagnosis and where that might leave Josh and him. She told him again that she hadn't stolen the hair straighteners, needing him to believe her. She still wasn't sure he did, that he imagined she might have taken them subconsciously because of the hair loss. The frightening thing was, she wasn't a hundred per cent sure he might not be right. She'd been distracted lately too, cleaning obsessively in an attempt to assuage her grief and her guilt; the gnawing suspicion eating away at her. Her mind felt like wet cotton wool half the time, incapable of concentrating on anything but her physical endeavours and the release exhaustion might bring. Sleep, though, only ever came to haunt her.

She'd hoped that Samuel might help her channel her energies, fill the void in her life. Adam had been right about that too. She was obsessing about him, or rather about Kim and what she was doing wrong. But Samuel wasn't her child. He was Kim's. Kim would want to do things her own way. She had to back off a little, allow Kim the space she needed, if she didn't want her to disappear from her life; for Adam to decide he'd had enough too. That thought truly terrified her, because without him and Samuel, she would have no reason to keep living.

She looked him over, her heart twisting with a combination of love and fear. She took in his strong profile, which was an indication of the type of man he was: reliable; driven by his powerful work ethic to be successful, but never afraid to take time out, to be there when his family needed him. He was a catch for any woman. He had no family now apart from her, and she was slowly torturing him. She had to stop. Pull herself together and be there for him. Assuming he still wanted her.

What was he thinking? He seemed far away, lost in his own thoughts. 'Penny for them?' she asked, placing a hand on his arm. 'I can see the wheels going round,' she added as he glanced curiously at her. 'You obviously have something on your mind.'

The serious look in his eyes caused her heart to stall. 'I do,' he said, after an agonising second. 'But I'm not sure whether it might have to be censored.'

Seeing the slow smile curving his mouth, Cassie's heart started beating again. 'Try me,' she said, reaching to graze his cheek softly with her hand.

'I was wondering…' Adam paused, catching her hand and pressing his lips to it, 'how you would react to my giving you a relaxing massage.'

Cassie scanned his eyes and saw a flicker of uncertainty, but also found what she was looking for: desire. 'Pleasurably.' She smiled. 'The thing is, how much do you charge?'

Adam laughed, with obvious relief. 'It's gratis,' he assured her, leaning in, his hand seeking the tie on her towelling robe. 'All part of the room service.'

'Remind me to give you a rating,' she murmured as his mouth found hers.

He was taking his time, kissing his way down the side of her neck, gently seeking her breasts, when her phone rang shrilly to her side.

Cassie's heart jumped. Instinctively she wriggled away from him to snatch it up.

'Cassie, it's me,' Kim said. 'Everything's fine, but…'

'But what?' Hearing the tone of her voice, as if she were preparing her for bad news, Cassie swung her legs off the bed.

'It's Samuel,' Kim went on, causing her breath to catch in her chest. 'He's fine now, he had a rash, but I had my phone off while I was at the hospital, and—'

'Oh my God.' Cassie's blood froze in her veins. 'Which hospital? Where are you?'

'*Dammit.*' She heard Adam cursing behind her as he rolled off the bed in search of his clothes.

'At my sister's.' Kim sounded defensive, as if she hadn't just told Cassie that her grandson had needed hospital treatment.

'You need to come back.' Cassie clenched her hand hard around the phone. 'I *knew* something like this would happen. What on earth were you doing, taking him away on some impulsive trip to—'

'Do you not want to know how he is?' Kim interrupted, now sounding belligerent, like a child, for God's sake. What was the matter with her? Did she not realise how worried Cassie would be?

'Of course I want to know how he is.' Cassie tried to keep the agitation from her voice. 'I'd prefer to *see* how he is, though, obviously.' A *rash*? If they'd discharged him, it wasn't what she'd first dreaded it might be, but doctors weren't infallible. 'Text me the address. I'll come and fetch you.'

'You're annoyed,' Kim said dejectedly.

Cassie drew in a breath. 'I'm concerned, Kim. I'm bound to be. If you'd wanted a break, I would have come with you. It's bad enough taking a baby away as a two-parent family, but on your own? And with Samuel so tiny…'

'But Adam was fine with it,' Kim countered. 'He wanted to take you—'

'Well Adam *shouldn't* have been okay with it.' Cassie glanced despairingly at him. 'You should have discussed it with me first, Kim. At least have let me know.' She stopped, cautioning herself to calm down. 'Look, let's just get you and Samuel back home and we'll talk about all this later.'

Kim didn't answer.

'Kim?' Hearing nothing but silence at the other end, Cassie's stomach turned over. 'Kim, are you still there?' But she wasn't. Cassie knew she wasn't. She'd ended the call.

Quickly Cassie called her back, glancing at Adam as she did. He looked as desperate as she felt. Her heart dropped like a stone as the call went to voicemail. 'She's not answering. She's not answering and we don't have her address!'

Keying in a text, she turned to dash to the wardrobe.

'Cas, calm down,' Adam said behind her as she yanked her clothes from the hangers. 'What's happened?'

Her heart thumping, Cassie grabbed her overnight bag from the wardrobe shelf and hurried past him to the bed. 'He had a rash. Lord knows what other symptoms if she was worried enough to take him to the hospital. She says he's fine, but how do we know they might not have missed something? I will never forgive myself if…' She gulped back a sob. 'I should never have let her go.' She turned back to Adam. 'You shouldn't!'

CHAPTER THIRTY

Joshua

April 2019

Josh's feelings were a mixture of bewilderment and exasperation as he waited again at the request of a woman. This time, ironically, at the front of the Plough and Dog pub at the end of the lane where he'd waited hopefully to meet Jemma, only to have her wish him dead. He'd managed to speak to her only once since then, when he'd asked her to at least let him see the baby, to allow him some kind of future contact, even if unofficially. She'd been staggered. 'And you think Ryan wouldn't find out then?' she'd said, sounding astonished that he would even suggest it. 'I'm sorry, Josh, I really am, but it's just not possible.'

'He'll find out if I'm forced to consult a solicitor,' Josh had pointed out, though he'd very much wanted to avoid going the legal route. That had gone down well. He could almost feel the resentment sizzling through the phone. 'Don't do this to me, Jemma, please,' he'd begged her. She'd ended the call, making it clear she felt absolutely nothing for him – leaving Josh wondering what he'd ever seen in her. She hadn't been like this, uncompromisingly hard, when he'd first gone out with her. Yes, she'd finished with him to go out with Ryan, but he'd still loved her, the person he'd thought she was, someone caring. Despite her dumping him, it had taken a while to accept what she was really like. He couldn't quite believe it, even now. He really was a prize idiot.

This time he was waiting to see Kim, who for some bizarre reason he was yet to understand clearly didn't want to be seen with him in public either, and had requested they sit at one of the tables outside the pub, rather than inside where it would be a damn sight warmer. Until he'd finally got hold of her on the phone last night, she'd been ignoring his calls – another woman who'd made up her mind to avoid him. Josh simply didn't get it. Was there something fundamentally wrong with him that he wasn't aware of?

Seeing her coming down the lane, he didn't bother to go and meet her. He'd had enough of being messed around. If the shoe were on the other foot he would be labelled a right bastard. Oh, he forgot. He was, according to Jemma. Maybe she was right. He must not be a very nice bloke.

He didn't stand to greet her either, waiting instead until she seated herself on the bench opposite him. No smile, he noted. Very little eye contact. He was intrigued to find out what he was supposed to have done to warrant the cold shoulder. 'Drink?' he asked.

Kim shook her head. She still wasn't looking at him, her gaze fixed downwards.

Josh sighed and took a swig of his pint. He'd clearly done something very wrong, not perfecting his mind-reading skills being his first big mistake.

Placing his glass back on the table, he twirled it pensively around and then took a fortifying breath. 'I'm confused, Kim,' he said, making sure to keep his tone even. 'I'm not sure what's happening here, but the last time we met you were all over me. Now, suddenly, you're avoiding me like the plague. I'd quite like to know why. Just out of curiosity.'

'You know very well why,' she said, her cheeks flushing.

Josh squinted at her, confounded. Her hands were stuffed in her jacket pockets, her shoulders tense, as if she was uncomfortable in

his company. Why? Was he public enemy number one, or what?
'Right.' He blew out a frustrated sigh. 'I'm obviously completely
bloody dense,' he muttered, 'because I really have no idea what
you're talking about.'

'Don't, Josh,' she said, still not looking at him.

'Don't what?' He laughed, disbelieving. 'I haven't *done* anything.'

'You're doing it now.' She looked up at him at last, her eyes
tear-filled and burning with accusation. 'Swearing. Being aggressive. I can't be around someone like that.'

'Aggressive?' Josh almost choked. 'That's bullshit, Kim. I've
never been aggressive in my life.' He stared hard at her.

Kim looked away. 'That's what they all say.'

'I think I should go,' Josh said shortly, his blood pumping with
anger he was struggling to keep in check. Why was she doing this?
Suddenly he felt like crying. But blokes didn't cry, did they, he
thought cynically. What was this? He'd never been aggressive, not
ever. What in God's name was going on?

'Kim, you need to tell me what's happening here,' he said,
trying hard to temper his tone. 'I really have no idea what you're
talking about.'

She was quiet for a minute, then, 'You used me, Josh,' she said,
looking at him reproachfully.

'*Used* you?' Josh was now utterly stunned. 'How?'

Her eyes flicked down. 'You're still in love with your ex. You're
still seeing her.'

So that was what this was about. Josh sucked in a tight breath.
The fact that he hadn't told her he loved her – because it would have
been a lie. As for Jemma, yes, he had still been in love with her when
he and Kim had slept together. Or he'd thought so. Now, he was
utterly confused. He didn't think sharing that with Kim would be
very considerate of her feelings, not that he felt inclined to be. 'I'm not
seeing her,' he said wearily. 'And I wasn't using you, Kim. I thought
you...' Hold on. How did Kim know he had seen Jemma? Unless...

'Have you been following me?' he asked suspiciously. 'Because I've only seen her once. Just once, Kim, and that was right here in this lane.'

'You really are a piece of work, aren't you?' Kim responded. 'I told you, I'm not that fucking desperate I would follow you around! I suspected you were seeing her, with good reason it turns out, since you've just admitted to it.'

So much for the objection to swearing. Josh eyed her warily.

'It's you who's got a problem, Josh,' Kim went on icily. 'Calling me every five minutes. Texting me.'

'Because I was concerned about you!' Josh retaliated, his anger rising. 'You just disappeared.'

'Concerned *why*? You don't love me. You manipulated me into having sex with you, but you didn't want anything else, did you?'

Josh's blood ran cold. 'I did no such thing,' he said shakily. 'That's absolute—'

'So you wanted a relationship with me then?' Tears filling her eyes, she glared at him. 'Hearts and flowers, the whole works?'

'Yes. No. I don't know,' Josh faltered. 'I wasn't sure you—'

'I'm pregnant!' she shouted. 'Are you concerned about that, Josh? Enough to marry me?'

Josh felt his world shift off kilter. *Christ.* She was joking. She had to be. He swallowed back his pounding heart. She'd said she was taking contraception. He'd asked her. When things were at the point of no return, admittedly, but... It just wasn't possible. Was it?

'No, I thought not.' Kim smiled bitterly as he stared at her uncomprehending. 'So there we have it. I'm having your baby and you don't want me. And you wonder why I would be upset.'

Shocked to the core, Josh had no idea what to say. What the hell to do. 'Are you sure?' he asked her. It was completely the wrong thing to say.

Her expression wounded, she looked at him with disappointment. 'It's not the kind of thing you make a mistake about, Josh.

And before you insult me more than you already have, no, I haven't slept with anyone else but you since my ex.'

'I didn't mean that. I…' How had this happened? He felt his blood run cold. Because he'd been careless of women's feelings. Jemma was right about him.

'It's because of who I am, I suppose,' Kim said, her voice quavering as she wiped a tear from her cheek. 'Common little Kim from the social housing estate. Oh, I did lie to you about that, I admit. About where I lived, my family. I thought that maybe if you thought I moved in the same social sphere as you, you would consider me suitable girlfriend material. Obviously you didn't.'

His thoughts a bewildered jumble in his head, Josh searched hopelessly for the right thing to say. 'I did. I do,' he mumbled. 'I just… You're right, I wasn't sure I was ready for a relationship, but I didn't mean to use you, Kim. I like you. I…'

'But clearly not enough.' She smiled sadly.

'That's not true. I—'

'You didn't want me to meet your mother,' she said.

Josh looked at her askance. He really had no idea now what she was talking about.

'When we went to the Italian restaurant, you said you should go and see her,' she reminded him. 'I offered to come with you, and you just shrugged and said *maybe*. I got the message, Josh. Loud and clear.'

Josh shook his head, astounded. 'I didn't mean anything by it. She hadn't been well. I told you. We'd argued and…' He groped for a way to explain that might limit the damage. 'Christ, I wasn't sure *I* would be comfortable going to see her. There was no way I would have wanted to put you in that position, make you feel uncomfortable. It was nothing to do with you. It was to do with *her*.'

He was making his mother sound like an ogre, and now he felt shitty about that. 'I wasn't even sure when I would be going. If I would.' He stopped, wondering if there was a way to win here.

Whether he would ever come out on top in a conversation with a woman.

Kim considered him thoughtfully. 'You know, it's a pity you aren't as caring of the women you have relationships with as your stepdad is,' she said after a second. 'You should really take a leaf out of his book. I doubt very much he would string someone along like you did.'

'I'll support you.' Josh pulled himself to his feet as she got to hers. 'Whatever you decide to do, I'll support you. I promise.'

Kim looked affronted at that, letting him know that he'd said the wrong thing again. 'Thanks.' She smiled shortly. 'But no thanks. Call me old-fashioned, but it's all or nothing, Josh. I do have my pride, unbelievable though it might seem. I won't be second best in a man's eyes. Sorry. Please don't call me again unless you have something worth listening to.'

His heart like a lead weight in his chest, Josh watched her walk away.

CHAPTER THIRTY-ONE

Cassandra

Having heard nothing from Kim for two days, Cassie was fighting the urge to crawl into bed and stay there. Kim was obviously making a point, refusing to speak to her – at least Cassie hoped to God that was what it was. Her stomach churned as she thought of all the other possibilities: that Samuel might have developed further symptoms. That it might actually be meningitis.

'*Anything* could have happened,' she'd said again to Adam, who'd tried to reassure her, though he was barely speaking to her either, leaving for work early, coming home late, coming to bed late, which was soul-crushingly hurtful. She didn't blame him. He was obviously hurt too, after her more or less blaming him for Kim going off, but he must see that she had been right to worry. Instead it felt like it was her in the wrong, again.

Attempting to focus her mind, she stripped the bed instead, thinking the smell of clean cotton might help her to sleep, though she very much doubted it.

Once the bed linen was in the wash, she went back upstairs with the vacuum. She had to do something other than sit around imagining worst-case scenarios. A graphic image of her son lying bleeding and helpless on the tracks emblazoned itself suddenly on her mind, and she reeled. Gripping the banister, she took slow, steadying breaths, and then carried onto the bedroom, where she tackled the carpet under the bed. It hardly needed doing. She was aware that she was obsessing, but surely it was better than trying to blot the 'what ifs' out with wine. Alcohol only ever fuelled her imagination.

Her heart leapt in her chest as she switched the vacuum off and realised the landline was ringing. She stumbled towards the stairs, but Adam had already reached it and had the phone pressed to his ear.

'Hello?' he said. Turning around, he glanced up as Cassie slowly descended the rest of the stairs. 'Hello?' he said again, a troubled frown on his face.

'Who was it?' Cassie asked, as he banged the phone back in its cradle.

'Same as before,' he said. 'Some joker on the other end hanging up. And before you start worrying, no, I don't think it was Kim. The last two calls were before she went quiet on us.'

Cassie nodded. He was irritated. She could see it in his eyes, hear it in his voice.

Sighing heavily, he ran a hand over his neck. 'Would you like some tea or coffee?' he asked, making an attempt to bridge the divide between them.

'No thanks.' Cassie offered him a small smile.

Once he'd disappeared into the kitchen, she darted into the lounge to grab her mobile from the coffee table. She'd known it wasn't Kim on the phone. She'd known exactly who it was.

Don't you think it's time to acknowledge what you did? It was a warning. A threat. Her past was creeping back to haunt her, seeping into her home. She had to do something. If Adam found out, on top of everything else, he would leave her in an instant.

How much? she replied, her hands trembling.

A beat, and then, *How much is a life worth?*

CHAPTER THIRTY-TWO

The despicable woman was playing some kind of game with her. Cassie wasn't sure why, what she hoped to achieve. She would gladly pay, if only there was a way to guarantee it would stop there. If the woman did find someone to buy her story, there was no doubt in Cassie's mind that her marriage would be over. Her life. There would be consequences for other people, though. Surely the woman must realise that. She couldn't know how devastating those consequences might be, but she would know that her son would be caught in the middle, that it might also destroy his life. Up until now, Cassie had felt nothing but guilty. Now she was angry. Yes, in not honouring the agreement they'd made, she'd wronged the woman. She'd taken advantage of the fact that she was incapable of looking after her own children. To have done nothing, though, to have simply walked away, would have been impossible.

After trying numerous times to contact her, with no success, Cassie left home soon after Adam the next morning. Having undertaken many a stake-out in her younger journalistic years, she'd decided to wait outside the care home the woman's profile said she worked at. It occurred to her after a while that she didn't know whether she was actually there. She wasn't. A phone call confirmed she was off sick, so Cassie drove to her house, from which the woman emerged around lunchtime with some man. She followed them to a city pub, where they went inside for a liquid lunch, and to satisfy a more urgent hunger. Cassie watched from her seat in a discreet corner of the lounge. She was no expert, but she recognised a deal going down, the small wraps of drugs changing hands. It was as she'd feared: the woman was using, a functioning addict but an addict nevertheless. And she would need money to fuel her addiction, more than she could earn as a caregiver, more than Cassie could earn even back at work full-time.

Leaving the pub, Cassie went back to her car and texted her. *I need to know how much. I need to put an end to this.*

I haven't put a price on it yet, the reply came back, leaving her in no doubt that whatever she paid, she would probably only be buying time. The woman would come back for more. Cassie needed to circumvent it, to tell her secret first. She needed to tell Adam.

But how? He would never understand what she'd done, how she'd handled it since. How could he? She didn't understand it herself. She'd found herself on a one-way road, no way to turn back. If only she could stop *her* telling.

Back home, the taste of fear thick in her throat, Cassie wondered what drugs the woman was taking as she busied herself cleaning the paintwork in the hall. How reliable her drug dealer was, what the heroin that she was ingesting or injecting into her veins might be mixed with. She knew from her research that to increase its street value, heroin was cut with all sorts of things: talcum powder and quinine, even laxative powder. Often, to produce a similar high, stimulants such as amphetamines, strychnine or caffeine would be added. Sometimes synthetic opioids were used; fentanyl, she recalled, had caused so many overdose-related fatalities the police had taken the unusual step of issuing a warning to users. Such drugs were easily available, she also recalled, if one knew where to look.

Feeling sick to her soul as she realised where her mind was taking her, that she was capable of even imagining such a dreadful thing, Cassie channelled her emotions into her cleaning. She didn't hear the front door open, didn't realise Adam had come home until he spoke.

'What in God's name are you doing, Cassie?' he asked, his tone a mixture of shock and exasperation.

Dipping her cloth into the bowl of water perched on the stairs, Cassie squeezed it out. 'Just cleaning,' she said lightly. Did he realise how exasperated she was with herself? How frightened? How much she was hurting as they grew further apart when she so needed him, when he so obviously needed the comfort of a loving embrace. *Though not hers.* She swallowed back a sharp pain as the thought popped into her head.

'Cassie…' Adam walked towards the stairs. 'The walls don't need cleaning.'

'They do. There are dirty marks above the handrail.' Cassie concentrated hard on those rather than look at him, see the familiar disillusioned expression.

She'd chosen the colour, ivory with a hint of pink. It was too light. Adam had said it was. It would show all the marks from sleeves rubbed against it, he'd warned, especially with Josh's mates charging up and down.

Her breath catching, Cassie paused. There would be no more dirty sleeves rubbing these walls. There was no one here any more. Just her and Adam, rattling around in a house that was too big for two. She swallowed hard and redoubled her efforts to remove a stubborn mark. It was one Josh had made when he'd been fetching his stuff before leaving. His arms had been full of clothes, his rugby bag slung over his shoulder.

Oh God, how she wished she could turn back time. Have her son back. She should have gone after him, made more effort. How she ached to go after him now, be wherever he was.

'Cassie, just stop, will you?' Adam asked, now sounding cautious.

She brushed a tear from her cheek with the back of her hand, and scrubbed harder.

'You don't need to do this,' Adam said more forcefully.

She glanced at him. He was clearly also working to control his emotions. She wasn't being fair on him. It wasn't his fault that Kim hadn't been in contact. None of what was happening was his fault. He'd been trying to reach out to her, but he couldn't. She didn't want to be here. Not without Samuel. Not without her son. Without Adam.

'Jesus, Cassie.' Adam mounted the stairs. 'This is nuts. You're taking the bloody *paint* off the walls.'

Cassie flinched as he caught hold of her wrist, her eyes skittering towards him. His were dark, full of confused shadows. 'Come down,' he said, his voice strained. 'I'll make us a drink and we'll—'

'I'm fine.' She attempted to pull away from him.

But Adam only tightened his grip. 'You're not fine,' he insisted. 'You're far from fine. You need to talk to someone. Get help. You're—'

'I don't want to talk to anyone.' Her heart hammering, Cassie struggled, stumbling up the stairs. It was him she wanted to talk to. Couldn't he see that? Couldn't he see that his seeming to be able to talk to Kim and not her was killing her?

'For God's sake! You're going to bloody well fall!' Adam caught her as her foot slipped. She saw the bowl she'd balanced so carefully on the stairs tip. Watched as it tumbled and rolled. Her throat closed as it landed on the hall floor, water splattering the walls and saturating the carpet.

Adam glanced down at it, and then back to her. 'You need to stop this, Cassie,' he repeated shakily. 'Please, come down with me.'

She didn't fight him as he moved to her side, his hold around her gentle, as if she were some delicate thing that might break, as if he cared for her. Did he? Could he still, if she told him all she needed to? Tears sliding down her cheeks, she allowed him to guide her down.

Feeling disorientated, she glanced at the stain bleeding into the carpet as they stood in the hall. And then at her husband. His eyes were troubled. Not sparkling. Not happy. Was his hair slightly greyer at the temples? She reached out, touching it delicately with her fingertips. He'd had enough. Her heart faltered. She wouldn't blame him if he did leave her.

'You need to slow down, Cas,' Adam said quietly. 'You're beginning to scare me.'

The truth was, she was scaring herself. 'I'm sorry,' she murmured. She didn't care about the mess. Only him. The one constant in her life. The man who'd stayed, who'd loved her, even at her lowest ebb when her body seemed to be failing her. She'd looked dreadful then. Still he'd loved her. She was sure of that much. Could he forgive her? She felt his arms around her, leant into him, rested her head on his shoulder. She wanted to stay like this forever, safe in his strong embrace.

'I'm sorry,' she repeated tearfully. 'So sorry.'

He squeezed her impossibly close. 'It's okay,' he said softly. 'We'll get through this.'

How? She looked up at him, her heart fracturing another inch as she saw the pain in his eyes. She had to talk to him. She had no one but him. She never had, her mother turning to God after her father's infidelity, turning away from Cassie and her brother, relentlessly cleaning, attempting to wash away the sins of her father, the shame… Just as Cassie was now. Adam might understand, if only she could find a way to explain. He'd cared so much for Josh, worried for him, about him. He worried still, convinced that Josh's death wasn't suicide, that he couldn't have fallen, that someone had hurt him. That by some miracle he could have saved him, kept him safe.

He would realise that that had only ever been her aim too, to keep him safe. She'd tried so hard. Breathing deeply, she braced herself. 'We have to talk,' she whispered. 'About Josh. There's something I have to—' She stopped as the doorbell rang behind her.

Adam held her gaze for a second longer, and then, a flicker of hope in his eyes, he looked beyond her to the front door.

Seeing his expression change to one of tangible relief, Cassie whirled around. Her stomach lurched as she took in the shock of fiery red hair.

Thank God. Relief coursing through her, she closed her eyes. She'd thought… imagined that Adam and Kim might be… She was losing her mind. Adam was right: she needed to stop her obsessive behaviour, rid her mind of her stupid suspicions. She would make everything right, whatever she had to do. She wouldn't let him down. Samuel either. She'd failed her son, but she would keep his precious child safe.

CHAPTER THIRTY-THREE

Kimberley

Kim felt a myriad of conflicting emotions as she walked into the lounge and saw Adam gazing lovingly at Samuel, who was nestled in the crook of his arm. Wonderment, sympathy, uncertainty. His marriage to Cassie was floundering, and suddenly Kim realised he would lose contact with the child he saw as his grandson as surely as he'd thought of Josh as his son. She'd made a promise to Josh, but she hadn't considered that Adam would be a casualty in all of this. Feeling for him, for all that he'd gone through, would still have to go through, she went across to him. 'He has his father's eyes, doesn't he?' she said softly.

Adam brought his gaze to hers. What Kim saw shocked her. Once again he seemed close to tears. She hadn't thought they existed, men who were truly in touch with their emotions.

'Undoubtedly.' His mouth curved into a smile of soul-wrenching sadness.

Watching him as he turned his attention back to Samuel, taking his small hand tenderly in his own strong one, exploring his features, Kim's heart broke for him.

'Where's Cassie?' he asked after a second, his face clouding with worry.

'She's warming Samuel's bottle,' Kim said. 'I hadn't realised she'd bought so much baby equipment.'

She saw a flicker of despair cross his face. And no wonder. Cassie had practically bought the entire baby section of Boots, online presumably. Kim didn't think she would dare show her face in the local store again any time soon. She had a bottle warmer and a thermal bottle carrier, though God only knew where she imagined she would be tripping off to with Samuel. She had bibs and burp cloths. Bottles in various sizes and milk storage containers. A stock of disposable nappies and baby wipes in the downstairs loo. Kim had yet to see the room she was turning into a nursery for when Samuel stayed over. She hadn't really thought that far ahead when she'd come to them, thinking she would take one day at a time. But she hadn't foreseen this. Her tummy twisted with nerves, imagining what the consequences of Cassie wanting to be so hands-on with the baby might be.

'Are you okay, Kim?' Adam asked, his eyes flecked with concern.

Kim nodded quickly. 'Fine,' she assured him. 'I was just, you know, thinking about stuff.'

Adam looked as if he did know. 'Do you want to take him back?' He offered her a small smile, and eased Samuel from his arms gently into hers.

'You might need to have a word with Cassie,' he suggested, as Kim drew Samuel to her. 'She's very keen to help out, as you've already gathered.' Running a hand over his neck, he glanced uneasily at her. 'Me too, but… I thought it might be a good idea if you worked out a schedule. You know, give her designated times when it suits you for her to come and visit.'

Kim stared at him, huge relief washing through her. He'd just given her the answer. It was the obvious thing to do: stipulate convenient times that would work for her and Samuel. Routine was important in a baby's life, after all. Cassie would see the sense in that.

'Or for you to come here,' Adam added. 'You're welcome any time, but…'

Kim glanced quickly over her shoulder. 'You're worried Cassie might get too attached?' she suggested.

Adam looked as relieved as Kim felt. 'She's always been a bit fastidious,' he went on with an awkward shrug. 'It got worse when she was ill because she wanted to be doing things but physically couldn't. I think losing Josh the way we did had a bigger impact on her psychologically than I realised.' He paused, allowing Kim to draw her own conclusions. 'She doesn't mean to be so full-on. It's just, she's been through a lot and it's left her a bit...'

'Stressed,' Kim supplied diplomatically as he searched for the right word.

'Definitely that.' Adam smiled sadly. 'She needs something else in her life other than this place. Something else to focus on.'

Kim nodded slowly. 'But you don't want her so focused she swaps one obsession for another.'

'Exactly. I know it's a big ask, but do you think you could be patient with her?'

'I think I can work something out.' Kim gave him a reassuring smile. 'She could come to the cottage and have him for an hour during the day, until I can get a job. I'm happy to come here too, that wouldn't be a problem.' She hesitated, glancing contemplatively down and back. 'I wouldn't want him staying overnight, though. At least not until he's older and...'

'Cassie's behaving more rationally,' Adam finished. 'I get it.' He nodded understandingly. 'I suspect she realised she'd overstepped the mark when you didn't return her calls. Hopefully she'll be more restrained in future.'

Dropping her gaze to Samuel, Kim eased his shawl from his little face. 'Sorry about that,' she said contritely. 'I know you were both worried about him, but he was perfectly all right. It was me panicking. I was only really ringing to let you know I was staying over a couple of extra nights. To be honest, I was a bit upset by her reaction. I felt as if she was… Well, it didn't make me want to rush back, if you can understand.'

'I do. Perfectly,' Adam said, pressing a reassuring hand to her arm. 'I can't say I blame you. I'm going to try to get her to see someone. I think she needs—'

Kim noted his gaze flick to the door and gathered Cassie was looming.

'I think it's the right temperature.' Cassie duly appeared, bottle and bib in hand. 'You'll need to test it, though, Kim. We wouldn't want to burn his little mouth, would we?'

'Thanks, Cassie.' Exchanging glances with Adam, Kim tried not to roll her eyes.

'My pleasure,' Cassie said, coming across to stroke Samuel's cheek. 'Isn't he just adorable?' she sighed longingly. 'He looks so much like his father…' She swallowed hard.

'Would you like to feed him?' Kim asked kindly.

'I'd love to,' Cassie said, looking delighted.

'Here we go then.' Samuel was beginning to fret for his feed. 'Keep an eye on him,' she warned. 'He's a little guzzler.'

'I will. There's no need to worry, Kim. I have done this before, haven't I, darling, hmm?' Cassie gazed adoringly down at Samuel as she walked across to the sofa.

Catching Adam's eye again, Kim gave him a smile, indicating that she was okay with it.

'He'll probably need a nap once he's had his feed,' Cassie said, once she'd encouraged Samuel to take the bottle. 'You too, Kim. You must be tired after your journey. Why don't you have a lie-down in the spare room and I'll sit in the nursery with Samuel for a while.'

'Um…' Kim glanced at her watch, a knot of panic taking root. She was happy to allow Cassie some time with Samuel, but she couldn't stay for the rest of the day. She had to get him home.

Clearly understanding her dilemma, Adam came to the rescue. 'I think Kim wants to get back home.' Crossing to the sofa, he glanced smilingly down at the baby and then leant to kiss the top of Cassie's head. 'She probably needs to sort herself out and settle Samuel back into his routine, don't you, Kim?'

'I do.' Kim nodded, relieved. 'I have Jack staying over too. My mum's taken him for a dental appointment but we're meeting up later, so I really should get off fairly soon.'

Cassie nodded, but she was clearly disappointed. 'I could come with you, put your washing on and keep an eye on Samuel while you and Jack—'

'No, Cassie,' Adam intervened, before Kim had a chance to answer. 'Kim needs her space, remember? Some time to herself.'

'To be honest, I do, Cassie,' Kim agreed, as Cassie gazed between them, her look a mixture of bewildered and crestfallen. 'You could come over in a few days, though. Maybe pop around for an hour or so. You could take him out for a walk if you wanted to, which would give me a break. What do you think?'

Cassie glanced at her thoughtfully. Then, offering a small, forced smile, she concentrated her attention back on Samuel.

Half an hour later, Adam walked Kim to the front door while Cassie went to wash her hands after changing Samuel's nappy. 'Thanks,' he said emotionally, giving her shoulders a squeeze.

'Thank *you*,' Kim said in turn, settling Samuel in the pushchair. 'I know you've been through a lot, and that you're still going through it. I just wanted you to know I really appreciate all you've done for me. You're a very special, caring man. Cassie's lucky to have you. Don't run yourself ragged, though,' she warned him, frowning. 'You'll be no use to yourself or anyone else if you do that. You have to look after yourself too.'

Adam smiled. It suited him much better than the confused look he seemed to wear around Cassie. 'I'll do my best,' he assured her.

His smile was one of surprise when Kim stretched to kiss his cheek and then give him a firm hug. He soon lost it, though, she noted, when he realised that Cassie was hovering at the top of the stairs, looking down at him stonily.

CHAPTER THIRTY-FOUR

Jemma

Jemma woke with a jerk, sweat saturating the sheets beneath her. The nightmares had plagued her since the day Josh had died. They'd grown worse since she'd realised Liam was the image of him. His eyes were Josh's eyes. The first time she'd looked into them, her heart had almost stopped beating. She'd been sure she could see the accusation there. Every night she heard his voice in her dreams: 'Don't do this to me, Jemma.' Over and over. She'd turned her back, ignored his plea. The squeal of the brakes, she heard that too, metal grinding raucously against metal, the high-pitched scream of primal terror rising above it. Then came the cloying darkness, deep, dark crimson turning to complete impenetrable black. She could feel it suffocating her, sucking her in and burying her along with him.

She would never forgive herself for the pain she'd caused him. She hadn't meant to treat him so cruelly. To hurt him so badly.

Gulping back a ragged breath, she pulled herself up, waiting for the frantic beating of her heart to abate, and glanced in the semi-darkness to Ryan's side of the bed. Her husband, solid and dependable. Holding her and comforting her when she couldn't go back to sleep.

He was scared too. Jemma had seen the puzzlement in his eyes when he looked at her, wondering why she couldn't bond with her baby. The midwife had told her to give herself more time. How *much* time? This wasn't normal. The palpitations and panic attacks… She'd had one in the supermarket once. She'd had to get out, leave her shopping. Her moods, which would alternate between lack of interest in Liam to extreme anxiety for him. If the nightmares didn't wake her, a deep-rooted fear that something had happened to him would, and she would climb out of bed and tiptoe into the nursery to make sure he was breathing.

This hollow hopelessness inside her was something she'd experienced before. Goose bumps prickling her skin, she rubbed her arms. The midwife had suggested she see her GP. She'd said he could refer her to someone to talk to if she was really worried. Ryan had thought that was a good idea, and Jemma had pretended to go along with it. She didn't dare tell him she hadn't gone to the appointment. How could she, when she was too petrified to tell anyone what she'd done?

Unable to make Ryan out under the tangle of duvet, she reached tentatively across to his side of the bed. Finding nothing but empty space, her heart lurched. He must have slipped out to see to Liam. She hadn't heard him. She hadn't heard her baby crying. *Again.* There *was* something wrong with her. She was some kind of monster. If Ryan knew how much of a monster, how badly she'd deceived him, he would leave her in an instant. She couldn't bear that. Couldn't be without him. Not now.

Scrambling out of bed, she crept to the landing. When she saw the soft glow of light spilling from under the nursery door, she felt a huge surge of relief. Also jealousy, she acknowledged, her guilt ratcheting up. Ryan had bonded with Liam. Liam had bonded with Ryan. His little mouth always curved into an excited smile when his huge blue eyes alighted on him. Why couldn't she feel the same connection? This was all she'd ever wanted, her own little family. To be a mummy. Yet she'd risked everything in a vain attempt to escape the pain of losing her first baby. She should have been honest. She should have told Ryan. Begged his forgiveness.

She couldn't tell him now. It would destroy him. She'd sealed her fate. Somehow she would have to live with her conscience.

Padding along the landing, she pushed the nursery door open to find Ryan nestling the child he thought was his son against his shoulder. Her heart broke for him as she watched him press a soft kiss to Liam's head before lowering him gently back into his cot.

Straightening up, he glanced back at her, pressing a finger to his lips as she crept closer. Comforted by the man who would always be his father in Jemma's mind, Liam was lying on his back sleeping contentedly, his eyelids fluttering as his mind chased his dreams, his little sausage arms splayed out to his sides. He really was beautiful. From his tiny toes to his button nose, he was a perfect baby. Jemma wanted to love him, but she knew she didn't deserve to, that she didn't deserve her baby's love. Ryan's love.

'He's out for the count,' Ryan said quietly.

'Sorry I didn't hear him,' Jemma whispered.

Ryan pushed his hands into the pockets of his tracksuit bottoms. 'You were out for the count too. Don't worry about it. You need your sleep. You're exhausted.'

She was, perpetually. She woke several times in the night when Liam was soundly sleeping, then slept too heavily to hear him when he woke. Never rested during the day.

'You had another nightmare,' Ryan said.

Jemma glanced away, trying to banish the images of Josh's broken body from her mind.

'You were crying out,' he added, and let it hang.

She could feel his eyes on her. She didn't look at him, reaching instead to brush Liam's peachy cheek with the back of her hand.

'Good-looking little bugger, isn't he?' Ryan commented after a second.

'He is.' Jemma smiled, marvelling at how peaceful he seemed, so different to the distressed tiny human being she could never seem to appease.

'Doesn't look much like me, does he?' Ryan said after another heavy pause – and Jemma's blood froze.

'He does.' She laughed nervously. 'He looks just like you. He has your nose, and I'm sure his eyes are going to be hazel.'

Ryan considered. 'I doubt it,' he said after a second. 'They're a really intense blue. I'm thinking they're going to stay that way.'

Jemma felt an icy dagger of foreboding pierce her heart. 'He still looks like you,' she offered weakly. 'He even sleeps like you. Look.'

Ryan was looking. A deep furrow in his brow, he was studying Liam intently. Her mouth dry, nausea churning inside her, Jemma waited. He didn't speak. The silence above the soft sound of her baby's breathing was so profound, she was sure she could hear the foundations of her life crumbling.

Ryan eventually moved, bending to tuck Liam's blanket gently to his chest. And then he turned to look at her, a long, penetrating gaze that chilled her to the bone.

Jemma tried to speak, but she couldn't get the words past her constricted throat. She reached a hand to his arm, desperately needing reassurance, but Ryan flinched and pulled away. Still he didn't say anything. Instead, he scanned her face for an agonising second, then turned to walk silently out of the nursery.

CHAPTER THIRTY-FIVE

Cassandra

It had been an innocent gesture. A show of affection. Cassie tried to dismiss what she'd seen in the hall, but the niggling thought that Adam and Kim were colluding against her, the feeling that she was on the outside looking in, just wouldn't leave her.

She was being paranoid. If she mentioned it, Adam would think she'd gone mad. He'd hugged the girl in a fatherly way, that was all. She tried to reassure herself as she prepared Samuel's bath. It was the kind of person he was. He'd always been hands-on with Josh, never shying away from physical shows of emotion. She was blowing things out of proportion because of her own insecurities. He could hardly have shoved the girl away when she'd thrown her arms around him. And Kim would hardly have been quite so demonstrative in front of Cassie if she had eyes on her husband, would she?

It was nonsense. Adam was old enough to be her father. But then you often heard of older men sleeping with much younger women. Never the other way around. Her brow furrowed in contemplation as she lifted the bath from the sink to the work surface. She didn't like the idea of the mixer tap anywhere near that darling little baby when she bathed him.

Her eyes flicked to the clock as she dried her hands and went to gather Samuel from his pram. What was keeping them? she wondered. Kim had arrived unannounced, telling them she thought the fuse box had blown and that she could smell burning, and Adam had dutifully gone to the cottage to investigate. Cassie wasn't sure why Kim had had to go with him.

Honestly, what was the matter with her? She would be certifiable at this rate. Despairing of herself, she went over to the pram. She was glad Kim had gone, to be honest. It would give her and Samuel a chance to share some time together. She'd barely seen him lately. 'Come on, little man,' she said softly, stroking his cheek and lifting him carefully from the pram. Samuel whimpered. From the smell wafting from his nappy, she guessed he needed changing. She didn't want Kim coming back and thinking she'd left him like that.

'Cleanliness is next to godliness, hey, my little angel?' she whispered, cuddling him close – and then stopping dead as she realised she was actually quoting her mother. Closing her eyes, she breathed through the panic. She wasn't anything like her. A cold shudder ran through her as she recalled the night of her father's adultery.

Her parents' bedroom door had been open. Cassie had soon realised that the young woman in the bed wasn't her mother. Shivering on the landing, she had glanced from the naked girl to where her mother was vigorously vacuuming. There were several long strands of blonde hair lying on the carpet, the kitchen shears abandoned there too. The rest of the girl's hair had been sucked up the vacuum, Cassie had guessed.

Unsure what to do, sorry for the girl but also scared, she'd hesitated, and then moved towards her. There were fat tears falling down the girl's face, snot running from her nose. With her shorn hair, she didn't look very attractive at all.

Now Cassie's hand went to her own hair. How unattractive must she look in Adam's eyes compared to a girl half her age, with pretty, delicate features and a lustrous mane of flame-red hair?

Shaking herself, she drew in a breath. She was wrong. Allowing her past to colour her thinking. Adam would never do something like that to her. But she'd never dreamed her father would do something like that either.

'Please make her let me go,' she heard the girl say over and over, fear in her voice. She remembered her young body, pale and naked and shaking. Recalled wondering where her clothes were. 'Please,' the girl had begged, her eyes wild as her gaze shot past Cassie.

To her mother, Cassie realised. Her heart flipping over, she'd watched in awe as her mother loomed over the girl, her face contorted with rage.

'Don't,' the girl sobbed, drawing her knees up, trying to make herself invisible.

Her mother stood tall. 'Dirty little *slut*,' she'd seethed, lifting the vacuum bag aloft, pausing for a second as if revelling in her victory, and then emptying the contents over her.

The rotating blue lights on the bedroom wall had told Cassie the police had arrived, her dad coming in close behind one of the uniformed officers. He was deathly white. Cassie guessed that he'd waited for the police before venturing back into the house. He'd been right to. Her mother didn't go quietly, screaming obscenities at him.

Cassie had soon discovered where the girl's clothes were. Poking around in the embers of the fire in the garden the next day, she'd found a strip of melted neon legging and one scorched pointy stiletto. Her father's clothes had largely fuelled the bonfire, she'd realised, which had been a big one. 'It's the children I feel sorry for,' she'd heard one of the neighbours whisper when she'd finally dared leave the house.

Was she like her mother? Her father had denied it when her mother had asked him whether he was seeing someone else. Told her it was all in her mind. The suspicion, the lies had driven her slowly *out* of her mind, until eventually she'd snapped. Cassie *wasn't* like her. She was stronger than that. Wasn't she? She had to be. She had to stop thinking like this. Samuel needed her. She hugged him closer.

'Silly Nana,' she chastised herself as she laid him down on the changing mat on the work surface. 'She needs to be a happy, smiley Nana, doesn't she? That's what you need, isn't it, darling, not a mixed-up, miserable Nana?'

Smiling down at him, she eased him out of his babygro and removed his nappy. Tutting as she dropped it, she bent to retrieve it, then went to the utility to fetch a nappy sack. Depositing the sack in the bin, she retrieved her hand gel from the shelf. Obsessiveness was one thing. Sensible precaution was quite another, she assured herself, quickly cleaning her hands.

'Shush, darling, Nana's coming,' she called reassuringly across to Samuel, who was working himself up to a good bellow.

She was grabbing the antibacterial spray from the cupboard when Adam yelled behind her, 'Cassie! What the fucking hell are you doing?'

CHAPTER THIRTY-SIX

Kimberley

Kim clutched the crying baby to her chest and watched the scene playing out before her with morbid fascination.

'Don't be so ridiculous,' Cassie laughed, bewildered. 'I might have been a bit distracted recently, which is no surprise if you take into account the fact that my son died, but I wasn't about to spray cleaning fluid anywhere near the baby. I'm not completely stupid, Adam.'

Kim winced at the reference to Josh as *her* son. That was just cruel. She glanced from Cassie to Adam, who'd obviously also picked up on it. He looked utterly crushed. 'Well what the bloody hell *were* you doing then?' he asked.

'I dropped the nappy on the floor.' Cassie looked at him as if she really didn't get it. 'It was the tiles I was about to wipe, not the work surface.'

'Jesus Christ…' Heaving out a sigh, Adam glanced away from her. The look in his eyes as he met Kim's was somewhere between despair and desperation.

'I was only cleaning the mess up. It's not a criminal offence, Adam. I don't understand what it is I'm supposed to have—'

'He was screaming his head off,' Adam grated, levelling a furious gaze back at Cassie. 'You left him balanced on the work surface.'

'Only for a second.' Cassie's voice quavered. 'I didn't move away from him long enough for him to roll over. I do have some experience of caring for a baby, Adam. Which actually you don't,' she pointed out defensively,

Kim's gaze shot to Adam, who looked as if Cassie had punched him. He didn't retaliate. Dragging his wounded gaze away, he kneaded his forehead hard, then turned towards the hall.

He met Kim's eyes as he approached the kitchen door. He looked so tired. Bone weary. And so, so angry.

'Kim?' Cassie said, looking at her. 'You don't seriously think I would ever do anything to harm Samuel, do you? I would die before hurting him.'

'No, I…' Kim hesitated, furrowing her brow.

Cassie looked at her uncertainly. 'Kim?'

'I should go,' Kim said. 'Samuel's upset.'

'But you'll come back?' Cassie asked, her expression fearful. 'Or I could come over to you, as we agreed. Tomorrow possibly?'

'Maybe.' Kim took her opportunity to back away as Samuel grew more fractious. He was probably starving. She'd brought a feed with her, but a tactical exit might be best.

'Here, let me take him,' Cassie offered, taking a step towards her.

'No,' Kim said quickly. 'I have to go, Cassie. I'll—'

She was interrupted by a loud crash. She whirled around, reaching the hall before Cassie, to find Adam quietly cursing and shaking his hand. There was blood dripping from it. Kim's heart caught in her chest. The mirror was smashed, broken glass sprinkled around like silver confetti. The blood had dripped onto the carpet, rich red against the pale cream. That wouldn't go down well.

'Adam?' Cassie said shakily behind her. 'What in God's name have you done?'

Adam laughed cynically. 'Broken a cardinal rule, Cas,' he said, his eyes blazing. 'Made a fucking mess.' Shaking his head, he turned to yank open the front door.

'Adam!' she called frantically. 'Come back. You can't—'

'Enough, Cassandra!' Adam exploded. 'For pity's sake, can you not just stop!' His shoulders tense, he hesitated for a second, and then strode out, slamming the front door behind him.

Hell. Kim had guessed he might blow at some point, but she hadn't imagined him walking out so suddenly. 'I have to go,' she said, grabbing Samuel's outdoor suit from the pegs.

Sitting in an armchair in the lounge, she fed Samuel's tiny flailing arms and legs into the suit in record time, shushing and soothing him as she did.

'Is there anything I can do to help?' Cassie offered. But she wasn't looking at her, Kim noticed. Her attention was on smoothing and straightening Samuel's blanket and pram cover. Kim's eyes boggled. Did she not care that she'd just driven her husband from the house, dripping blood? It hadn't seemed to occur to her that he might be seriously injured. It obviously hadn't occurred to her that Josh had been seriously upset when she'd driven him out too. It was no wonder the men in her life were so bloody conflicted.

'You could grab his bottle,' she suggested, biting her tongue and jumping to her feet to place Samuel in the pram, then wheel it into the hall.

Cassie hurried into the kitchen. 'I'll call you tomorrow, shall I?' she asked, reappearing to hand her the bottle.

Kim tucked it in the pram tray. 'Do that.' She forced a smile. 'But not before nine,' she added, a new wave of panic sweeping through her. 'Samuel's awake a lot in the night at the moment, but he sleeps quite late, so I—'

Cassie seized on that. 'I could come early. You could have a good lie-in then, and I could—'

'No,' Kim said adamantly, and walked around the pram to open the front door. 'It's nice of you to offer, Cassie,' she added, attempting a cordial tone, 'but I have a friend coming in the morning. Thanks, though.'

'What friend?' Cassie asked, her sharp tone sending a shiver down Kim's spine. 'I mean, is it anyone I know?' she added, more lightly.

'I shouldn't think so, no.' Kim didn't look at her as she tipped the pram back, negotiating the step and then hurrying down the driveway.

'Are you sure you want to walk? It looks as if it's about to rain,' Cassie called after her. 'I could give you a lift if you like.'

'Positive,' Kim called back. 'The exercise will do me good.'

Turning the corner at the end of the road, she spotted Adam's car parked a short distance off. Relief flooded her veins. She'd thought he might have gone permanently, and wasn't sure where that would leave her. Cassie didn't appear to have completely lost it yet, but she did seem perilously close to the edge.

Adam climbed out of his car. 'Sorry,' he said, looking sick to his soul as he walked towards her. 'I shouldn't have stormed out like that. I just…'

'Had to get out before you lost your temper?' Kim finished. 'It's okay,' she said kindly. Flicking the pram brake on, she checked on Samuel, whose sobs had mercifully quieted, and then walked around to press a reassuring hand to Adam's forearm. 'I understand. I think you did well to hold your temper at all, to be honest.'

'I'm not so sure I did.' Adam smiled ruefully.

Kim's attention went to his injured hand. He'd wrapped a cloth around it, one he must carry in his car. It wasn't very clean. Cassie would have a fit if she saw it, and would probably be right on this occasion. The hand was still bleeding.

'She wasn't always like this.' He sighed wearily. 'When I first met her, she was house proud, yes, but she was fun to be around.'

Kim nodded understandingly.

'She loved to go out,' Adam went on, his voice edged with despair. 'Theatre, concerts, music festivals. She would dance, let go and enjoy herself. But now… I just don't get what…' His voice cracked.

Tentatively Kim reached for his injured hand. 'It needs a proper dressing on it,' she said softly. 'This cloth is probably crawling with bacteria.'

Adam looked nonplussed for a second. Then, seeing her teasing look, he laughed, a strangled laugh, before swallowing hard.

'She didn't mean the things she said, Adam,' Kim ventured. He was clearly in utter despair about his wife, but Kim realised she had to tread carefully. She wanted him to think of her as sympathetic and understanding, not someone who would cheerfully dig the knife in. 'She's unwell,' she went on cautiously. 'This obsessiveness, her distraction, her mania... She's obviously trying to soldier on, but she's been through so much: her illness, losing Josh. I think she might need to see someone. A professional counsellor possibly?'

Adam sighed again, heavily. 'I know. The thing is, how the hell do I convince her? I've tried, but it's as if she's not hearing me. She insists she's fine. She doesn't seem to be aware of what she's doing.'

'Maybe if you tell her she needs to do it for Samuel's sake,' Kim suggested. 'You could tell her I'm worried about leaving him alone with her unless she makes an appointment.'

'Are you?' Adam asked, his look one of trepidation.

Kim took a second. 'To be honest, with all that's happened, I am a bit.'

He nodded.

'If she agrees to get help, she'll be admitting she has a problem, won't she? We can work it out, Adam. She needs support, that's all.'

'I'll talk to her,' he said, sounding less despondent.

'Do that.' Kim gave him a reassuring smile. 'And don't forget, if you ever need to talk, I have an ear. Two, actually.'

This time he managed a half-hearted smile in return.

'You need someone to be there for you too, you know,' she said carefully. 'We all need that.'

Adam glanced down, his troubled gaze now on the thumb she was gliding across his injured knuckles.

'You're human, Adam. It's not a weakness to admit it. You'll get through this,' she assured him.

Adam eased his hand away. 'I'd better get back,' he said, nodding past her to where Cassie was hurrying anxiously towards them. 'I'll call you and let you know how things go.'

CHAPTER THIRTY-SEVEN

Cassandra

Straightening up from where she was kneeling digging in the garden, Cassie wiped the back of her hand across her forehead and gazed towards the patio, where Samuel gurgled happily on his play mat. She was so relieved that Kim had accepted her apology, which she had been more than willing to offer to ensure future contact with Samuel. They'd been right, of course. She shouldn't have left him, not even for a second. She wasn't sure what she'd been thinking.

Adam had been less forgiving, insisting she should talk to someone, for the sake of her relationship with Kim if nothing else. Cassie couldn't help but wonder whether it was *his* relationship with Kim he was concerned about. Still, she'd bitten her tongue, agreed to make an appointment and apologised to him too.

'Thanks,' he'd said, relief flooding his face. 'For agreeing to make the appointment, not the apology. I don't need that, Cas. I just need you to be well.'

Hearing another gurgle from Samuel that was almost a chuckle, she smiled sadly. She didn't think counselling would help. She'd done what she'd had to do to buy her some time with her grandson.

And she had clearly won Kim's trust. She'd had Samuel here three times over the last two weeks. The first time for just an hour, while Kim went to a dental appointment. Cassie had suspected it had been concocted by Kim and Adam, a trial of sorts to assess whether she was well enough to look after him. She had smiled quietly at the obviousness of it. She might be neurotic and obsessive at times, but she wasn't blind. She hadn't missed Kim smiling girlishly at Adam when he'd offered her a lift to her cardio dance class on his way into work.

She hadn't missed what she was wearing either: white leggings and a white sports top with flesh-revealing mesh panels that showed off her slim figure. She was lucky not to have carried much weight while she'd been pregnant, Cassie mused. She herself had piled on the pounds.

Despite her fears that Kim's workout might not be the sort that generally took place in a gym, Cassie was happy to let her go, leaving her to tend the garden and look after little Samuel. In allowing her access to him, Kim knew where her interests lay. She always had, Cassie was in no doubt of that. She'd come to them distraught, with Josh's baby. A vulnerable young thing, guilty of nothing but falling in love with a man and being too poor to bring up his child on her own when tragedy struck. Cassie wasn't as gullible as she appeared, however. She was very aware that Kim wasn't the picture of innocence she pretended to be. It had taken a certain amount of guile to approach them in the first place. She'd had an agenda. She'd needed money up front to secure her house. She'd wanted furnishings, financial support for the foreseeable future. Cassie had been fine with that. Everything was a means to an end, after all, and the girl had been owed that much in her mind, if not more. She'd brought Samuel into her life, and Cassie would be eternally grateful for that. Now, though, it was apparent she wanted more. The question was: was Adam obliging? Cassie hadn't seen much affection in his eyes for her lately. Concern, yes. His affection for Kim, though, that was obvious. All that whispering and touchy-feely body language between them… He couldn't keep his hands off her. Had he had sex with her yet?

Her heart lurched as she imagined him sharing that kind of intimacy with the mother of her son's child. A woman who was not much more than a child herself – ripe forbidden fruit, all the better for being so.

She turned her face skywards. The late-autumn sun was warm, the smell of freshly mown grass piquant on the air. The last cut of the year? she wondered. Seasons changed, plants withered and died, giving way to vibrant new buds; such was the cycle of life. Josh had gone. *Ashes to ashes.* She stopped breathing, her trowel grating against the grit and dirt as she jabbed it into the freshly dug earth. His child lived. Cassie would do whatever she had to to make sure he stayed in her life. She would keep quiet for the moment, but she too would make plans, as Kim and Adam possibly were. She would not let them, or the woman who was texting her, threatening her, take her grandson from her. He was all she had left now.

Finding her preparation of the ground for the new rose bushes she intended to plant therapeutic, Cassie continued digging, images of Josh as a young boy floating through her mind. She pictured him tramping through the mud in his red wellington boots, rosy-cheeked and happy as he helped her tend their vegetable garden. Everything had been so perfect. How did it all go so wrong? Wiping away a salty tear, she concentrated on her manual labours. She was tugging at a particularly persistent weed when her mobile rang from the patio table.

Damn. She pulled off her gardening gloves and headed quickly to the patio. Having finally contacted Jemma via text, she'd meant to keep the phone by her. Wetting her dry lips with her tongue, she hesitated before picking up. They'd agreed to have no contact unless it was absolutely urgent. Jemma had been desperate not to, in fact. Sure now, though, that Kim had lied about knowing her, Cassie had no choice but to speak to her. She had to know whether Jemma had shared anything they'd both sworn to keep secret.

'I have to tell him,' Jemma blurted, as soon as Cassie answered.

Caught off guard, Cassie tugged in a sharp breath. 'But… why?' she stuttered. 'What good can it possibly do now?'

'He has a right to *know*,' Jemma said, going back on everything she'd said previously: that she would do anything to stop Ryan finding out. 'I can't keep lying to him, Cassie. I just *can't*.'

Cassie felt a kernel of anger tighten inside her. Jemma wanted to do this now? After all that had happened? She'd denied herself contact with the child, fearing she would grieve the loss of him too. She'd made a clean break, for all of their sakes. Better that than try to maintain contact, which might have alerted Ryan. It had almost killed her. Had Jemma considered that?

'Just like Josh had rights, Jemma?' she asked, a hard edge to her voice. 'Feelings? Did you consider those when you decided it would be a fun thing to lead him on? Have sex with him without once thinking what the consequences might be?'

'That's not fair, Cassie. I wasn't well at the time. You know what I'd been through.' Jemma's voice trembled.

Cassie did know. Jemma had blurted the whole story out when she'd first come to her, telling her about her miscarriage, her depression. Cassie had sympathised. How could she not, having been there herself not once, but twice?

It had been too late to try to convince her not to have the baby. She'd been too far into her pregnancy and had clearly wanted it. Though it broke her heart, Cassie had had to do all she could to help Jemma save her marriage and to protect Josh. They'd agreed that the only way forward would be to prevent Josh being involved in the child's life. If there'd been a DNA test, the truth might have come out. It would have been devastating for everyone: Josh, Ryan, Adam, Cassie herself. Jemma had understood why. Cassie hadn't pressurised her – the girl had been aware that if the facts became known, her relationship with Ryan would stand no chance of surviving. She'd been grateful for the money Cassie had given her, which she'd hoped would at least ensure the child had a secure future. And now here she was, out of the blue…

Josh was *dead*. She couldn't let Jemma drag it all up. Her own marriage might be crumbling, but Cassie intended to fight for it, to fight for contact with Samuel. If the truth came out, it would be fodder for Kim to use against her. She couldn't let her.

'You can't tell him, Jemma. It would be suicide after all this time, don't you see?'

'But why?' Jemma asked tearfully. 'Things have changed, haven't they, with Josh…' She faltered. 'I'm sorry. I don't mean to be insensitive. I just want to be honest with Ryan. I have to.'

'It's *insanity*, Jemma. Think about it. Do you really think he would want to know? What will it do to him now he's bonded with the child? Allowing him to think the baby was his was the cruellest of deceptions, but telling him the person you cheated on him with was more than just a friend…?'

'I wasn't going to tell him that. I was going to tell him—'

'What? More lies, dressed up as the truth? If you start down this road it will all come out. He will *never* forgive you. How could he? You'll lose everything,' Cassie warned her, her heart pumping with fear. 'Your husband, your house. *Everything*. I can't let you do this, Jemma. I won't. Jemma? *Jemma?*' she said frantically, but Jemma had gone.

CHAPTER THIRTY-EIGHT

Jemma

The phone still in her hand, Jemma gazed out of the bedroom window, seeing nothing of the pretty view over the open fields opposite. Her silence had afforded her this. Thinking it was a way to save her marriage and provide the home she and Ryan could never otherwise have afforded, the home that Ryan had craved after spending his childhood in care, she'd been hugely relieved when Cassie had offered to help her. It was the least she could do, Cassie had said, to make sure the baby's future was secure. She'd been so understanding, as only a woman who'd been through a similar bereavement could be, and had come up with a way forward for Jemma when she'd been flailing.

Jemma had thought her marriage was over until she'd found Ryan at the cemetery grieving the loss of Noah as deeply as she was. That was when they'd both realised they didn't want it to be over. Ryan had been desperate for a family, somewhere he belonged. How could she have told him she was pregnant with another man's child? She'd guessed that in offering her financial help, Cassie had wanted to be sure of her silence, and she'd readily agreed. If Ryan had ever found out, it would have broken his heart into a thousand pieces. If he'd found out on top of that what Cassie had told her about Josh, it would have destroyed him.

She hadn't bargained on Josh wanting to be involved in the baby's life, determined to put his responsibility as a father above his friendship with Ryan, above anything he'd ever felt for her. He'd loved her. Even when she'd been as vile as it was possible for a woman to be to a man, she'd suspected he still did. She'd been sure that he would hate her when she'd insisted she wanted nothing to do with him, that he would walk away, as any other man treated so badly would have done. She'd been shocked when he'd contacted her.

She didn't know how to handle it. Cassie told her to deny him access. She'd tried, but Josh only grew more determined. He'd cared, genuinely. Recalling how gently he'd held her when, not long after losing Noah, she'd sobbed in his arms, she gulped back a deep sense of shame. She'd misjudged him. Hurt him so badly.

When he'd died, even as she mourned him, she'd prayed it would all go away. That she could bury what had happened between them and carry on as normal. How could she have been so naïve? Ryan knew something. How much, Jemma didn't know, but she'd sensed a change in him. He'd been withdrawn, watchful. She'd been calling out in her sleep, he'd said. How much had she unwittingly told him? She'd caught him several times lately standing over the cot staring at Liam. Not in wonderment, but studying him hard, as if analysing his features. The comment he'd made about his eye colour had made her blood run cold. What should she do? If she told him, she would lose him. If she didn't, she felt she was losing him anyway.

Goose bumps prickling her flesh, as if the ghost of Josh had walked over her grave, she rubbed her arms and turned from the window, and her heart leapt in her chest.

'Shouldn't you be at work?' Ryan asked from the doorway.

'God, you almost gave me a heart attack.' Jemma attempted a smile.

Ryan didn't smile back.

'I… rang in sick,' Jemma stammered. 'I didn't feel too well this morning.'

Ryan nodded, but his eyes were narrow, his expression inscrutable. 'Feeling better now?' he asked after a second.

'A bit.' Jemma broke eye contact, smoothing a non-existent crease in the duvet as she walked towards him. 'I think it's that bug that's going—'

'Who were you talking to on the phone?' Ryan cut across her.

'No one,' she said quickly. 'I mean, no one important. Just a friend. Kelly, from school.'

A frown crossed Ryan's face. 'Not Cassie then?' he asked bluntly.

'I…' Jemma scrambled for something to say. 'She did ring, yes,' she offered lamely. 'A moment ago. She wanted to chat about—'

'Josh?' Ryan enquired, his expression darkening.

Jemma's blood froze. 'No. I mean… Yes, she did mention him, obviously she would—'

'I *heard*, Jemma!' Ryan glared at her. 'Every word.'

Jemma's mouth ran dry. Silence hung heavily between them for an agonising second. 'It didn't mean anything!' she cried hopelessly, moving towards him.

Ryan stepped back, his thunderous gaze rooting her to the spot. 'Right.' He locked eyes full of contempt hard on hers. 'You created a fucking child together and it didn't *mean* anything?'

Jemma took another stumbling step forward. 'Ryan, please, let me explain.'

'*Explain?*' He laughed incredulously.

'I made a mistake.' Jemma ran her tongue over her parched lips. 'A terrible mistake. One I'll—' She stopped, letting out a yelp of shock, as he slammed his fist hard into the door frame.

'Ryan!' She flew towards him.

'*Don't.*' His chest heaving, he warned her off. 'When were you going to tell me, Jemma?' He wiped his bloodied hand across his mouth. 'Not when he was born, clearly; you were hoping I was gullible enough to accept him as mine. When he was ten? After I'd given a speech at his fucking wedding? *When?*'

'I *was* going to tell you,' Jemma lied. 'I wanted to.'

'Yeah, right.' Ryan sneered scornfully. 'When was that then? After you'd made the "terrible mistake" of shagging my mate? Or when you realised you were pregnant with his child?'

She dropped her gaze. 'I… don't know,' she whispered, wrapping her arms about herself. She felt so cold. So cold and lonely and ugly inside. She'd thought this was her way of having everything. The family she'd so badly craved. A beautiful little house they could live happily ever after in. Instead, she had nothing. Dirty secrets swept under the carpet, that was all.

'I get that you wanted to keep the baby.' Ryan spoke after a minute, his voice choked. 'But this? The deceit? The lies? *Why?* What did I do that was so *wrong?*'

'I'm sorry,' Jemma murmured uselessly. Ryan didn't move to hold her as the tears cascaded down her face. He would have done once. Would have always been there for her, but she hadn't wanted him, couldn't bear him near her, his pain and his grief only exacerbating hers. 'When did you know?' she asked him, swallowing back the knot of guilt expanding in her throat.

He glanced away. 'About the affair? A while,' he said with a disconsolate shrug. 'It might have been an idea to delete the texts he sent you every five minutes, you know?'

She could feel his humiliation, the heat from his eyes as he looked back at her.

'Did you want to be with him?'

She shook her head.

'Right, so you were heartbroken at his funeral because…?'

Confused, she squinted at him. 'He died, Ryan, horribly.'

'Yeah.' Ryan shrugged again, indifferent, and turned towards the stairs. 'And as far as I'm concerned, the bastard deserved all he got.'

Jemma's head snapped up. 'Ryan?' She followed him, dread pooling in her stomach. 'What do you mean?' she asked as he thundered down the stairs. 'Ryan! What are you *saying?*'

He didn't answer, didn't look back.

'It was an accident!' she shouted, over the slam of the front door. 'He fell!'

CHAPTER THIRTY-NINE

Kimberley

Kim was walking back through the playing fields behind the gym towards the main road. Her mind on Cassie, wondering how she was managing to remain so together after all that had gone on; she didn't take much notice of the man walking behind her, until he started whistling. It was a bit of an odd melody for this time of year.

Rain was beginning to spit down, and a chill ran through her as he whistled on, 'Auld Lang Syne' echoing mournfully across the open ground. Scanning the field, only to realise she was alone apart from him, she glanced back and her heart stopped dead. She stared hard at him, and slowly her heart started pumping again. He was the same height, the same colouring, wearing a similar leather jacket to the one she'd last seen Josh in, but it wasn't him. She was imagining things, 'Auld Lang Syne' and her guilty conscience conjuring up his ghost.

His hands thrust deep in his jacket pockets, the man stared back at her. Kim was about to say something, anything to break the ice, but there was something about the intent way he was looking at her, his face hard and expressionless.

Acutely aware of what she was wearing – leggings and a cropped sports top, the tracksuit top she'd been about to put on still in her sports bag – she turned round and walked on. Panic took root when he recommenced his whistling, and she quickened her pace and fumbled for her phone in her bag. God, where *was* it?

Glancing quickly back again as she pulled the bag from her shoulder, she realised he was keeping up with her. Following her.

She dug deeper in her bag, a hard lump clogging her throat. She held it by one handle, delving in the pockets and right to the bottom, and finally her hand met hard plastic. She yanked the phone out and glanced over her shoulder once more. *Shit.* He was gaining ground.

She looked towards the gate. It was miles off. *Shit. Shit.* Her chest hammering, she veered to the right, breaking into a run towards a hedgerow at the perimeter of the field. He was still behind her. She dropped her bag and ran faster. He came after her, shouting something, Kim couldn't hear what. Pressing her thumb hard to her phone, cursing the cheap casing, she struggled to switch the bloody thing on.

She was almost at the hedgerow. The road into the town centre was just beyond it. There would be people, cars.

'Oi!' he yelled behind her. 'What yer running for? I was chasing my dog, not you!'

What dog? Kim hadn't seen a dog. Did he have a lead? Not daring to look back, she sprinted on, through the thicket fronting the hedgerow, ready to launch herself over it.

'Silly cow,' the man threw after her. 'Do yerself a favour, luv. You'll cause yourself an injury.'

Kim's heart hammered. He'd stopped a few yards off and was turning around, walking away. Her legs weak from the exertion, trembling with fear, she resisted sinking to her haunches. Keeping her eyes fixed on him, she made her way along the hedge until she spotted a gap big enough to squeeze through.

On the other side, she debated for a second and then called Adam, who she knew wouldn't hesitate to come to her rescue. 'Adam?' she said tearfully when he picked up. 'I'm really sorry to bother you while you're working, but—'

'What's happened?' Adam was immediately concerned. 'Are you all right? Is it Sam?'

He'd grown attached to the baby, shortening his name affectionately. Kim was both touched and saddened by that. 'Sam's fine,' she assured him. 'I checked with Cassie as I left the gym. I was on my way back, but…' She gulped in a wretched breath.

'Jesus. What? Is it Cassie?' Adam's voice was a combination of wary and fearful.

'No, nothing like that,' she said quickly. 'It's just… I've got a bit of a problem. I was running from this man and—'

'What man?' Adam stopped her, his tone shocked. 'When? *Where?*'

'In the playing fields at the back of the gym. I was taking a shortcut. I heard him behind me, and I—'

'Are you still there now?' Adam cut in, his tone tight.

'I'm on the road outside, leading into town.' Kim sniffled, and wiped a hand under her nose.

'Are there people around?' Adam asked, clearly worried.

'Yes. Lots. I'm just heading to the roundabout by Morrisons.'

'Go to the supermarket entrance,' he instructed her. 'Wait there. I'll be ten minutes. Try not to worry.'

Kim heard his hurried footsteps, a door opening and closing. Wherever he was, he was clearly exiting fast. 'I won't,' she assured him shakily. 'Not now I know you're on your way.'

CHAPTER FORTY

Kim watched, impressed, as Adam screeched to a stop in the car park directly opposite the supermarket doors. A second later, he was thrusting his door open and climbing hurriedly out to meet her as she ran towards him.

He'd obviously noticed her torn top. She saw his eyes flick to her torso. She guessed her make-up would be smudged, tear tracks wending their way down her face. She must look a right state.

Noting his concern, she launched herself at him, pressing her face hard into his shoulder. 'I'm sorry,' she whispered. 'I didn't know who else to call.'

Seeming uncertain what to do as she clung to his neck, Adam hesitated for a second, then wrapped his arms gently around her. 'There's nothing to be sorry for, Kim,' he assured her.

'I shouldn't have dragged you out of work.' Kim eased away from him, gulping back a sob and wiping a hand across her cheek. 'It's just, when I realised I'd lost my bag and that my purse was inside it…'

'It's fine.' Adam gave her a reassuring smile. 'What's that?' he asked, his eyes darkening as he looked at her throat.

Kim's fingers fluttered towards the raw scratch she knew he was referring to. 'I got caught up in some brambles near the hedgerow,' she said, her hand trembling as she wiped at a fresh tear spilling down her face. 'I was trying to get away from him and—'

'He was following you?' Adam's eyes darkened to thunder.

'Yes,' Kim said in a small voice. 'I might not have noticed, but he started whistling behind me, as if he wanted to scare me. I started to walk faster, and then he walked faster. And then I panicked and ran, and he ran, and…' She stopped, averting her gaze and swallowing hard.

'And?' said Adam.

'He was shouting something. I'm not sure what,' she went on, wrapping her arms around herself. Noticing her shivering, Adam tugged off his jacket.

'I looked over my shoulder to see how far away he was,' Kim went on as he draped the jacket protectively around her, 'and that's when I realised he was almost on top of me.'

'Jesus Christ.' Adam wiped a hand angrily across his mouth.

'I was all tangled up in the thicket by then, and he…' She faltered and drew in a breath. 'He…' Closing her eyes, she stopped.

Her eyes sprang open as Adam placed his arm around her. 'It's okay,' he said softly, drawing her closer and guiding her towards the passenger side of his car. 'Let's get you inside and warmed up a bit, shall we? You're shaking fit to rattle something loose.'

Helping her into the passenger seat, he closed the door with another reassuring smile, and then went around to the driver's side. 'Okay?' he asked, climbing in.

Twisting towards him, she nodded. But she guessed from Adam's furious expression as he swept his gaze over her that she looked anything but. She noted him looking again at her torn top, the flecks of blood on her breasts.

An agitated tic playing at his cheek, he pulled his gaze back to her face. 'Did he…?' He stopped, his hands going to the steering wheel, his fingers tightening around it.

Kim got the gist. 'No. He…' she wavered, 'assaulted me, but he didn't… He ran off when I managed to scream. He took my bag. My purse was inside it. That's why I called you. I… wasn't sure what else to do.'

Adam clutched the steering wheel hard. '*Bastard!*'

'I'm all right.' She reached to place a hand over his. 'Honestly, Adam, I'm okay, I promise.'

He emitted a short incredulous laugh. 'Have you called the police?' he asked, his voice choked as he glanced at the phone she was clutching.

Kim shook her head. 'I tried when I was running, but my phone was off. I couldn't turn it on. The panic, I think.' She looked at him uncertainly. 'I've been in this kind of situation before,' she said, her voice tremulous. 'That's why I was so terrified.'

His face paling, Adam eyed her questioningly.

'This guy…' she dropped her gaze, 'he stalked me. I got away from him eventually, but… something similar happened.'

Adam sucked in a terse breath, held it. Then cursed again, half under his breath. 'You should report it, Kim,' he said, sounding sick to his soul – for her. 'This bastard shouldn't get away with what he's done. Then there are the other women he might prey on, possibly already has.'

Kim looked back at him. 'I will,' she said, nodding. 'Just… not now. All I want is to go home to my baby.'

Adam blew out a sigh, but nodded understandingly. 'Do you want to talk about it?' he asked her cautiously. 'What happened before?'

Kim's eyes flickered down again. 'I would love to. I've never really spoken about it before, but I actually think I could, to you. Maybe not here, though,' she added, with the tiniest of smiles. 'Right now, I think I just need someone to hold me; no agenda, you know?'

Adam hesitated for a second, and then placed an arm around her, allowing her to rest her head on his shoulder. He held her for a while, until her sniffles subsided, and then eased gently away. 'We should get back,' he said, his eyes searching hers. 'Are you sure you're okay? Would you like me to take you to the hospital?'

'I'd rather not. I'm okay. Just shaken,' Kim assured him. 'I really would rather get back to Samuel.'

Adam nodded, but didn't look convinced.

'You know, I've never met anyone like you, someone so genuinely caring,' she said as he started the car. 'Whatever happens in the future, between you and Cassie, I mean, I want you to know that I'm always there for you, Adam.'

CHAPTER FORTY-ONE

Cassandra

Sitting in the garden with Samuel nestled against her shoulder, finally contentedly sleeping, Cassie was surprised to see Adam come through the patio doors.

'You didn't mention you'd be back early,' she said, careful not to wake Samuel as she got to her feet. He'd tested his lungs mightily after she'd fed him and tried to put him down. The little man had ideas of his own, a strong personality, undoubtedly. Strength of character was no bad thing, though. God knew he would need it to survive in today's world.

'No, I wasn't planning to be.' Adam stepped out onto the patio as she laid Samuel carefully in his pram. He didn't stir; he was obviously all cried out, poor mite.

Walking across to the pram, Adam smiled fondly down at him. Cassie felt a stab of sorrow that she hadn't been able to give him his own child. God really did move in mysterious ways, though. After Josh had gone, this child had come miraculously into their lives. She'd hoped that he might help them to find a way through the grief that shrouded them and find some contentment again. She was realising now that might not be possible. Adam had been growing increasingly irritated, simply because she'd forced herself onwards rather than give in to the dark depression that had wrapped itself around her like a cloying grey blanket; unable to allow the dirt to build up around her, which would only depress her further. He'd never really seemed open to discussing the shoplifting incident, seeming to believe that she was guilty, presumably because of the previous incident. She'd wondered, as she lay awake in the small hours wishing she could reach out to him, if he hadn't been content for a while. They'd had no common bond once Josh had gone, after all. And then Kim had crash-landed into their lives. No doubt she'd reminded him he could still have a family, if only he were with a younger woman.

'Kim called me,' he said. Cassie smiled ironically. 'She, er, had a problem in town. I went to fetch her.'

'Oh?' Raising an eyebrow, Cassie glanced back to the house. There was no sign of Kim. She wondered whether she was in the downstairs toilet, repairing her make-up. Cassie had noticed she'd been titivating a lot lately.

'And she called you?' she enquired casually, and started to tidy up the paraphernalia on the patio table. It was growing chilly. She would have to take Samuel inside.

'She lost her purse,' Adam said, his expression distracted as he turned to face her.

'I see. That's unfortunate.' Cassie frowned. She'd spilled some juice on the table, she noticed, moving her glass. She would have to clean that up. It would attract wasps. 'How on earth did she manage to do that?'

'It was in her sports bag. The bag was stolen.' Adam was watching her carefully now, baffled by her apparent indifference. But Cassie wasn't indifferent, far from it. If Adam was oblivious to the attention Kim paid him, her subtle manipulations, Cassie's radar was on red alert.

'But not her phone?' she asked, bending to pick up her gardening tools. Tugging a baby wipe from the pack still on the table, she used it to wipe the mud from her trowel.

'No,' Adam said uncertainly. 'She must have been carrying it.'

Cassie noted the furrow in his brow as she glanced at him. 'Well that was lucky, wasn't it?' She gave him a short smile. 'That she had your number to hand, I mean. And that you were able to drop everything and ride like Sir Galahad to her rescue.'

'What in God's name are you talking about, Cassie?' He looked angry. But she was also angry. Fed up with being treated as if she were a fool, as if she were mentally unstable. No doubt the growing rift between them would suit Kim, whom Cassie was beginning to think wouldn't hesitate to step into her shoes.

'Nothing,' she said lightly, and turned her attention to wiping her secateurs. 'Just that I'm not as naïve as I may seem, that's all.'

'Jesus,' Adam muttered, and glanced skywards. 'Would you like to tell me what's going on here, Cassie?' he asked, an edge to his tone, 'because I really have no idea.'

Cassie ignored him in favour of removing a particularly stubborn chunk of mud.

'Cassie!' Adam snapped. 'For God's sake, will you stop that!'

'Stop what?' She blinked at him, perplexed. Was she inconveniencing him in some way, she wondered. By breathing, possibly? She swallowed back the tears building inside her.

'Talking in riddles. Cleaning everything in sight! What the *hell* is wrong with you?'

She ignored that, too. Plucking a fresh wipe from the pack, she channelled her energies into cleaning the tabletop vigorously instead.

'She was attacked!' Adam raised his voice.

Samuel stirred in his pram. Cassie stopped wiping.

'Some pervert was following her across the playing fields.' Seeing he had her attention, Adam went on more quietly. 'Naturally she would call me, knowing you were here with Samuel.'

Cassie took a minute to assimilate what he was saying. 'Did he catch her?' she asked, trying to dissect her emotions. Why didn't she feel anything? Horror? Sympathy? She did feel something:

disbelief. She didn't believe Kim, though Adam clearly did. Cassie was struck by an overwhelming sadness as she considered that.

Adam eyed her, confused. 'I've just said.'

'So you did.' Tilting her head to one side, Cassie looked him over. He was clearly working to restrain himself, but still his fury was tangible. Outrage for Kim, rage directed at *her*. Why? Her heart twisted with hurt. She took a long breath. 'Has she reported it to the police?'

'No.' Adam sighed. 'She doesn't want to. I can't say I blame her, given what she'll have to go through. I was hoping you might persuade her.'

Cassie paused to take stock. 'I could try,' she said. 'I can see why she would be reluctant, though, considering what she was wearing.'

Adam squinted at her. 'What?'

'The clothes she was wearing,' she repeated calmly. 'They're designed to attract attention after all, aren't they?'

Adam baulked. 'You have to be joking.'

Cassie didn't answer. Walking across to Samuel, who was fretting, she rocked his pram, shushing him gently.

Adam shook his head. 'Are you telling me you think she *deserved* to be attacked?'

Cassie answered with an enigmatic smile. He really couldn't see it, could he? That the girl was playing him like a fiddle? 'That's not what I said, Adam,' she replied evenly. 'I merely observed that she was aiming to attract attention.'

He laughed incredulously. 'I don't fucking believe this.'

Cassie turned to face him, her anger bubbling to the surface. '*Your* attention, Adam, quite obviously. And she has it. Doesn't she?'

He stared at her, a long, penetrating gaze. 'You're insane,' he muttered, and turned to walk away.

Cassie swallowed back the hard lump in her throat. 'I know what you're doing!' she yelled after him.

Adam stopped and ran a hand agitatedly through his hair. 'Which is what, exactly?' he asked, his tone weary, which only added to her humiliation.

'You know *very* well.' She laughed. Was he about to go the denial route?

Sighing heavily, he turned to face her. 'No, I don't. You're losing it, Cassie,' he said, kneading his temples. 'You need help.'

Cassie felt her blood boil. 'So it's all in my muddled little mind, is it?'

'Yes.' He locked his eyes on hers. 'You're obsessing, Cassie. There's nothing—'

'The amount of time you spend at her cottage, the touchy-feely body language between you, all in my overactive imagination?'

'Cassie, will you just slow down and *listen*? There's nothing going—'

'The lingering eye-contact?' Cassie's voice rose. 'It's blatantly obvious, for God's sake! Are you going to add insult to injury and stand there and *lie* to me?' Moving towards him, she reached to snatch her phone from the table, catching the juice glass as she did.

'For fuck's sake!' Adam shouted as the glass shattered against the slabs. 'There is nothing going on! You need to talk to a counsellor. Now! Get help, before you drive—'

'How *dare* you?' Cassie eyeballed him furiously. 'How *could* you? After all I've been...' Seeing Kim coming towards the patio doors, she trailed off.

'What's happening?' Kim asked, turning beguiling tear-filled eyes on Adam.

It was an act. Cassie looked from her to Adam, stunned. Couldn't he see it? It took all her willpower not to go across and slap the girl, which would go some way to venting her fury. And would also give Kim immense satisfaction. She was playing Cassie too, her aim to make her look like a raving lunatic in front of her husband. 'As if you didn't know,' she seethed contemptuously.

'Cassie?' An alarmed look on her pretty face, Kim took a step towards her. 'I don't know what you're thinking, but I overheard some of it, and—'

Cassie whirled around to walk away from her, cutting her off mid-sentence.

'Cassie, you've got it wrong.' Kim caught up with her as she reached the pram.

'I'm leaving,' Cassie informed her.

'No you're not.' Striding across to her, Adam caught hold of her arm as she bent to lift Samuel from the pram. 'Not with Samuel, Cassie. That's not going to happen. You need to calm down and listen.'

'Listen? Ha! Do you honestly expect me to stand here while you and your little trollop lie through your teeth to me? No! I won't have it. I won't let you—'

'That's *enough*, Cassie!' Adam yelled. 'Kim has been through enough without this.'

'She's *lying*. Why can't you see what she's doing?' Cassie emitted a disbelieving laugh. 'Silly question, I suppose. Love being blind and all that. Or should I say lust? You're disgusting. You're old enough to be her father!' She attempted to yank her arm from his grasp.

Adam only tightened his grip. 'Look at her,' he said, steering her around to face Kim. 'She's injured. Her clothes are torn. What more do you need to convince you to stop this bloody insanity?'

With no choice, Cassie did as he wanted, looking Kim over slowly and derisively. Kim was now crying actual tears. She was good, Cassie had to admit. She should win an Oscar. 'Couldn't wait to get them off her, hey, Adam?' she asked, gaining marginal satisfaction from Kim's muted sob as she pressed a hand to her mouth.

'That's it, I'm done with this.' Adam released his hold on her arm. 'Kim, get Samuel's things together. I'll drive you—'

'Ask her what Josh's favourite cake was,' Cassie demanded. 'Go on, *ask* her.'

Adam said nothing; simply stared at her, looking pig sick.

Not half as sick as Cassie felt. 'He was allergic to dairy products, you lying, scheming little bitch!' she shouted, stopping Kim in her tracks as she started across the patio. 'Pity you didn't know that, isn't it?' she added, over a silence so profound you could hear a leaf drop. 'You might have put him out of whatever misery he suffered with you sooner.'

CHAPTER FORTY-TWO

Joshua

July 2019

Since it was pouring with rain, Josh supposed he should be grateful that Kim had suggested meeting inside the pub, though why she insisted on the same pub, which was just outside the village he would rather avoid, he couldn't fathom. She had friends in the village, she'd said. He couldn't think who. It was a small community. He certainly didn't have many friends there any more. Jemma hated his guts. As for Ryan… Well, he wouldn't be very friendly once he found out that the child Jemma was carrying was his so-called mate's, which he was bound to whether or not Josh pursued access.

He'd consulted a solicitor, only to be told that he couldn't establish the baby was his until it was born, when he would have a right to ask for paternity testing. The technology to establish paternity before then did exist, but would require the consent of the mother, which was highly unlikely to be forthcoming. In any case, Josh didn't want to go that route. In short, he could do nothing but wait. 'Try to build a sensible relationship with the mother,' the solicitor had advised. Fat chance. 'Oh, and if you do have to pursue access through the courts, you might want to think how you're going to fund it,' he'd added. He would need a shedload of cash, basically, which he simply didn't have.

He sighed and knocked back his pint. As for the situation with Kim, despite the messages he'd sent he'd had no contact from her whatsoever. He'd been taken aback when she'd called him out of the blue. She hadn't turned up for the morning train in a long time, although he was sure he'd glimpsed her a couple of times at Birmingham New Street. He'd felt as if she was bloody well haunting him at one point, when, waking hot and sweaty, he'd gone to open the window and noticed a slim figure standing on the opposite side of the road. He couldn't be sure it was her in the pitch black, but he'd had a weird feeling it might be. When he'd pulled the front door open two minutes later, shaking his head free of sleep, the figure had gone. His housemate reckoned it was a thief sussing the area. Josh supposed he was right; there'd been a break-in nearby the week before.

Feeling more guilty after that, he'd tried harder to find her, but she seemed to have disappeared. Part of him selfishly hoped she'd been mistaken, that she hadn't been pregnant and had simply moved on. She wasn't mistaken, as he gathered when she told him she couldn't talk on the phone because she was due at her antenatal class. She would be well into the pregnancy now, and Josh had no idea what to do, other than what he was obliged to. He didn't like himself much for it, but he really wasn't sure whether he believed the child was his. He must be the unluckiest man on earth if it was.

About to go and get another drink, he glanced towards the door to see that Kim had arrived, finally. She was definitely pregnant. He noted the bump under her long jumper and felt a turmoil of conflicting emotion: regret, uncertainty, shame.

Checking his watch, feeling unnerved by the half-hour she'd kept him waiting, he picked up his glass and got to his feet as she approached.

'Sorry I'm late. I do hope it didn't inconvenience you too much. I felt a bit faint before I came out. The baby turning, I think.

Not that I imagine you would be interested,' she said, sweeping a derisory gaze over him.

He guessed she'd caught him looking at his watch. 'Of course I'm interested, Kim. I checked the time instinctively. It's force of habit; I do it a hundred times a day in school. I didn't mean anything by it.'

Kim didn't look impressed.

'So, how are you?' he asked uncomfortably.

She gave him a short smile. 'Pregnant,' she answered curtly.

Josh pulled in a breath. He guessed he'd asked for that. What else was she going to say, after all? 'Drink?' he asked her as she sat down at the table.

She shook her head.

Deciding to pass himself, given that this was hardly a social occasion, he placed his glass back on the table and sat down opposite her.

Kim dragged her ever-escaping tendrils of hair from her face and glanced around. She looked pale, Josh noticed. Settling a hand on her tummy, she turned her gaze to him. 'So, did you have something you wanted to say to me?' she asked him.

He knitted his brow in confusion. 'You called *me*,' he reminded her.

'Because I hoped that now you've had time to think about things, you might have something to say that's worth listening to,' she said, her expression somewhere between reproachful and hopeful.

Josh's heart sank. He might have asked what it was she wanted him to do, but he already knew. She'd said it succinctly enough when he'd offered his support the last time they'd met. 'All or nothing,' she'd said, leaving him in no doubt that she wanted the whole wedding thing. But how could he do that? He didn't love her. He didn't even know her that well, nor she him. Wouldn't marrying her out of some misguided attempt to do the right thing be a recipe for failure? Instead he would offer to be there for her whenever she needed him, be a friend to her. Right, and how lame did that sound? It would be her bringing the child up – on her own. *Christ*, when he messed up, he really did do it spectacularly.

'I will support you, Kim,' he repeated. 'I'm not trying to shirk my responsibilities, I promise. I'm happy to co-parent.' He paused, wondering at the irony of his desperately wanting to do that with Jemma. Because he'd been in love with her, which obviously influenced his thinking about the baby. How fair was that on an innocent child? Perhaps he needed to stop thinking about his own emotions and concentrate on what was really important here, he thought soberly.

Kim scanned his face. Her eyes were glassy with tears, Josh noted, his gut twisting. 'That's very noble of you,' she said eventually. Then, two bright spots blooming on her cheeks, she looked away.

Now what did he do? His guilt intensified. She didn't even have a place of her own. She'd said she was staying with a friend, he recalled, as it dawned on him that perhaps he actually *was* being a bastard. He had no reason to think she was lying about the baby being his. Why would she? She must know paternity could easily be proved. Him suggesting they get a test would make him even more of a shit in her eyes. In his own eyes too – he wasn't his own biggest fan right now. Whatever happened in the future, the fact was, she was having a baby, and she was also homeless, or as good as. He was house-sharing. The guy he was living with would be moving out soon, but even as things stood, there was room for another person. If she couldn't meet the rent on her student income, he'd cover it. He would have to. He needed to help her keep her life on track, be there for the baby, end of.

'Look, Kim, I'm not sure whether—' he started. And then stopped as she got abruptly to her feet.

'Right, well, that was short and sweet, wasn't it?' she said, picking up her bag. 'Thanks for nothing, Josh. Like I said, you can keep your financial support. I can manage without it. There are millions of single mothers out there who do, thanks to the men in their lives not stepping up. I suppose I'm just going to be another statistic. But that's not your problem, is it? Because *you* can just walk away.' Wiping angrily at her eyes, she turned for the exit.

'Kim, wait.' He stood to follow her. 'I was going to—'

Kim whirled around. 'No, Josh. I won't wait to hear you spouting more rubbish. You manipulate me into having sex with you and then think you can treat me like an *inconvenience*?'

Josh's heart plummeted to the pit of his stomach. 'That's absolute bullshit, Kim,' he seethed. 'You *know* it is.'

'There was no love there, was there?' she challenged him. 'Even though you told me you loved me.'

What? Josh stared at her, flabbergasted. 'I never said I loved you,' he protested, realising how that sounded, but not caring. 'I liked you, felt sorry for you. I was scared for you after all you'd been through, but I was never anything but honest.' And now, seeing the look in her eyes, hearing the rubbish she was spouting, he was bloody well scared *of* her.

'You forced me!' She eyeballed him furiously. 'As good as. Coercion is a crime, Josh, or haven't you heard? You knew how vulnerable I was after my previous relationship. That I would be too frightened to say no.'

Josh felt the blood drain from his body. Saw heads turning, every gaze in the room burning into him. 'What in God's name are you *talking* about?' He stared at her, disbelieving.

'You *used* me,' she cried. 'All you wanted from me was sex. What do you think your parents would think about that, hey? Your mother, who you keep bleating on about being ill, as if that's an excuse for her instilling nil respect for women in you.'

'*What?*' Josh squinted at her. 'That's enough, Kim. You are way out of—'

'Adam, who's so caring and obviously ten times the man you are,' Kim talked over him, 'what do you think *he* would think?

Do you think he'd turn his back on a woman who was carrying his baby? Treat her the way you seem to believe you can treat me? I think not. Don't you?'

Josh's mouth ran dry. 'Don't you dare, Kim,' he warned her, a hard knot of anger tightening inside him. That was the reason for this charade, he realised. Her reason for wanting to meet here. So she could threaten him. *Coerce* him. Into doing what, for fuck's sake?'

'You probably hoped I'd get rid of it, didn't you?' she said, narrowing her eyes. 'That would have solved your problem, wouldn't it, me killing my baby?'

He was scarcely able to believe what he was hearing. 'Don't be ridiculous. I would never—'

'It's people like *you* who should be got rid of!' She glared at him. 'You're despicable.'

'Just stop this, Kim, will you?' Josh said shakily. 'I don't know what it is I'm supposed to have done, but whatever you're thinking of doing, please don't. My mother really hasn't been well. My parents both have enough on their plates without my problems.'

She didn't answer, notching her chin up instead.

'Kim, please come back and sit down,' he begged. 'Let's try and work this out calmly.'

She cocked her head to one side, studying him now as if she felt sorry for him. 'No need, Josh.' She looked away. 'You've said all I need to hear.'

Bewildered, Josh watched her leave. With all eyes on him, he didn't dare follow her. Didn't have a clue what to do. She actually said he'd *forced* her. Jesus. She'd instigated what had gone on between them. She'd been all over him. What in God's name was he going to do? His career would be over before it started, his life ruined. His mother… Kim wouldn't go and see her, would she? Speak to Adam? *Why* would she? But Josh had a sick feeling in his gut. She'd grilled him about Adam, said he sounded like her sort of guy. He pictured again the figure standing outside his house.

Would an opportunist thief really have just stood there, knowing they'd been seen? She'd witnessed his meeting with Jemma. She'd denied it, but… The hairs rose on his skin as he recalled her tearful apology after falling down the station steps: *My ex accused me of all sorts of things. He said it was me stalking him, when it was the other way around. He told my friends I was obsessed with him…*

How was it she'd always been on the same train he was on? That he'd seen her outside his school, somewhere else she claimed not to have been? Jesus Christ, had she been stalking *him*? It seemed incomprehensible, but what if it wasn't? What if she had moved on and was targeting someone else now? He might be way off the mark here, suffering from delusions himself, but was it possible she'd made up her mind to extract from Adam what Josh plainly couldn't offer her? Not just support, but security for the foreseeable future. He needed to talk to his stepfather. At least to make him aware.

CHAPTER FORTY-THREE

Kimberley

Noting the absence of Cassie's car on the drive, Kim approached the house. Adam had been frantic when he'd rung, telling her that Cassie had gone off somewhere after the awful scene on the patio and he had no idea where. He'd wondered whether she might have been in contact with Kim. Kim imagined that she was the last person Cassie would contact when she believed she was having an affair with her husband. Poor Adam. He would be distraught with his mentally unbalanced wife gone missing. He hadn't asked her to come over, but she guessed he would need a shoulder.

Taking a fortifying breath, she knocked on the door.

'Hi.' She offered him a tentative smile when he opened it, his expression distracted. He looked worryingly pale, with dark circles under his eyes. Kim was sure there was another worry line etched into his brow. He would be better off if Cassie stayed away. He needed someone to look after him for a change, not someone who heaped endless worry on his shoulders.

'Hey.' He mustered up a smile and stepped back to allow her in. 'Sorry, my mind's all over the place.'

'I'm not surprised.' She gave him a sympathetic smile back. 'Has she been in touch?'

He nodded. 'She's safe,' he said, heaving out a sigh. Kim couldn't tell whether it was one of relief or despair. The latter, probably.

He must be at his wits' end with his wife becoming progressively more unstable.

On which subject, she braced herself to broach something that was bound to have been troubling him since Cassie had made a big point of it. 'I need to mention something, Adam.' She glanced warily at him.

Adam nodded apprehensively. 'Go on,' he said.

'What Cassie said about Josh's allergy… I knew about it, obviously. I could hardly not when we ate together most evenings, but…' She paused, making sure to convey that she was reluctant to bring it up. 'She never mentioned it to me. As far as I can remember, we've never had a conversation about cake.'

Adam looked troubled, scrutinising her carefully.

'I'm not that bothered. I know Josh's death will have derailed Cassie, emotionally and mentally. She was obviously confused,' she pushed on, 'but when she hinted that she thought I was making him miserable…'

She paused again, her eyes fixed down, communicating how miserable Cassie had made *her* feel.

'I'm sure she didn't mean it,' Adam said, after an interminably long pause, during which Kim began to panic. 'She said a lot of things she's probably regretting. I'm hoping she is anyway, that once she's had time to think…' He stopped and tugged in a breath.

Kim answered with a small nod. 'I did make him a dairy-free chocolate mousse once,' she said, looking up with a cautious smile. 'He didn't like it. Mind you, it was awful.'

Adam laughed at that, albeit sadly. 'He was probably too polite to tell you he wasn't much into chocolate,' he said, nodding towards the lounge.

'I gathered.' Kim rolled her eyes good-naturedly and followed. 'So you know where she is then?' she asked.

'In Herefordshire. We have a holiday place there.'

'That must be nice,' Kim said, her gaze going to the photograph albums scattered on the coffee table and sofa. He must really be feeling down if he was raking through old memories, no doubt wondering where it all started to go so wrong.

'It is. Josh loved it there as a child.' Adam smiled. 'He was into nature even then. He'd walk for hours over the open countryside with his dog.'

Hearing the deep sadness in his voice, his obvious loneliness, Kim felt terribly sorry for him. He was clearly suffering in all of this, and he'd done nothing to deserve it as far as she could see. 'Are these photos of him?' she asked, nodding towards the albums.

'They are,' Adam confirmed. 'Have a look if you like. I'll go and put the kettle on. No Sam?' he added curiously.

'He's with my friend for a few hours.'

'Oh, right.' He nodded thoughtfully. 'She's obviously a good friend. With you being able to leave him with her so often, I mean. We haven't met her, have we?'

'No, not yet,' Kim said, walking across to the sofa. 'Like I said, she has a little boy of her own, so she's happy to mind Samuel.'

'Handy friend to have around,' Adam commented.

'She is,' Kim said quickly, wanting to put his mind at rest. 'With all that's happened, I needed a break, to be honest, so I was really grateful she could take him.'

'Of course,' Adam said. 'Sorry if I appear to be grilling you. I…'

'You're concerned,' Kim finished sympathetically as he trailed off. 'Don't worry. I get it with all that's going on. I'd be the same. Samuel is your grandson, after all.'

Adam smiled. 'So, how are you?' he asked, his expression a mixture of apprehension and embarrassment, as it would be after the cruel things Cassie had said.

'Fine,' she assured him, 'thanks to you. I did report the man who attacked me, by the way. I'm going to give a statement tomorrow.'

'Well done, Kim,' he said, with admiration in his voice, causing a flicker of guilt to run through her. 'Let me know if you need someone to come with you.'

Her eyes flitted away. 'Thanks, Adam, I think I'll be fine, but that's really kind of you.'

'No problem at all. I'll go and make that tea,' he said, heading for the door. 'Unless you'd prefer something stronger?'

'A glass of wine would be lovely,' she said tentatively. 'I wouldn't normally, but as I'm off duty for a while…'

'One glass of wine coming up,' Adam said, looking less tense than he had when he'd invited her in. 'Red or white?'

'White. Thank you.' Glad that he was relaxing a little, she smiled at him and settled down to look through the photos.

He'd been beautiful even as a child. Kim's heart dipped heavily in her chest as she browsed the photographs. She had loved him with her whole heart and soul. She'd been so sure that when he discovered she was carrying his child, he would realise how much he loved *her*. Clearly, though, his past relationships, his experience of other women, had influenced his thinking. His mother's treatment of him, and of Adam, was hardly a shining example of how fulfilling a loving relationship could be. He'd been damaged. Kim could have changed all that, if only… He'd been so hostile that night in the pub. He'd hurt her so badly. She'd wanted him dead. She'd never imagined in a million years she could feel that way about him.

Mentally reiterating the promise she'd made him, the promise she'd made to herself to make amends, she turned the page, and froze. A photograph of Cassie looked back at her. One arm around Josh's shoulders, she looked happy and radiant, as in pregnant radiant. Her other hand rested on her tummy. There was no mistaking the bump under her top. Kim's gaze flicked to the photograph on the page alongside it. A grainy black-and-white image; there was no mistaking that either. It was a scan. A twenty-week scan, meaning she must have had a late miscarriage. She felt a pang of guilt, closely followed by disappointment for Adam. If he'd been poring over these, he plainly still had strong feelings for Cassie, despite the woman showing her true colours.

Aware of Adam coming back from the kitchen, she closed the album, pushed it aside and grabbed another. Then bowed her head and wiped a hand across her eyes.

'Kim? Are you okay?' Adam asked worriedly.

She nodded, but didn't look up. 'I'm fine,' she whispered. 'It's just…'

Placing the wine on the coffee table, Adam moved towards her. 'The photographs.' He sighed in despair. 'That was thoughtless of me. They were bound to upset you.'

Kim smiled and got to her feet. 'I'm okay, honestly,' she assured him with a stoic smile. 'Do you mind if I…' Picking up her bag, she ran a hand under her nose and nodded towards the hall.

'No problem.' Adam smiled apologetically back. He was reaching to gather up the albums as she walked to the door. Caring, he was always that. She couldn't imagine him being anything but. She hadn't been mistaken about him. She hadn't been mistaken about Josh either. He'd been caring. He'd cared for her. His thinking had been clouded by his past, that was all.

Once in the hall, she glanced back to the lounge, making sure Adam wasn't about to emerge, and then to the stairs. Steeling herself, she went quietly up them. Adam wouldn't think it odd if he found her up here. She'd often been up to fetch something from the abundant baby supplies Cassie stored in the nursery. Walking past it, she hesitated, then placed her hand on the main bedroom door and pushed it open.

Crossing to the bed, a king-size with pristine white linen, she paused. It was beautiful. She ran her hand over it. Like something out of a show home. Not very practical, though. A woman as neurotic as Cassie would be bound to spot the slightest blemish in an instant.

CHAPTER FORTY-FOUR

Careful not to thrust the bathroom door open and hit Adam with it, Kim tapped and then poked her head around. 'All done?' she enquired.

'All done,' said Adam, straightening up from where he'd been fixing the leak that had sprung out of nowhere from under the bath. 'It was the P-trap come loose, though I can't quite fathom out how. Fitted incorrectly, I suppose.'

'Thanks, Adam. I wouldn't have had a clue what to do if you hadn't come to my rescue. I didn't know who else to call. It's so risky for single women picking a plumber off some random site, isn't it? You never know who might turn up.'

Wiping his hands on his cloth, Adam nodded. She could tell by the combination of sympathy and annoyance flitting across his features that he got what she meant. 'There's a safe site that lists reputable services,' he said. 'I'll let you have the link. You can always call me, though, you know that.'

Noting the earnest look in his eyes, she smiled her appreciation. 'I know I can, Adam, thanks. I don't like to disturb you at work, though.'

'It's not a problem. I'm self-employed. I can always take time in an emergency, and I owe it to Josh to make sure the property you and his son are living in is comfortable.' Adam offered her a smile, but still looked distracted, as he had since he'd arrived.

Kim guessed why. He hadn't been at work when she'd called. He'd been at home. She gathered he'd been trying to get hold of Cassie, who apparently hadn't been returning his calls. It struck Kim that where Adam was abundantly considerate and helpful, Cassie was totally self-absorbed. Opposites attracted, she supposed, but she really did wonder what he was doing with the woman when it was obvious he would be much better off without her.

'No news yet?' she asked him, her tone sympathetic.

Adam sighed and shook his head. 'Her phone keeps going to voicemail. I was wondering whether I should drive over there.'

He was obviously worried sick about her. Nodding thoughtfully, Kim knitted her brow.

'You don't think it's a good idea?'

'Maybe,' she said with a shrug, 'but…'

Adam eyed her quizzically.

'I know you're worried about her,' Kim went on. 'I am too,' she added quickly, 'but… I'm wondering whether you might do better to give her some space. She knows you're concerned, after all. You must have rung and texted a thousand times. I'm thinking if you just turn up, it might seem as if you're trying to control her.'

Adam arched an eyebrow, then frowned contemplatively. 'I suppose.' He nodded slowly. 'I hadn't thought about that.'

'From a woman's perspective, you might do better to give her some time to think things through. She'll be back when she's cooled down, I know she will.' Kim reached to give his arm a squeeze. 'You're a catch, after all.'

Adam smiled wryly. 'You reckon?'

'Um, let me see. You're caring, not too bad-looking, handy to have around. Yup, definitely a catch.'

Adam laughed. 'I must remember to remind myself of my attributes more often,' he said, turning to survey his handiwork.

Yes, and so should someone else, Kim thought tetchily.

'I replaced the taps while I was at it,' Adam said, nodding towards the bath. 'You should get a decent flow of water now.'

'Thank God for that.' Kim eyed the ceiling. 'I'm just about coping bathing Samuel in the kitchen sink, but I'm struggling to fit in it myself.'

'I can see that would be a bit of a problem.' Adam glanced back at her, amused. 'I'll check out the plumbing in the kitchen sometime,' he offered. 'It looks a bit dodgy.'

'Brilliant, thanks, Adam.' Smiling, Kim smoothed down the short fuchsia-pink slip dress she'd chosen from Miss Selfridge for just this occasion.

'You're off out, I take it?' Adam asked, turning to pick up his tool bag.

'Just to the pub with my friend,' Kim answered, heading out onto the landing.

'Not the friend who minds Samuel, I take it?' Adam asked, following her down the stairs.

'No. You don't know her,' Kim answered, leading the way into the kitchen. Glancing back at him, she noted a puzzled look cross his face. 'Samuel's with the girl who normally minds him, don't worry. She texted me just now to tell me he's fast asleep. She's dropping him home on her way back from taking her little boy to school in the morning.'

'Oh, right. Good.' Adam nodded contemplatively.

'Coffee?' she asked, giving him a bright smile.

'Yes, why not? Just a quick one, thanks.'

Aware of him watching her carefully as she filled the kettle, Kim felt a bit flustered. She needed to change the subject. He'd been asking one or two pointed questions, wearing that same quizzical expression he'd had when he'd asked her about her trip to Boots on the day of Cassie's shoplifting spree.

'Ooh, I've just thought.' Flicking the kettle on, she went to grab her phone from the work surface. 'We should have a photo.'

Scrolling to her camera, she threw her arm around his shoulders, taking a couple of quick shots at arm's length before he had a chance to object.

Heading back to the kettle, she beamed him another smile over her shoulder. 'I hope you don't mind. It's just that after seeing your albums, I thought I should start one of my own. You know, as a keepsake for Samuel,' she gabbled on while she made the coffee. 'I'd much rather have pics of his new family than my dysfunctional one.'

'Er, no. I don't mind,' Adam said, sounding unsure.

Kim realised she'd dropped a bit of a clanger with his own family looking pretty dysfunctional at the moment. 'Black, no sugar.' She twirled around and offered him a mug. 'I put some cold water in it so you wouldn't burn yourself.'

'Cheers.' Adam smiled, but his eyes were still curious. 'So, this friend who looks after Samuel…' He went straight back to the child-minding subject. 'Sorry, I didn't catch her name.'

'Freya,' Kim said, turning away to retrieve some clothes from the washing machine. 'She's an old school friend.'

'You've known her a while then?' Adam asked as she headed to the conservatory to hang the washing on the clothes rack she'd put in there. He was grilling her again. Kim didn't like it.

'Since we were eleven,' she shouted back. 'She's as mad as a hatter, but we'd trust each other with our lives. Like I say, she has a little boy of her own, so I know Samuel's in safe hands.'

Coming back into the kitchen, she stopped in her tracks.

'It's a decent photo,' Adam said, his eyes flicking from her to the phone he'd picked up from the work surface.

Shit. Kim cursed silently. She hoped he hadn't bloody well checked her texts.

CHAPTER FORTY-FIVE

Cassandra

Realising she couldn't hide away in Herefordshire forever, a place full of happy memories that only exacerbated her loneliness, Cassie had decided it was time to come home, to be honest with Adam. What she would say to him, how she would begin to explain, she didn't know, but she had to try. First, though, she knew she had to confront the woman whose threatening texts had added to the weight of the problems that were crushing her marriage, crushing her and Adam both.

She glanced at her dashboard clock and then looked back to the pub doors, wondering whether to go in, where she might be able to follow the woman to the toilets. She had to find a way to talk to her alone. Reaching for the door handle, she stopped, relief flooding through her, as the man the woman had gone in with emerged without her.

She decided to give it a little longer before going inside. Even if she managed to get her on her own at a table, she would much rather have this conversation in private. Her patience was rewarded when, ten minutes later, the woman also came out, pulling her cigarettes from her pocket, lighting one up and blowing smoke agitatedly into the air.

Cassie had been in the wrong, she was well aware of that. She'd hated what she'd done, though she couldn't possibly have foreseen the tabloid she'd had articles lined up for folding. If the guilt she lived with had been her punishment, she'd paid for it ten times over, a thousand times since Josh's death. Now, though, mixed in with the guilt and the grief was an anger so potent she could taste it.

She watched as the woman answered a call on her mobile. Pressing it to her ear, she took another draw on her cigarette and then growled, 'Tell him he's old enough to get his own bleeding dinner. I'm his mother, not his fucking servant.'

Cassie felt bile rise in her throat. She hadn't been wrong. By whatever means she'd done what she'd done, she'd been right. Seeing a scene play out in her mind's eye, she clenched the steering wheel until the whites of her knuckles showed. Seconds was all it would take. Every sinew in her body tense, she willed herself not to release the handbrake, press her foot down hard on the accelerator and rid herself of the problem, the woman's family of *their* problem.

Breathing in deeply, she closed her eyes, seeing him, as she always did, her boy. Hearing it as she did in her dreams, the sickening impact. Felt it as if the pain were her own, her son's bones splintered by unforgiving steel against steel. She could see his face, such a perfect face, so innocent as a child. He wanted to know why. She could see the question in his eyes when he knew it was inevitable he was going to die. His warm blood speckling her own face, she would wake screaming.

'Sue!' someone yelled from the pub entrance, and Cassie snapped her eyes open, expelling the rage that had consumed her in one harsh breath. 'You forgot your shopping bag.'

'Typical. I'd forget me head if it wasn't screwed on.' The woman rolled her eyes and about-faced. 'Thanks, Debs,' she said, going back to retrieve the bag. Checking the contents, she turned, tossed her cigarette down, grinding it out with her foot, and walked straight into Cassie.

'Watch where you're going, darling,' she grumbled, giving her a cursory glance up and down.

Cassie presumed she wanted her to step aside. She stood her ground, holding the woman's bloodshot eyes instead. 'What do you want?' she asked.

The woman scowled. 'Yer what?'

'The texts!' Cassie bit back the anger rising dangerously inside her.

'What texts?' The woman's scowl deepened. 'You're out of your tree, darling,' she said, looking guardedly at her. 'I don't have a clue what you're on about.'

'But you contacted me. You…' Cassie faltered, disorientated, as the woman stepped off the kerb to go around her, the expression on her face a mixture of wariness and pity.

She felt the ground shift beneath her as she watched her go. It wasn't her. She hadn't been wary because she was frightened, meeting her on her own in the street. She'd been wary of being approached by a rambling lunatic. She hadn't even recognised her.

It wasn't her. Then who?

Cassie's stomach turned over as she realised she knew.

CHAPTER FORTY-SIX

Relieved that Adam appeared not to be home, Cassie pushed through the front door and dumped her overnight bag on the hall floor. Picking up the post, which he clearly hadn't bothered to do, she tossed it on the hall table and headed for the kitchen. She tried to leave the bag where it was, but couldn't. Her compulsion to put her clothes in the wash and tidy her toiletries away, making sure everything was in its proper place, was too strong. She needed to get her life back in order.

Swallowing the tight lump clogging her throat, she stepped back and picked up the bag. She was growing tired, weary with her own obsessive behaviour. Had she actually created the very situation she'd always dreaded *before* Kim had appeared? Had she been so sure Adam would leave her one day that she'd ended up pushing him? That was the thought that had been nagging her as she'd driven here. Now that she'd established – or at least thought she had – that it wasn't the woman from her past sending the texts, was it possible that she might somehow be able to salvage her relationship?

She'd accused him of sleeping with Kim. The Adam she knew before their lives had fallen apart would never have cheated on her. But now... She was as certain that Kim was coming on to him as she was that it had been her sending those texts. He couldn't fail to have noticed. Could he? She had to ask him outright, talk to him calmly, not rant like some demented witch. She would have to apologise, whatever her suspicions. If he *was* attracted to a woman so much younger than she was, a prettier woman with flame-coloured hair, then she might be fighting a losing battle, but she would fight. Adam had been her whole life. She loved him. Would love him until the day she died. She needed him to know that.

Heading up the stairs, she tried to work out what she would say to him. Where to start to explain the terror gnawing at her insides, the voice in her head that constantly told her she was about to lose everything. That she deserved to.

Going into the bedroom, she ran a hand through her hair, which needed a good wash, and was reminded how short it still was. Cursing herself for being obsessed now about her appearance, she walked towards the bed. She was about to drop her bag onto it when she hesitated. Something didn't feel right. Her gaze travelled over the Egyptian cotton duvet cover and her heart lurched.

The appliqué frill was at the bottom of the bed. The duvet was on upside down. She tried to think rationally above the panic mushrooming inside her. Adam had slept in it, obviously he had, and hadn't made the bed properly. Her hand went to the indent in his pillow. But why was there an indent in the other pillow? *Her* pillow?

Her mouth ran dry as she spotted the evidence of what she already knew. Her heart rate quickening, she stared stupefied for a second, and then plucked it from the pillowcase and dangled it between her thumb and forefinger. One long flame-red hair.

She snatched the pillow up, nausea rising like corrosive acid inside her as she pressed it to her face and breathed in a perfume that wasn't hers, floral, musky, warm and sweet, the smell of another woman. Would he tell her *this* was all in her mind? Her world crumbling, she stood rooted to the spot, recalling the smouldering anger in Adam's eyes when he'd told her she was imagining things. The disillusionment. She'd tried to convince herself he was right.

She'd sensed the sexual charge in the air when Kim had been around him, felt it, yet she'd doubted her instinct, doubted her sanity. Sloped off like some spurned woman, allowing them to carry on behind her back, undoubtedly aroused by the illicit thrill of it. Right here. In the bed she and Adam shared together. Had they talked about her? Laughed at her whilst lying together in their post-fucking afterglow? Raw with pain, with the knowledge that this nightmare she'd been living was indeed her reality, she wrapped her arms tightly around herself, a primal moan escaping her as she rocked to and fro.

How could she have been so *stupid*?

Anger and humiliation rising hot in her throat, she clutched hold of the corner of the duvet and, summoning the last vestiges of her self-esteem, tore it from the bed. She didn't know whether to be more insulted by what he'd done, right under her nose, or by the fact that he would think she wouldn't notice. Perhaps he wanted her to. Knowing her as he did, surely he would have been more careful if he'd wanted to cover his tracks. Plainly he didn't care.

Her chest heaving, she grappled for the fitted sheet and attempted to pull it from the mattress, catching a fingernail in the process, tearing it to the quick. The pain was excruciating, the droplet of blood stark against the pristine white of the sheet. Blood from the wound of her marriage that had opened the day she'd lost her baby.

Trying to oust the images from her head – her husband and the mother of her grandson grinding and moaning in *her* bed – she bundled the duvet and sheet into her arms. Carrying them along the landing, tripping over them as she went, she heaved them higher and, almost blinded by the tears cascading down her face, picked her way carefully downstairs.

She was passing the open lounge door when she saw them. The photograph albums, stacked on the coffee table. Images of their life together, a happy life, she'd once thought, her life with her son.

Why would he have fetched them from the loft now? He would hardly have been going through them, his heart breaking, when he didn't give a damn about his marriage, about her. He clearly didn't care about Josh either, if he was sleeping with the mother of his child. Drinking wine with her. Cassie's blood turned to icicles in her veins as she noticed the two washed wine glasses on the plate rack in the kitchen. She went to the fridge and found an open bottle of white wine. Adam didn't drink white wine. Kim did.

Stultified, she carried on to the utility room. Placing the bedding on the floor, opening the washing machine door, she wondered what temperature to choose. Forty degrees? Or thirty, bearing in mind the environment? Or sixty, considering how soiled they would be?

Sixty, she decided, reaching for the washing capsules.

A ragged sob rose inside her. She couldn't do this. *Couldn't*. She pressed a hand to her mouth, sinking to her knees on top of the Egyptian bed linen. Kim was stealing her husband, her life and her memories. Cassie tried to stop the choking sobs, but still they kept coming, racking her body. Sobs for her stolen babies, who'd never breathed independently of her; for her beautiful son, all grown, yet still such a child; for her husband. She cried until she thought her heart must surely break.

Her *grandson*… they would steal him from her too.

No. She would not let that happen. She would not allow Adam and the whore who'd slept with her son and her husband to do this to her.

Grasping the washing machine door, and then the work surface, Cassie pulled herself up, straightened her shoulders and tried to stand tall. She would do their dirty washing. In public. She would stop them.

It would scorch the lawn, she realised, heaving the bed linen outside. Her pretty garden, which she tended so meticulously, would be scarred. But she didn't care. Her mother had been right:

this was a far more satisfying way of cleaning up the dirt and mess her husband had created. Her anger growing steadily, she went back to the kitchen and found the matches she kept in a drawer to light the candles at Christmas. They wouldn't use them again now. There would be no more family Christmases. No more family.

Plucking the matches out, she banged the drawer shut and headed to the lounge, fuelled with purpose. She scanned the drinks cupboard and then grabbed the cognac – Courvoisier, Adam's tipple of choice when he was celebrating or stressed. He would certainly be stressed when he realised that though it was he who had destroyed their marriage, she was the one who was lighting the funeral pyre.

CHAPTER FORTY-SEVEN

Flames dancing in her eyes, Cassie watched the bed linen burn, waited to feel the thrill of satisfaction. There was nothing. Nothing but a hard rock in her chest. She watched a while longer, her arms wrapped tightly about herself, the warm glow of the fire scorching her cheeks but doing little to force the chill from her bones, and then went back to the kitchen for the bleach.

Hurt and anger burning inside her as surely as the fire outside, she went back upstairs into the bedroom and stood over the bed. It was a good bed, comfortable. It contoured their bodies perfectly, Adam had once said. Had *she* lain in his embrace? Had he pulled her close to his midriff, her body fitting perfectly with his?

Swallowing hard, Cassie held the bottle of bleach high, hesitated for a heartbeat, and then upended it. She couldn't wash away the sins of her husband, but the mattress would be germ-free at least. She swiped at a tear from her cheek and turned to the wardrobe, where Adam's shirts hung. Resisting the urge to press her face to them, breathe in the scent of crisp clean cotton suffused with his citrusy aftershave, she tugged them from the hangers. The majority of them had been selected by her, ironed by her.

His suits too? she wondered. Yes, she decided, piling as many as she could over her arms and making her way downstairs. If he was leaving, he could go with all that he'd left her: nothing.

Her step faltered, her heart stalling as she recognised Adam's silhouette through the glass in the front door. 'You're home early,' she commented, gliding her eyes over him as he let himself in, and then carrying on to the kitchen. He was looking very pale, she noticed. And just the tiniest bit nervous. Now why would that be?

'Cassie? What are you doing?' she heard him ask worriedly.

She ignored him. She really didn't think it was he who should be asking the questions.

Heading into the garden to drop his clothes on the fire, she gathered he'd got the gist when she heard him gasp, 'What in God's name…?'

Still she ignored him, turning instead to go back to the house. His face was white almost to the point of grey as he stepped aside, allowing her into the kitchen – wisely.

'Cassie, what are you doing?' he repeated, plainly shaken.

'Just obsessing,' she answered him blithely, squeezing her tears back.

'You've burned my clothes?' he asked incredulously as he followed her.

'And the duvet and the sheets,' she confirmed, concentrating her attention on dragging the bin from under the work surface. Checking the contents, she pulled the inner bin out and carried it to the hall.

'Why?' he said, astounded.

'Good question.' Pausing, Cassie frowned. 'To vent my emotions, I suppose,' she said, wiping her perspiring brow as she climbed the stairs, dragging the bin behind her.

Once in the bedroom, she surveyed the bleached mattress with bittersweet regret, then picked the bin up and upended the contents onto the carpet.

'Cassie! For fuck's sake!' Adam grabbed her arm as she plonked the bin back down. 'What are you *doing*?'

'Currently?' Her anger unfurling dangerously inside her, Cassie locked her eyes hard on his. 'Contemplating sinking my teeth into your hand if you don't let go of me.'

A slow swallow sliding down his throat, Adam hesitated for a second, then heeded her warning.

'Thank you.' She headed back to the door, the empty bin in tow.

It took Adam a moment to come after her. 'What's happened?' he asked, his voice tight.

'Apart from me coming home to find you'd fucked that manipulative little slut in our bed, nothing much,' she said lightly, walking into the kitchen to reassemble the bin. Her heart was pounding, the tears brimming. Still she tried to hold on. 'Oh, I got some shopping on the way back.'

Adam shook his head as she looked at him, his expression a mixture of bewilderment and fear. 'I did *what?*'

'I think you heard,' Cassie said, her hands shaking as she pulled open the kitchen cupboards to survey the contents.

'Jesus Christ, Cassie. Are you serious?'

'Deadly,' she assured him, dropping a plate on the floor, closely followed by another.

'I have no idea what you're talking about,' Adam shouted. 'I haven't even *slept* in the bloody bed! I've been sleeping on the couch, for Christ's sake.'

'Unfortunately, I left it in the boot of the car.' Contempt rising like bile in her throat, Cassie followed the plates with a tumbler, sending a thousand slivers of glass shooting across the floor. 'The shopping,' she clarified. 'I do hope it's not too warm for it in there. I got fish for dinner, by the way. Sea bass.'

Bending down, she examined a chip in one of the ceramic floor tiles, and then straightened up with an indifferent shrug and headed to the utility room, leaving Adam staring stupefied after her.

He approached her with caution as she retrieved the vacuum cleaner from the cupboard. 'You're scaring me, Cassie,' he said, backing away again as she wheeled it towards him.

'Really?' She widened her eyes in mock surprise. 'Good.' She trundled it on, through the hall to the lounge. She'd almost added, *Be scared. Be very scared*, but fancied that might have been a touch overly dramatic.

'I have no idea what's going on, Cassie. None whatsoever,' Adam said shakily as she extracted the dust chamber from the vacuum. 'Please stop this. Just calm down and—'

'It holds an awful lot of dust, doesn't it?' She pressed the button and released the lid, then, gulping hard, proceeded to sprinkle the contents of the chamber arbitrarily around. 'You can see why the place needs vacuuming regularly, can't you?'

'Whatever you're imagining I've done, Cassie, you're wrong,' Adam stated categorically. Cassie could hear the suppressed anger in his voice, which only exacerbated her own fury. 'There's nothing going on between Kim and me. I've never even *thought* about—'

'*Liar!*' Cassie screamed, her rage and devastation spewing over.

Adam stepped back, almost falling over the armchair, as she advanced towards him.

'You brought her *here*!' she sobbed. 'Deliberately. Trashing everything we ever had! You complete—'

'Cassie…' Adam took another step back, holding his hands out defensively as she grabbed the closest object to hand and hurled it at him.

The framed wedding photograph they kept on the mantel shelf, she realised, her heart dropping as it glanced off Adam's forehead to clatter to the floor.

She looked down to where it had landed at his feet, the glass smashed, the photograph spilling from the frame. Now everything was broken, truly.

'For Christ's sake,' Adam grated, pressing the heel of his hand to his bloodied head. 'What the *hell* are you doing? Are you completely insane?'

Cassie saw red. 'Don't you dare,' she warned him. 'Don't you *dare* try and tell me this is all in my head. You fucked her in *my* bed! Right under the nose of the neighbours! I bet she just loved that, didn't she? Seeing the nets twitching.' She flailed a hand in the direction of the window. 'And won't they just revel in it, hey? The gossipers whispering in corners about my dysfunctional family.'

'That's nuts, Cassie,' Adam tried, daring to step towards her. 'No one is gossiping. There is nothing to gossip *about*. I don't know why you think anyone would be interested—'

'I don't gossip about them, do I? Have I ever revelled in other people's misfortune? No! Because I know what it's like to be the source of the gossip!' Tears spilling from her eyes, she pictured her mother, going further and further into herself, fixating on the dirt in the house, the dirt people dished about her adulterous husband, the judgemental looks, the gossip. 'My family is not dysfunctional!' she screamed, banging a hand against her chest. 'I will *not* let anyone drag me down to their level, not you, not Josh, not anyone!'

Adam looked her over, his expression now a combination of disbelief and shock. 'Josh didn't drag you down to any level, Cassie,' he said quietly. 'He did everything he could to be whatever it was you wanted him to be. It wasn't enough. Did it occur to you to wonder whether that was why he left?'

Cassie wasn't hearing him. She didn't want to hear him. She hadn't meant to say that. She *hadn't*. She had to get out. She couldn't breathe.

'Cassie, *wait*!' Adam followed her as she flew to the hall. 'Where are you going?'

'Out.' She looked frantically around for her car keys. Where had she left them? 'My keys,' she wiped a hand across her nose, tried to breathe,' where are they?'

'I don't know.' Adam moved around her, clearly trying to stop her opening the door. 'Cassie, don't. Please. You're in no state to drive.'

They were here. She'd dropped them here. She knew she had. She scrabbled around the hall table, scattering the post, sweeping it frantically to the floor. 'Have you moved them?' She glared accusingly at him. 'Have you taken my keys?'

'I haven't taken them, Cassie,' Adam said carefully. 'I'm only concerned—'

'It won't stop me,' she warned him. 'I won't let you take my grandson.'

'For *fuck's*…' He glanced at the ceiling. 'No one's trying to take your grandson,' he said, his tone softer.

'Lies,' Cassie hissed.

'Right.' Kneading his forehead, Adam dropped his gaze. 'Can we not just go and sit down?' he asked gruffly. 'Try and talk—' He stopped, his face draining of colour.

His eyes flicked to hers, and then back to the post on the floor. Quickly he bent to retrieve it, but Cassie was quicker, snatching up the letter before he could.

CHAPTER FORTY-EIGHT

Cassie reeled as she read the words stamped in blood red across the top of the envelope: *The DNA People*. Did he know about the secret she'd kept from him all these years? Had he always known? Guardedly she looked back at him. He appeared more terrified than she did. Her mouth running dry, she tore the letter open with trembling fingers.

'Cassie…' Adam took a step towards her as she scanned it.

'No!' She stepped back. Tried to make sense of what might as well be hieroglyphics: indecipherable tables, genetic systems, combined paternity index, figures relating to case number, alleged father, alleged mother… Nausea almost choking her, she scanned it again. She couldn't digest the information, couldn't understand it. Couldn't grasp why Adam would have requested it – until she reached the maternity test conclusions.

Oh dear God! This wasn't right. This *couldn't* be right. Pressing a hand to her mouth, she dropped the letter as if it might bite her.

'What?' Apprehension crossing his face, Adam looked from her to the letter as she took another stumbling step back, then bent to scoop it up.

Her heart booming against her ribcage, Cassie watched, petrified, as he read it. 'You knew.' She stared at him, uncomprehending.

'No. I didn't. I…' He looked back at her, his complexion deathly pale. 'I suspected. I—'

'You *requested* it. You *knew* and you didn't—'

'Cassie, I didn't know, I swear.' Adam looked sick to his soul. 'I felt something wasn't right when I realised she'd been in Boots the same day you… When she was so vague about who she'd left Samuel with. I kept wondering. I wanted to talk to you, but—'

Cassie stopped listening, snatching up Adam's car keys instead and dodging past him.

'Cassie, no!' Adam spun around after her. 'Cassie, don't! We have to talk.'

No time. There was no time. Cassie flailed out a hand, sweeping the heavy Japanese statue from the table and then groping for the door as it crashed to the floor.

Panic threatening to choke her, she flew out, pressing the key fob as she went, and threw herself into the car.

'Cassie!' Adam yelled as she dropped the locks and started the engine. 'Cassie, wait!' He banged his hand against the driver's-side window. 'We need to—'

Step back. Please step back. The car lurched forward, and she pressed her foot down hard.

He'd fallen. Her heart hammered as she glanced in the rear-view mirror, then relief flooded every vein in her body as she saw him pull himself to his feet. Rake his hand through his hair in frustration as he watched her go. She couldn't wait. She had no idea why Kim was doing what she was doing. What Adam had done or not done. Her one certainty was that an innocent child needed her.

Josh's child… not Kim's. The maternity test conclusions showed no genetic link to Kimberley Summers. She wasn't the mother. Samuel wasn't hers.

CHAPTER FORTY-NINE

Jemma

Jemma sat on the edge of the bed, her hands clamped to her ears in an attempt to block out the sound of her baby screaming his lungs out. *Please stop. Please, please make him stop*, she begged, lifting tear-filled eyes to the ceiling.

Liam only bawled louder, raucous, heart-rending sobs.

Choking back a sob of her own, she pulled herself to her feet, wrapped her arms tightly around herself and padded barefoot out of the bedroom. Resting her hand on the handle of the nursery door, she prayed again for God to give her strength; then, breathing deeply, she pressed the handle determinedly down. His cries cut through her as she stepped in, grating on the inside of her skull, paralysing her where she stood. She swallowed hard, ran her tongue over her parched lips and tried to quell the fear churning inside her. She was scared, not of him, but of herself, her inability to cope.

His little arms and legs were flailing. She forced herself forward, her heart thumping wildly. He was distressed and she had no idea what to do. For months she'd carried this child, carried her secret with him; felt those little limbs flexing and kicking her womb. She'd been so relieved, overjoyed, feeling him growing stronger inside her. She'd wanted him so much. And now she didn't know how to help him. How to be with him.

Rubbing at the goose bumps prickling her arms, she tentatively approached him. 'Liam, what is it, baby?' she asked him tearfully, as if he could answer. But he *had* answered. He hadn't wanted the feed she'd offered him. Hadn't wanted her. That had been his answer, loud and clear. He wanted his daddy. He wanted Ryan. But Ryan had gone. He despised her. How could he not after what she'd done? And now she had no one except the baby of the man who'd died because he'd fathered her child.

Shivering despite the mild weather, Jemma felt it again, the soft tread of footsteps over her grave. She wiped a salty tear from her cheek, recalling how vile she'd been to Josh, the bewilderment and devastation in his eyes when she'd been adamant she didn't want him involved in the baby's life. Yet he'd done nothing but what any woman in Jemma's situation would be desperate for him to do. He'd wanted to be there for her. There for his child. And now there was nothing but the ghost of him, haunting her day and night. She never really stopped thinking about him, the fact that his life had been snatched away so horrifically. He was always right here after all, a constant reminder of him in the eyes of her child. She should have told him. Yes, she would have been sharing a secret she'd sworn to Cassie she never would, but she couldn't help thinking that Josh might have understood why she'd agreed to keep quiet. *Please forgive me*, she begged him silently.

As if he'd heard the thoughts in her head, Liam's wide blue eyes, scrunched closed a moment ago, swivelled towards her.

Icy fingers trailed the length of her spine as she wondered whether Josh could hear her too. 'Please stop, baby,' she pleaded, her voice catching. 'Please stop crying for Mummy.'

His cries only grew louder. His little cheeks were red raw, his whole body rigid.

'What is it, sweetheart?' Sniffling hard, Jemma reached a hand cautiously into the cot, placing the flat of it against his tiny heaving chest. His heart was beating fast, like a frightened pigeon.

Her own heart wrenching with unbearable guilt, she plucked him from the cot and pressed him close to her shoulder. Tears and snot running down her face, she jiggled him, tried desperately to soothe him. Moving him to the crook of her arm, she rocked him, walked him around the room, along the landing to her own room, showing him all the pretty things in her wardrobe, on her dressing table, jewellery and ornaments and brightly coloured scarves. He didn't seem to hear her. Wasn't interested.

She went downstairs, clutching him tight to her and treading carefully. Nothing enticed him. He didn't stop crying. Finally, frustration knotting her stomach and twisting her nerves, she climbed the stairs back to the nursery, where she picked up his toys, waggling them one by one in front of him: his Jellycat Fuddlewuddle, his pompom penguin, his green dragon, which Ryan had coaxed his first chuckle from him with. She activated his Peter Rabbit musical mobile, stroked his back and attempted to shush him as it gently rotated and played its calming lullaby.

It didn't work. Nothing worked, his howls of anguish only increasing.

Jemma's heart banged against her ribcage. Cold fear and nausea constricting her stomach, she laid him back in his cot. Still he wailed, his mouth wide, like a gaping wound. She ran her hands over her face, dragged her fingers through her hair, grabbed two handfuls of it and tugged it hard.

Stop, she begged. *Please stop. Please stop.* Over and over she repeated it. Then, 'Stop!' she screamed, snatching him back up. 'I don't know what you want! What *is* it? What do you want me to *do*?' Her hands under his arms, Liam held high above her, she was an inch away from shaking him when she caught herself.

Horrified, she lowered him carefully back down and, a hand clasped to her mouth, backed stumbling out of the room.

Her breath ragged, she closed the door, placed the flat of her hand against it, then slid slowly to her haunches. She could have hurt him. Dear God, she might have… Burying her face in her hands, mortification settling like ice inside her, she stayed there, crying along with her baby.

Eventually, when Liam's cries quietened to an exhausted hiccuping whimper, she pulled herself shakily to her feet and pressed her forehead against the door, feeling the solidity of it between them. 'I'm sorry, baby. So, so sorry,' she whispered.

She wanted to go back in to him, kiss his Cupid lips and say goodbye to him. She couldn't allow herself to do that. Couldn't trust herself to be anywhere near him.

Turning silently to the bathroom, she stepped in and opened the cabinet. They were still there, the antidepressants she'd been prescribed when she'd fallen apart, her emotions spiralling out of control, after losing her darling little Noah.

CHAPTER FIFTY

Adam

Staring in disbelief at the letter, Adam felt his gut twist. He closed his eyes, swallowing back the acrid smell of smoke suffused with alcohol that permeated the house; the guilt, which was lodged in his throat like a stone. His fault, all of it. Up until Cassie had mentioned Josh's allergy, he'd been refusing to acknowledge what his instinct had been telling him. Yet he'd known. Deep down somewhere, he'd known. When he'd learnt that Kim had been in the very same shop Cassie had been accused of shoplifting from, he'd wondered. Every time she'd mentioned the friend they'd never seen, he'd been wary. They'd never seen her because she didn't fucking well exist. There was no text from Freya. No one called Freya in her contacts.

Even after checking her phone, he'd wondered why he was doing it, skulking around stealing samples to send off to some DNA lab. To prove what? he'd wondered. It seemed impossible that Samuel wasn't Josh's son. Cassie had been right: he was the living, breathing image of him. Still he went ahead and did it, if only to confirm his own neurosis. Samples hadn't been hard to obtain. Kim's brush in the bathroom had many strands of hair to choose from. He'd even taken a glass she'd drunk from.

He'd thought that obtaining a sample from Josh would be problematic. Not so. He'd felt his heart crack wide open when he'd taken the lock of hair Cassie had kept in one of the family albums.

So here they were, the results. Scarcely able to comprehend it, he read the letter again. *There is no genetic link to Kimberley Summers*, the report clearly stated. *Kimberley Summers is therefore excluded as the biological mother.* How had this happened? How had he let it? Why in God's name hadn't he mentioned his concerns to Cassie? She'd also sensed something wasn't right. That had been abundantly clear when she'd had what he'd feared was some kind of mental breakdown that day in the garden. His sympathies had been with Kim, whom he'd thought had been attacked, and who seemed to be under attack all over again. He'd refused to listen to his own wife, insinuated she was paranoid when in fact she was half out of her mind with grief and suspicion. And now… He had to find her. Reach her before she… Christ, what would she do?

Pressing his phone hard to his ear, he willed the taxi firm he was calling to pick up, cursing when it didn't. Wiping his hand over his face, he googled another, all the while scanning every conceivable place for Cassie's car keys. They were nowhere to be seen. What the *hell* should he do? She would be almost there by now. Panic climbing inside him, he contemplated ringing Kim. He would have to say there was an emergency, ask her to come over here, rather than alert her to the fact that they were aware of what she'd done… to what end? Why would she have feigned a pregnancy, claimed another child as her own? To get to them, obviously. She done that masterfully. But *why*? She'd said she'd loved Josh. They'd believed her. She knew things about him she couldn't possibly know unless she'd been close to him. But was it possible she'd hated him for some reason? Fallen out with him? That she'd been trying to exact revenge for some kind of wrong she imagined he had done her?

He sucked in a breath, the same impotent anger crashing through him that always did when he tried to work out who would have wanted to harm Josh. He couldn't make himself believe he'd been so drunk he'd fallen onto the tracks and just lain there. It didn't make sense. Josh had drunk in his youth, as most kids did, but never to excess. He could have knocked himself unconscious – Adam had held onto that. Prayed that Josh had been out of it in those last seconds of his life. He couldn't bear to imagine what would have been going through his mind if he hadn't been.

Bile rose in his throat as he recalled what the officer had said about possible suicide. He couldn't make himself believe that either, that Josh had been so depressed he was contemplating ending his own life. He'd tried to move on, to forget, but he simply couldn't. The inescapable fact was that what was left of Josh's wallet had still been in his bloodied pocket. His broken phone by the side of the tracks. If someone had attacked him, then robbery hadn't been the motive. So failing a random attack by some kind of psychopath, it had to have been someone who knew him. Someone who'd wanted to hurt him.

Kim, who had to be insane to have coldly done what she'd done? But she was petite. Would she have had the strength to push a grown man who didn't want to be pushed onto the tracks, to be pulverised by the approaching train? He pressed his fingers hard to his temples, then breathed a sigh of relief when the next taxi firm picked up.

While he waited for the cab, he bolted up the stairs to check the bedroom for the keys. It was carnage up there. He understood now why Cassie had done what she'd done – Kim had been playing him, playing them both; why hadn't he been able to see that? – but the fact that she had obviously mistrusted him shook him to the core.

Halfway down the stairs, his gaze shot to the front door as the bell rang. He stopped, his body tensing, then hurtled down the rest of the stairs and swung it open.

'Hi. Is Cassandra home?' the young man on the doorstep asked. 'I need to speak to her.'

'No, she's not,' Adam said shortly. 'Can I help?'

'Not sure.' The guy looked him over warily. 'Ryan,' he took a breath and introduced himself, 'Josh's mate from school. I was hoping Cassandra might know where Jemma is. She's not at home and I can't get hold of her.'

'Why would she?' Only half listening, Adam glanced past him to his car. He was about to ask him for a lift when he realised he recognised him. 'I saw you at the funeral, didn't I?' he asked. 'With your wife.'

'We were there.' Ryan smiled uncomfortably. 'We're actually not together any more.'

'Oh?' Adam felt a ripple of apprehension run through him and wasn't sure why. 'That's a shame. I thought you were…'

'Expecting a baby? We were. That is…' Ryan trailed off with an awkward shrug.

Shit. This wasn't the time or the place, but… 'Is there a problem?' Adam couldn't help feeling for the man.

'You might say that.' Massaging his forehead, Ryan glanced down and back. 'Look, there's no easy way to tell you this… It's Josh's. Liam, Jemma's baby, Josh was the father.'

Adam stared at him, astounded, for a second. Then, *Samuel*, he thought, his heart almost stopping.

'He had an affair with my wife,' Ryan went on, as Adam's mind raced. 'We were going through some stuff at the time. The details don't really matter. The thing is, I think Cassandra knew about it. I'm not proud of it, but I checked Jemma's texts.'

Adam shook his head, his bewildered thoughts reeling back to the last conversation he'd had with Josh. Was this what he'd wanted to talk to him about? Why he'd been on a deserted station platform late at night having been drinking? And Cassandra *knew*?

'There's something else.' Ryan hesitated. 'There was a sum of money deposited in Jemma's account. It allowed us to buy our house. We could never have afforded it without it.'

Adam's gaze shot to his. 'Money? What money?' His mouth ran dry as he realised he probably knew the answer.

'It came suddenly out of nowhere,' Ryan supplied. 'Jemma said it was left to her by some distant relative who'd died. It was bullshit. I checked her online banking. The deposit was made by Cassandra. I think she paid Jemma to keep quiet about the baby. I'm not sure what she told Josh, but…' He stopped, clearly choked.

Cassie paid her off? Paid her to keep quiet; to keep the information from her husband? *Why?* Adam had no idea. What he did know, though, a jagged picture forming in his head, was that *that* had somehow led to *this*. That realisation hit him like a sledgehammer.

'Jesus Christ.'

CHAPTER FIFTY-ONE

Cassandra

Samuel wasn't where she'd imagined he might be. She'd gone straight to Jemma's house having found no one at the cottage. Jemma hadn't been home. The place had been in darkness, no cars on the drive. She'd come back to the cottage, but there was still no one here either. Peering through the rivulets of rain that ran down the conservatory window, Cassie could see the place was empty. An icy drip of water snaked its way down her spine as she surveyed the upstairs windows. She wouldn't easily gain access that way, not without the next-door neighbour seeing her. Shivering, chilled to the bone, she made her way to the back door. She would get in by whatever means. Kim had to come back sometime. She would wait all night if she had to. Victory was never won without a battle. And Cassie knew how to fight. She'd fought all her life.

The back door was solid. She was about to try the kitchen window when a thought occurred to her. Going around to the front of the cottage, she pulled out Adam's key ring – and there it was, the spare key Kim had given him so he could let himself in to finish the wardrobes. Cassie had wondered about that, why she would trust him with a key to her house – as Kim had known she would. She'd planted her seeds of doubt well. Insidious little things that they were, they'd taken root and grown until Cassie couldn't see anything past them but the suspicion that had turned her into the monster Kim had wanted Adam to see. She'd wanted him to leave her. Had she wanted him for herself? Cassie wasn't sure. She was certain, though, that Kim hadn't wanted *her* to have him, the only thing worth having in her life… apart from Samuel. Kim had guessed that after losing Josh, she would bond with him. She'd lied about her friendship with Jemma, Cassie had known she had. Why in God's name hadn't she confronted her then?

Pushing the door open, she slipped silently inside and quickly checked the downstairs rooms. There was no one there, no sound but for the slow drip of the kitchen tap. Ignoring the crumbs on the work surface, the baby bottles that hadn't been swilled, she made her way upstairs, instinctively checking the nursery first. He wasn't here, her beautiful grandson. Crossing the room to place the flat of her hand on the empty cot mattress, she felt a deep sense of bereavement. Had he ever lain here at night, in the nursery she'd so carefully chosen the woodland theme for?

Her chest tightening, she shoved Kim's bedroom door open. Casting a glance around, she noted the pink satin dress abandoned on the floor, the frilly underwear adorning the bed. Had Adam succumbed to her charms? Cassie had been so sure he'd cheated on her. The signs were all there. The body contact, the coy glances, the hair on the bed. But who had initiated the contact? The coy glances were all Kim's. The hair, how else might that have got there?

Realising how easily she'd jumped to conclusions, nausea swilled inside her. She still didn't know whether they were wrong or right, how far Adam might have been tempted, but she would never forget the fear and confusion in his eyes when she'd viciously turned on him. Swiping tears from her face, she closed the door and went along the landing to push open the door to the small box room.

Stepping in, her heart jolted – and then stopped dead.

She couldn't quite take it in at first, the cork tiling decorating one of the walls, the many photographs pinned to it. A montage of photographs, mainly of her son. Josh out walking. Shopping in

his casual clothes. Waiting at Worcester train station in his smart
work clothes, disembarking at Birmingham.

Her breath caught painfully in her chest.

Bewildered, she studied them. They'd been taken over a period
of time. She could tell by the changing seasons, by the length of
his hair. It needed cutting in some. She would have nagged him
to do that. Her eye was drawn to one she recognised, one she'd
taken herself, the photograph that had gone missing from her hall.
She had wondered about Kim that first time, when she'd found
the photograph missing after she'd gone. But then, she'd imagined
that Kim was as upset as she was, that she might have taken it as
a small memento of Josh.

Her eyes drifted to the train timetables also pinned to the
wall. That first visit, the emotional letter that followed it… Kim
had wheedled her way in. She'd stalked Cassie's son, manipulated
him. She'd stalked *them*. Cassie took in the other photographs.
She herself appeared in some of them, coming to and from the
house. Mostly, though, they were of Adam. He was smiling in one
or two, a sad, contemplative smile but one that still reflected his
caring nature. In others he was pensive, distracted. She recognised
the look. His mind would have been on Josh, his insufferable loss.

Tempted to rip the photographs from the board, to tear everything of Kim's to shreds, tear her flame-red hair from her head,
she swallowed the hatred burning her throat and backed quietly
away instead. Her jaw clenched, her heart thrashing wildly, she
was heading back to the stairs when her phone vibrated.

She needed to switch it off. She needed to be quiet, invisible
until she was ready to make her presence known. Instinctively she
checked it, and laughed, a short, hysterical bark. Kim, creative little
thing that she was, had thoughtfully sent her another photograph.

Why would she do that, she wondered, send her a photograph
of herself in her short, tarty pink dress with her arm draped
around Adam's neck? She was evidently unaware that the man

she'd mercilessly manipulated, cared nothing for, had been on to her. This photograph was presumably designed to be the final push that would send Cassie over the edge. Not content that she'd already turned her into a demented, screaming harridan in front of her husband, she wanted to rob her of everything, including her sanity. Did she not realise this might be the final straw that would break her back? That Cassie, driven as far as she'd been, would cheerfully snap her neck?

CHAPTER FIFTY-TWO

Kimberley

'Bloody rain,' Kim cursed as she pushed through the front door of the cottage. God, what was the matter with the weather? Huffing irritably, wishing she'd remembered to take her brolly, she banged the door to and went straight through the lounge to the dining room, selecting Jemma's number on her phone as she did. She cursed silently as it went straight to voicemail, again. 'Great time to do a disappearing act, Jemma,' she muttered, moving nearer to the large mirror she'd propped on the mantel shelf until she'd figured out where to hang it, wiping the mascara from under her eyes.

The woman didn't deserve a reliable child-minder. She didn't deserve a child. She had no idea how to be a mother to him, barely had time for him, in between her job and bleating on about her post-natal depression. She should try Kim's life on for size. Some people didn't know they were born. Jemma had everything: her own little family, a beautiful house. Kim was buggered if she knew what more she could want.

She'd almost felt sorry for her when she'd first made contact. She'd been watching her in the nightclub, trying to work out what it was Jemma had to offer compared to her, what it was that had Josh so besotted. Not a lot, as far as she could see. The woman had been a mess, dancing like someone possessed on the dance floor, knocking back vodka shots, so many Kim had been surprised she'd made it to the exit, let alone to the street outside, where she'd puked out her guts.

Feeling a smidgen of sympathy as Jemma had retched and sobbed, Kim had gone to her, held back her hair, wondered if it might be to her advantage to befriend her. When she'd blurted that she was pregnant, Kim had feigned sympathy and surprise. Listened attentively as she'd told her what a terrible person she was, that the baby wasn't her husband's. This much Kim knew. She'd smiled kindly. 'You're not a bad person,' she'd told her reassuringly. 'You wouldn't be sobbing your heart out if you were.'

Jemma had said Kim had saved her, joked she was her green-eyed guardian angel as their friendship had deepened and she'd taken such good care of her baby. And now this was how she repaid her, too self-centred to even return her phone calls.

'Jemma, it's me,' she said, making sure to keep her voice concerned as she left a message. 'I'm worried about you, wondering if you're okay. I'm a bit worried about Liam too, to be honest. Call me back, sweetheart, as soon as you can.'

Like now. Where on earth was she? Kim had got no answer when she'd gone over there and knocked on the door, and now she really was growing worried. She couldn't keep telling Adam the baby was with a friend. She was sure he was beginning to wonder. She'd had to ad lib like mad the last time he'd quizzed her.

Sighing, she examined her eyelashes at close quarters, trying to decide whether to get a lash and brow tint, and then, catching a movement in the mirror behind her, she stopped, her blood freezing.

Shit. Fear slicing through her, she whirled around. There was someone there. She was sure there was. Her heart pumping manically, she scanned the darkness beyond the French doors that led to the conservatory. She'd seen something grey and ghostly flitting by past the…

Josh! Had he come back to haunt her?

She took a step forward – and then almost had a heart attack as a great fat wood pigeon swooped upwards from the garden to land with a claw-scraping thud on the roof.

Twit. She chastised herself and took a deep breath, trying to slow her rapid heartbeat. She was beginning to get the jitters being here on her own. Not surprisingly when she saw Josh every night in her dreams; the way he'd looked at her that time in the pub when she'd hinted she would tell his parents what he'd been up to – as if she'd punched him. Bits of his body pressed to the train tracks like dog meat, that was what had woken her screaming last night.

Feeling hot and clammy, despite being soaked to the skin, she stepped towards the conservatory. Her imagination had obviously gone into overdrive, but she would be happier if the lights were on in there. Jemma going quiet on her hadn't helped her nerves. If she wasn't careful, she'd end up as neurotic as Cassie. She wondered how the woman was faring out there in deepest Herefordshire. She would be a bit lonely, she expected, especially if she'd seen the photo Kim had sent her. It was a good one of Adam, who really was worth his weight in gold. He'd obviously thought he should remain loyal to someone who was nothing but a drain on his emotions, just because he was married to her. Kim doubted he'd be feeling so devoted now. Judging by the venom Cassie had been spitting on the patio when they'd argued, she was willing to bet the woman would go apoplectic when she got back from her little holiday to find everything less than immaculate in the bedroom. She was banking on it, in fact, sure that Adam, however caring he was, would throw his hands up in despair and realise he'd had enough. And then poor deranged Cassie would be all on her own, which was no less than she deserved after all she'd done. If it wasn't for her, Josh would still be here. He would have had his eyes opened to what a selfish creature Jemma Anderson was and been with Kim instead, someone who would love him in spite of his flaws, who would be there for him, prepared to devote her whole life to making him happy.

CHAPTER FIFTY-THREE

Adam

Adam couldn't help overhearing the work phone call Ryan had taken on his hands-free as they drove. His mind on Cassie, he wasn't taking much notice until Ryan mentioned rolling stock and trains. 'Tell him it's in his job description,' he said to the colleague who'd called him. 'He's on call-out to attend to emergency maintenance and repair of trains. If he doesn't like it, he's out of a job, end of.'

He worked on the railways. Adam felt every sinew in his body tense. The man had known that Josh had had an affair with his wife, that Josh was the father of the child she'd been carrying. His mind raced, apprehension tightening his stomach as he realised the possible implications. What would Ryan's state of mind have been when he'd found out? He would have been furious, consumed with jealousy. How could he not have been?

A frightening scenario unfolding in his head, Adam breathed in hard. He had to pursue it. He had no choice but to. He just couldn't escape it, the feeling gnawing away at his gut that Josh hadn't simply fallen that night. 'Problems at work?' he enquired, forcing a casual tone.

'Usual crap.' Ryan emitted a heavy sigh. 'Some idiot looking for excuses not to do his job. I end up going out myself half the time.'

Adam nodded understandingly. 'The joys of being in charge,' he said, glancing sideways at him. Ryan kept his gaze fixed forwards. He

wouldn't offer up information about his job, surely, if he'd had anything
to do with what had happened to Josh. He would be more vague about
what he did for a living. But still Adam had to ask. 'When did you
find out about Josh and Jemma?' he ventured, while he tried to get
his thoughts in order. 'Were you aware of the affair before he died?'

Ryan didn't answer, glancing guardedly at him.

'I just wondered whether you'd wanted to confront him,' Adam
pushed on. 'I know I would have.' He saw Ryan's grip on the steering
wheel tighten, gathered he was getting the gist of where this was going.

'I was his mate,' Ryan reminded him. 'I came to his funeral.'

Yes, and Adam would have done that too, had he wanted to
deflect suspicion from the fact that he had confronted him. A
confrontation that had possibly ended disastrously, whether by
accident or design.

'In answer to your question, no, I didn't know for sure then,'
Ryan went on, definitely sounding guarded now. 'I suspected she
might have been seeing someone. She was going out a lot, drinking
a lot. It's a small community. The jungle drums tend to go into
overdrive when there's something to gossip about.'

Adam smiled wryly at that.

'She was desperate to keep it from me, as you can imagine. It
took me a while to piece things together.'

Adam's heart stalled. *How* desperate? he wondered, his mind
swinging to Jemma, and how much she might have had to lose.
He had to get to Cassie, work out what the hell was going on.
Whatever this mess was about, it had started the day Josh had
died. Someone was responsible. He was determined to find out
who and why. Calling her number again, his head snapped up as
an unmistakable blue light swept the interior of the car.

'*Shit*,' Ryan muttered as the inevitable siren wailed behind
them, beckoning them to pull over. 'My brake light's out. You'd
think they'd have something better to do, wouldn't you?'

Christ, just what they didn't need. Adam cursed agitatedly.

CHAPTER FIFTY-FOUR

Kimberley

Kim stepped out of the conservatory, scanning the garden as she snapped the doors closed behind her. The thought had occurred that Cassie might be here, snooping around, but that wasn't likely, she realised, the frantic beating of her heart abating a little. As far as she knew, Cassie wasn't back. In any case, she never went anywhere near the garden without being kitted out in the right gear: gardening gloves, knee pads… She would hardly be standing about in the dark getting soaked without good reason.

She did have a reason, though. She was probably trying to scare Kim off. Her heart rate skittering up again, Kim decided that calling Adam might be her best bet. If the woman had gone completely off her trolley, he needed to come and get her. Selecting his number, she headed back into the dining room, kicking off her shoes and continuing on to the lounge – where she stopped dead, her heart slamming full force into her chest.

'Cassie.' She gulped and smiled weakly as the woman stepped out from the shadows.

'Kim.' Cassie smiled sweetly back, which sent goose bumps the entire length of Kim's spine. 'How are you?'

'Fine.' Looking her over warily, wondering what she was up to, how the hell she'd managed to get in, Kim swallowed again and took a step back.

'Where is he?' Cassie asked, her tone calm, her face neutral, which did nothing to appease Kim's growing apprehension.

'Who?' she asked, her eyes swivelling in the direction of the conservatory as she backed into the dining room. Should she lock herself in there? She tried to still the panic climbing her chest and think what to do. Should she bolt for the back door?

'My grandson!' Cassie yelled suddenly, causing Kim to almost leap out of her skin. 'Where *is* he?'

'Not here!' Kim yelled back, nerves knotting her stomach. 'He's not here,' she repeated more quietly, her legs trembling as Cassie came towards her. 'He's with a friend. She's babysitting. I—'

'What friend?' Cassie asked tersely.

'Just a friend. Freya. She's an old friend… from school,' Kim stammered, taking another stumbling step away. 'You don't know her, but Adam's met her,' she lied.

Smiling cynically, Cassie took another step towards her and then stopped, her gaze shooting to the phone Kim still held in her hand. 'Give that to me,' she said. 'The phone, give it to me.'

You must be joking. Kim sidestepped as Cassie held out a hand, palm up. 'I just want to talk, Kim,' she said, attempting a reassuring tone, though it was anything but. 'We're friends, aren't we? We can sit down and have a nice cosy chat.'

'He's not here, Cassie,' Kim repeated gently, her mind ticking feverishly as she tried to reason with her. 'Even if he was, you can't take him.'

Cassie blinked in puzzlement. 'Why ever not?' she asked. 'It will free you up, after all, if you think about it. You'll have plenty of time to titivate then.' Her face darkened. 'And sleep with my husband.'

Shit, she'd dug her own grave. Cassie had seen the bed, obviously. She'd come to confront her. Her heart pelting in her chest, Kim moved fast, swiping the ornaments from the mantel shelf as the woman continued to advance on her.

Cassie faltered as the ornaments fell at her feet. Kim grabbed her chance. Reaching quickly for the mirror, she heaved it from the shelf, summoned all her strength and swung it hard sideways, hitting her target with a dull thud.

The glass smashed satisfyingly. Cassie stumbled, staggering slightly as the broken shards tinkled to the floor.

Kim froze for a horrified second, taking in the rich red blood oozing from the cut on Cassie's temple, and then she flew, heading back towards the conservatory.

Shit! She'd locked the doors. Her stomach clenched violently. She could almost feel Cassie's breath on her neck as she fumbled with the key.

CHAPTER FIFTY-FIVE

Cassandra

Cassie watched Kim as she stood with her back pressed to the conservatory doors. Kim broke eye contact first, glancing quickly towards the kitchen and then taking a faltering step sideways. Cassie shadowed her, and Kim froze. 'What do you want?' she asked tremulously.

'My grandson,' Cassie answered, her tone even, her temper simmering dangerously.

'He's not *here*! I've *told* you,' Kim cried, her voice catching. 'Please leave me alone, or...'

'Or what, Kim? What will you do? Send me a threatening text?' Cassie narrowed her eyes. *I know all about you*, the first text had said. Others had followed. *Don't you think it's time to acknowledge what you did? You took everything that was worth anything away from me.* How much did Kim know? How much had she learnt stalking them, storing up information to use in her twisted little plan? *I haven't put a price on it yet*, she'd replied when Cassie had asked her how much she'd wanted.

She had, though. She'd wanted to take everything.

'Why did you send them?' she asked, out of curiosity.

'I *didn't*. I haven't... I don't know what you're talking about!'

'Why have you done all of this?' Cassie ignored her. 'To drive me mad? Convince Adam that I was crazy? Is that what you did to Josh? Played mind games with him, tried to manipulate him?'

The colour drained from Kim's cheeks. 'You need to leave.'

'Do you know how close I was to murdering the person I thought had sent those texts?' Cassie watched her interestedly. 'I was an inch away from mowing her down in my car. I even considered giving her fatal drugs.'

Kim's eyes widened with shock.

'Did you factor that in when you started out? That you might be dealing with someone who is every bit as capable of evil as *you* are?'

'You need to go!' Kim shouted.

'Where *is* he?' Cassie growled. 'Where has Jemma taken him?'

Kim's eyes skittered again to the kitchen, Cassie could almost see the wheels going around. 'I'll call the police!' she warned her.

Cassie saw her hand tighten around her phone, gripping it as if her life depended on it. The way Cassie was feeling, it might. 'Will you, Kim?' she asked her, with a doubtful frown. 'Will you really?'

The air between them crackled for an instant, and then Kim moved, darting with remarkable agility towards the back door.

Cassie spurted after her, skidding to a halt as Kim stepped outside and then stopped, a yelp of pain spilling from her mouth. She'd stood on some glass, Cassie realised as the woman gingerly lifted one foot. Presumably it had spilled from the split binbag Cassie had seen dumped untidily outside the back door. Kim really might have done better to clean it up, she thought with a flash of satisfaction.

Kim hobbled on, leaving a red snail's trail behind her. Cassie raised an eyebrow in surprise. Obviously her adrenalin was fuelling her flight. She was terrified. As she should be. Anger twisting her chest, Cassie followed her. The back gate was locked, fortunately.

Reaching it, Kim emitted a woeful sob and looked desperately back. She'd deduced, presumably, that Cassie would be on her before she was able to scale it. Turning slowly, she surveyed Cassie fearfully for a second, her face deathly pale under the glow of the security light, and then, her gaze darting sideways, took off again, across the garden this time to scramble over the neighbour's fence.

Cassie's own adrenalin kicked in, launching her into action. Kim wouldn't get far once she reached the lane. Grit biting into the bare soles of her feet, along with the wound, should slow her down. Cassie prayed it did. The car was parked a little way up the lane. She needed to get to it. She couldn't lose her. She had to find Samuel, find out how much Kim knew about Josh.

Climbing over the fence, she'd almost caught up when Kim wrenched open the neighbour's gate, squeezing through the gap and sprinting off. Cassie noticed the limp as she fled. A toxic mixture of anger and contempt burning inside her, she hardened her resolve and raced after her.

Passing Adam's car, Kim glanced frantically over her shoulder, a look of stone-cold terror on her face.

Cassie pressed the fob as she approached, flinging herself inside and starting the engine as she yanked the door closed. Kim was fleeing for her life. Cassie's incentive was so much stronger: the life of Josh's child. A chance to save her marriage once she'd shown Kim's true colours. She didn't know how Adam felt, but she aimed to grab that chance. She had to try.

She drove slowly, determinedly, the slim figure of the woman running in front of her fixed in the beam of her headlights. She felt that same primitive urge she'd had once before, to vanquish her nemesis, her tormenter, now the tormented. Imagining how easy it would be, her heart pounded, blood whooshing in her ears as she fought her desire to press her foot lower on the accelerator. She could simply drive away. But she *couldn't*. She needed to know where Jemma was. She needed to find Samuel.

Repeatedly Kim glanced over her shoulder, her expression terrified. Clearly she believed that Cassie was intent on mowing her down.

Squinting through the windscreen wipers that sloshed ineffectually against the lashing rain, Cassie willed her to stop. She must know she couldn't hope to escape.

Kim looked over her shoulder once again, her pale face a mask of terror, and then, as if finding a last reserve of strength, she veered suddenly towards the woods.

God, no. Panic wrenching her stomach, Cassie slowed the car, watching as Kim wove through the tall beech trees that bordered the lane. With no street lights away from the cluster of cottages, the woods were dark, thick with foliage. She had to go after her. Kim would keep running. Wherever the path through the woods took her, she would keep going. Cassie *had* to follow. There was no other way to find Samuel. Jemma was running scared. It was the only explanation Cassie could think of. She wasn't at home. Wasn't answering her phone. She and Kim had to be in league together, possibly trying to extract more money from her. She didn't know what madness had driven all of this, but she did know that keeping up with Kim might be her only hope of finding her grandson.

Quickly she checked the glove compartment, hoping against hope that Adam might keep a torch in there. Nothing. Flipping the boot lock, she hurried to the back of the car and rummaged through his work things. His toolbox was there, his high-vis jacket, decorator's dust sheets. Finally, tucked to the side of the well, she found what she was looking for. Thank God. Always practical, always dependable; she'd known he would have one.

Breathing deeply, she swung around, ducked under overhanging branches and made her way into the woods. She trod tentatively at first, pointing her torch if even a raindrop plopped from the trees, and then moved faster, branches and brambles tearing at her flesh and her clothes as she followed the only visible track.

Where the hell was she? She couldn't see her. *Fuck!* She stopped. Panting heavily, cursing liberally, she didn't hear the twig snap behind her a split second before something thudded hard into her back.

She hit a fallen branch sharply as she went down, felt a weight drop on top of her, winding her; a knee forced painfully into the small of her back, pinning her down. 'You think you're so clever, don't you, Cassie,' Kim hissed close to her ear, 'with your journalist's badge, your fancy house, your airs and graces. I gather you've worked it all out, with the help of your poor gullible husband, who you're actually *not* clever enough to hold onto. I bet you haven't worked out why, though, have you?' she went on, applying more pressure, pressing the heels of her hands between Cassie's shoulder blades. 'I'll tell you, shall I?'

She waited, as if Cassie was capable of answering. Then, 'I know what you did,' she whispered.

Cassie felt her heart turn over.

'He was *talking* to me, Cassie, on the phone. I *heard*. Everything!'

'What?' Cassie gasped. 'What did you…' She stopped as Kim increased the pressure, compressing her ribcage until she felt the air being forced from her lungs.

'Would you like to know what we were talking about?' Kim asked. 'He was begging me to see him. He was telling me how much he loved me.'

Liar! Cassie screamed inside. Kim had had a relationship with Josh, Cassie didn't doubt that. What kind of relationship, she didn't know. A one-night stand? An obsessive relationship that was all in her imagination? Josh hadn't loved her. He'd loved Jemma. To her bitter regret, Cassie hadn't realised how much.

'*Love*, Cassie. You know, that thing I seriously doubt *you* know anything about,' Kim continued, dripping vitriol. 'He loved *me*! I loved *him*. Unlike that bitch Jemma, who used him, hurt him, *crushed* him, thinking she could rob him of his child. Unlike his fucking bitch mother, who made him utterly miserable, emotionally damaged him, robbed him of his ability to *trust*! That's what you did, Cassie. I hope you're proud of your achievements.'

She was insane. Cassie's heart boomed. 'I can't breathe,' she gulped, grazing the flesh from her cheek as she twisted her head to one side.

'Good,' Kim snarled. '*Die!*'

Cassie's blood froze. Was that what she wanted? To kill her?

'I made Josh a promise.' Kim babbled inanely on, unaware of Cassie creeping her hand closer to the torch, which had landed beside her. It wasn't much of a weapon, but it was something. 'I promised at his graveside that I would avenge his death. That I would make everyone who'd wronged him in life suffer the same kind of loss that he had, that *I* had.'

Panic gripped Cassie's stomach. She had to talk to her. Try to reach her. Play for time. 'I know how much you loved him, Kim,' she said carefully. 'I know when you lost him, you—'

'You know nothing!' Kim raged. 'Samuel should have been mine! Mine and Josh's, not *hers*. We were meant to have a baby together, destined to be together. She *never* loved him. She doesn't love his baby. She doesn't even know how to look after him!'

'But you do,' Cassie tried, her voice parched, from the pressure, the dirt and the rain. 'It's obvious how much you love Samuel, but this isn't going to help him. We don't know where he is.' She took a gamble and prayed hard. She hadn't been able to get hold of Jemma. If Jemma had realised how deranged Kim was, it was possible that she was running from her, rather than from Cassie. 'He might be in danger. She might be hurting him, Kim. For God's sake, think before you do anything. We have to talk, think of all the possible places he might be. We have to *find* him.'

Feeling the pressure on her back ease a little, she moved her hand another fraction.

'Do you have any idea where she might be?' Kim asked, now sounding uncertain.

Cassie hesitated. She had to make this convincing. 'No, but if I can send her a text, I know how to persuade her to part with him.'

'How?' Kim asked doubtfully after a second.

'Money.' Cassie held her breath, prayed in earnest. 'Jemma will give him up to someone who loves him, who can care for him properly, as long as she knows she can slip quietly away. I can help you too, Kim, if you—'

'I don't want your fucking money!' Kim screamed. 'I *loved* Josh. I would have followed him anywhere! Followed him onto the tracks!'

'I know!' Cassie's fingers curled around the torch. 'I know you would.'

It took all of her strength, all of her willpower, to buck her off and swing the torch.

As Kim flailed backwards, Cassie scrambled away, her heels slipping and sliding in the soft earth beneath her as she tried to lever herself up. Once on her feet, nausea and terror swilling inside her, it took a second for her mind to process what had happened.

Kim wasn't moving.

Cassie's world stopped turning, the whisper of the wind through the trees fading as she sank slowly back to her knees.

Move, she willed herself. *Go.* But she couldn't. She couldn't move. Her mind raced feverishly. She had to find Samuel. They would take him. The authorities… After everything… She dragged herself up, took a stumbling step backwards, swiping the blood and the rain away from her face – and then stopped, her gaze lighting on the phone at Kim's side.

Her breath stalled in her throat. Sick trepidation clutching her stomach, she willed herself forward, faltered as if the devil might reach up from the bowels of hell and drag her down with him, then took another cautious step and snatched the phone up.

Gulping back the fear lodged like a shard of glass in her windpipe, she hesitated over the keypad, fingers trembling.

CHAPTER FIFTY-SIX

Adam

'Anything?' Adam asked Ryan, glancing back to where he stood trying to get hold of Jemma on the phone.

'Nothing. She's still not answering.'

'And you're sure she wasn't at home?' Adam asked futilely. Ryan had said the lights were all off, that Jemma's car had gone from the drive. In which case, where was she? Was Kim with her? Had they realised that he and Cassie had found out that Samuel and Liam were one and the same and run?

Cursing the time they'd wasted after being stopped by the police, Adam turned back to the cottage. There were lights on here, which must mean that Kim had been here this evening. The conservatory lights were also on, judging by the glow he could see over the back gate. Was she in there, listening to music with her earphones on maybe?

There were no lights on upstairs. He scanned the windows again. Where in God's name was she? More worryingly, where was Cassie?

He went to the lounge window, glad that he'd put off the job of replacing it. It took no more than a few shoves before the ancient sash gave. Praying he hadn't alerted the neighbours, he hitched himself up and climbed inside. Ryan was close behind him, as desperate as he was. After Adam had told him about Kim and what she'd done, he guessed that finding the child he considered to be his son was Ryan's priority. He felt like a thief, but this was an emergency. How much of an emergency he wasn't sure, but the sick feeling churning his gut told him something was very wrong.

'Kim?' he called, attempting to keep his tone calm. Despite the anger that had possessed him when he'd realised she'd faked her pregnancy, he didn't want to scare her. He needed to know what the hell had been going through her mind, what her end game had been, apart from to milk the situation for all she could get, destroying what was left of his family in the process. He badly wanted to understand what she'd hoped to achieve in the long term, but that could wait. Right now, he needed to find her – and fast.

Going through to the dining room while Ryan checked upstairs, he ground to a halt. *Christ.* Fear slicing through him, he took in the scene before him: ornaments swept from the shelf, the mirror smashed, jagged pieces of glass all over the floor. His gaze shot to the conservatory, where the lights were blazing. Striding across to the French doors, he tried them. 'Locked,' he said to Ryan, who'd appeared behind him. 'Anything upstairs?'

'Nothing,' Ryan said. 'Apart from a whole bunch of photographs of Josh on one of the bedroom walls. Weird photos, not personal, you know? Some of you and your wife too.'

Fuck. Adam raced to the kitchen. The back door was open. What the hell had gone on here? He ventured onto the patio, dreading what he might find out there.

Something crunched under his foot as he stepped out. He bent to retrieve it. A shard of glass. Apprehension knotted his stomach as he pressed two fingers to the dark stain underneath it. It was thin and watery after the rain, but it was definitely blood, stark against the pale grey of the patio slabs. Whose?

'They've gone!' someone shouted across the garden as Ryan joined him, his phone torch picking out other random splatters of crimson. Ryan shone the beam in the direction of the voice. The old woman next door, Adam realised.

'Came right across my garden without so much as a by-your-leave,' the woman went on indignantly. 'Arguing, they were. I could hear it through the walls as plain as day.'

'Who?' Adam stepped forward. 'When?'

'I'm not sure. Three quarters of an hour… an hour ago. I can't be certain who the other woman was – my eyesight's not what it was, you know – but one of them was definitely her who lives here. Nothing but trouble, that one, I can tell you that for nothing. I knew it as soon as she moved in.'

He should have listened more closely to the damn neighbourhood gossip, Adam thought agitatedly. He turned to Ryan. 'When you went home, did you check the house thoroughly?'

'I… No,' Ryan said, his expression apprehensive. 'I checked downstairs. I called out, but… The car wasn't there. I'd already rung her a few times by then. I thought—'

'The pushchair? Was that there?'

'No. I don't know. Jemma puts it in the utility when it's raining. I didn't check. We'd argued. I thought she might have left. Gone to stay with her mother for a few days possibly, although…' he paused, his look now one of consternation, 'that's not very likely. They don't get on. Why? What are you thinking?'

'We should go back there,' Adam said. Trepidation was rising inside him. He'd thought the blood might be Cassie's. The state Cassie had been in, though, consumed with fury, it could equally be Kim's.

And learning what she had, what might she have done if she'd called at the Andersons' house before coming here and found Jemma home?

CHAPTER FIFTY-SEVEN

Cassandra

Please ask Cassie to look after Liam and love him as I would. I'm sure she will when she sees him. It's not his fault. It's mine. Josh died because of me. I can't live with that guilt any more. With the knowledge that I robbed my baby of not one father, but two. Thanks for being there for me, Kim, for taking such good care of my baby. I found more than a child-minder in you. I found a true friend. Please tell Liam I'm sorry and that I love him, even though I can't make him smile. I can't comfort him. I can't even feed him. He'll be better off without me. Jemma x

Her heart thrashing, Cassie read the text on Kim's phone over again. Glancing up at Jemma's bedroom window, she could see there were no lights on inside. Jemma's car still wasn't on the drive. With the house in darkness the first time she'd come, it hadn't occurred to that the car might be in the garage. Now, peering through the mottled glass in the side door, she realised it was. Jemma was inside the house, Cassie was sure of it. Samuel too. She would never forgive herself if…

Her stomach clenching as she realised it might be too late, she made her way painfully to the back gate, thankful for the cover of darkness and praying the gate was open.

It was, mercifully. The back door, though, was locked. Growing desperate, Cassie glanced frantically around, and then snatched up the broom propped against the wall and used the wooden handle to jab a small pane of glass from the door. The key was in the lock on the inside. She breathed a sigh of relief, unlocked the door and stepped in.

Trying to ignore the incessant throbbing in her knee, she hurried through the kitchen and her heart stalled. He was here. He was crying – she would be able to identify his cry in a nursery full of wailing babies. He was clearly distressed. Her chest expanding with fear, she grabbed hold of the banister and swung up the stairs. Faltering at the main bedroom, she glanced in and felt her heart almost stop beating as she saw the limp figure lying on the bed. Guilt choking her, she went tentatively in. All of this was her fault. She should have stopped running from her past, stopped trying to bury the secret she couldn't hope to hide indefinitely. Been honest with Josh, instead of weak and scared. She'd killed him, she could never escape that fact. It was too late now; all the grief and guilt in the world couldn't bring him back.

'I'm sorry,' she whispered, reaching to smooth Jemma's hair from her face. Then, swallowing hard, praying harder, she leant over her, pressing her ear close to her mouth. Feeling shallow breaths brushing her face, relief surged through her. She was alive. But what about Samuel? Might she have…? Torn with indecision, she pulled her phone from her pocket and keyed in 999. As soon as she'd relayed the information she needed to, she cut the call and hurried to the nursery.

'There you are.' Seeing his little arms and legs flailing, she swallowed back a lump of emotion and went to him. Tears almost blinding her, she smiled reassuringly as she reached to lift him from his cot. 'It's all right, sweetheart,' she said, pressing a kiss to his head, which was wet with sweat. 'Nana's here. Nana will look after you. I'll make everything warm and safe for you, I promise.'

She wasn't sure *how* she would keep him safe, where she would go, but she had to do it. She needed to open the front door, be ready to slip out the back once she was sure the ambulance had arrived, and get as far away as possible. Take Samuel away from all of this. That was the only way to keep him safe. That was her promise to Josh. She'd hoped there might still be some chance for her marriage, that Adam might understand if she explained. Now, though, realising the horrendous consequences of the decisions she'd made, she couldn't see how he could ever forgive her. If it all came out – when it did – she would be denied access to Samuel. She couldn't live her life not seeing him grow up. He might end up in care. She couldn't bear that. Couldn't allow it. She had to keep fighting, but now her fight was for him.

Shushing and soothing him, his cries abating to a bewildered whimper as she did, she made her way back along the landing. *Hold on*, she willed Jemma, pressing the baby closer as she paused at the master bedroom. *Please hold on.*

CHAPTER FIFTY-EIGHT

Adam

It hadn't been difficult to work out where she was. They'd passed his car parked askew a little way up the road. Meeting Cassie descending the stairs as he came into Ryan's hall, Adam stopped and looked quickly at the child, who seemed unharmed. His gaze going to Cassie, he eyed her warily as he took a short step back. 'Hand the baby over to Ryan, Cassie,' he suggested quietly.

Her gaze darting to Ryan standing in the doorway, Cassie drew the baby closer to her.

'Cassie! Hand him over!' Adam raised his voice, causing Cassie to jump and Liam to start in her arms. He had no idea what was happening, but with the chaos at the cottage, and now seeing Cassie drenched to the skin, a gash to her forehead, and her jeans soaked in rich red blood, he wasn't taking any chances.

'*Now*, Cassie.' He moderated his tone as Liam squealed. 'I can't let you take him.'

Her eyes desperate, Cassie's gaze shot again to the door; then, glancing behind her, she took a precarious step back up the stairs.

'Cassie, *don't*,' Adam warned her. 'If you care about that child at all, don't.' He locked his eyes hard on hers. 'I won't let you take him away from here, Cassie. You know I won't. Just give him to his father.'

At that, Cassie stifled a sob. 'He's not his *father*.' She held the baby still closer.

'Jesus! He's been his father since the day he was *born*! For God's sake, hand him over, or I call the police, right here, right now.'

She seemed to waver at that. Adam had thought she might. He thought he knew why, too, and it was tearing his heart from inside him. Glancing down at Liam, she lowered her head to kiss his cheek. Then, meeting Adam's eyes, wariness in her own, she passed him to Ryan, who hugged him tight. One hand defensively over the back of the child's head, he moved past Adam, carefully past Cassie, and climbed the stairs.

Adam waited until he'd reached the landing. 'Where's Jemma?' he asked Cassie, trying for some level of calm.

Cassie looked flustered. 'In the bedroom,' she answered, a new fear beginning to take root inside Adam as she spoke. 'She's…' Her eyes grew wide with alarm as she faltered.

'Jesus Christ! Adam!' shouted Ryan.

Hearing the terror in his voice, Adam grabbed hold of Cassie's arm and steered her up the stairs in front of him.

As soon as he saw the slim figure lying unmoving on the bed, he realised that something was very wrong. 'Shit,' he muttered, grappling his phone from his pocket and jabbing 999 into it. She'd known. Was she going to leave her to *die*? His heart pumped with anger and confusion. 'Ambulance,' he said.

'I've called them,' Cassie said tearfully as the operator told him they'd already had a call from this address. 'I've called them,' she repeated, desperation in her voice.

'She's unconscious,' Adam said. 'We're not sure what to do.'

'Stay on the line, caller,' he was advised.

'She must have taken something. I can't make her wake up!' Ryan said hoarsely as he laid Liam gently down on the duvet.

'Is she breathing?' Adam asked, repeating what the call handler was telling him. Clamping hard on his fury, he manoeuvred Cassie ahead of him and kicked the door closed behind them.

'I don't know.' Ryan's voice was filled with panic, his hand shaking as he brushed his wife's hair from her face. 'I—'

'Look at her chest,' Adam instructed him urgently. 'Look to see if it's rising and falling. If not, listen for breaths over her nose and mouth.'

Ryan did as he was told. 'She is!' Straightening up, he swiped a hand over his face. 'She's alive.'

Adam felt himself go weak with relief. *Thank God.* His eyes back on Cassie, he nodded her towards the dressing table stool on the opposite side of the room, hoping she would get the message: there was no way he was about to let her out of his sight.

'Turn her on her side.' He repeated another instruction to Ryan, going across to the bed to make sure the baby was safe. 'You need to put her in the recovery position.'

Ryan nodded shakily and eased his wife onto her side.

'Do we know what she might have taken?' Adam asked, feeling as desperate as the man looked.

'No. There's nothing here.' Ryan's gaze skimmed the bedside table as he straightened up. He was crying openly, wiping his tears against his shoulder.

'*Fuck!*' he said suddenly, and raced to the en suite. 'Antidepressants,' he shouted, swinging back into the room. 'And sleeping tablets, it looks like. *Fucking hell.*' His voice was wretched with fear as he stopped short of the bed, his chest heaving, the packets clutched in his hands.

Adam stayed with them until the ambulance arrived, keeping his gaze hard on Cassie, who sat mutely, her expression inscrutable as she gazed towards the window, where the rain lashed prophetically against the panes and the dark night beyond them was as bleak as his soul.

CHAPTER FIFTY-NINE

'Talk to me, Cassie,' Adam begged, as Cassie sat silently in the passenger seat beside him.

She didn't answer. Her gaze was fixed forwards, her expression closed.

Wearily Adam shook his head. She'd refused to go to the hospital, despite the cut to her forehead, which had obviously bled profusely, as well as the deep grazes on her cheek and the injury to her leg. Did she realise he was a millimetre away from calling 999 again? The ambulance wouldn't be the service he required this time, though. Did she care? It was as if she was seeing and feeling nothing.

'Where's Kim?' Fear settled like ice in the pit of his stomach. If Cassie had gone to the cottage, Kim would have run. Where was she now? Seeing the state Cassie was in, he was desperate to know she was safe. 'Please talk to me, Cassie. Tell me where she is.'

Cassie looked at him at last, a frown crossing her face. 'I don't know. I haven't seen her,' she said distractedly. 'Why? Are you missing her?'

Hearing the sadness in her voice, Adam glanced down, pressed a thumb hard against his forehead. He'd been naïve. He shouldn't have allowed the closeness she'd witnessed developing between him and Kim. He couldn't undo it, but he wished she would believe that he'd never considered sleeping with another woman.

'How did you know where Samuel was?' he asked her, his throat tight.

Cassie looked at him guardedly. 'Because of the text,' she said.

Adam had seen the text. Ryan had found it on Jemma's phone and shown it to him. A text sent to Kim, not Cassie. 'The text on Kim's phone?' he checked, treading carefully.

'Yes, the text on Kim's phone.' Cassie lowered her eyes, and Adam's heart dropped like a stone.

'How did you know about the text, Cassie?' he asked, fear settling like ice in his chest as he replayed what she'd said when she'd found the so-called evidence of his infidelity in their bed. Evidence he now realised had been manufactured by Kim. *My family is not dysfunctional!* she'd screamed. *I will* not *let anyone drag me down to their level, not you, not Josh, not anyone!*

He'd felt the hairs rise on his skin as she'd said it. There'd been something in her look, a challenge, almost as if she was conveying that she was capable of doing whatever she had to in order to put a stop to what she imagined was going on. *Was* she capable?

She hadn't been at home on the evening Josh had died, he recalled, hopelessness spreading through him. She'd been out on some work-related thing, returning home shortly before the police arrived.

'How did you come by Kim's phone if you haven't seen her?'

Cassie looked stumped for a minute. He watched as she blinked rapidly, her eyes flooding with panic. 'I went to the cottage,' she blurted, as if seizing on an explanation. 'The phone was there, in the kitchen. I… saw the mess, checked the phone instinctively.' Lies. All lies, Adam knew it. 'I was scared. I…'

So was Adam. He was terrified.

'I thought that Ryan had been there,' she stumbled on, looking anywhere but at him, her hand trembling as she pressed the back of it to her nose. 'It was obvious there'd been an argument. I thought he might have lost his temper, that something might have happened to Samuel.'

'Why did you think he might have lost his temper, Cassie?' Adam managed, though he felt like breaking down and weeping. 'Because you knew that Samuel and Liam were one and the same? Because you realised that Ryan might have found out?'

'No! I didn't *know*,' Cassie protested adamantly. 'Not until I read the text. I couldn't let them take Samuel, don't you see? I had to—'

'But you knew that Josh was the father of Jemma's child!' Adam shouted over her. 'You paid her to keep quiet, for *fuck's* sake. *Why?* Why wasn't that child important to you when you were so desperate to have Samuel in your life?'

'He was!' Cassie turned to him, her eyes beseeching. 'But I thought it was best if… Jemma and I thought it was best if I didn't see him. Ryan might have suspected. Josh might have found out. There might have been blood tests. When I saw the letter from the DNA people, I—'

'Found out *what?*' She was making no sense. Adam ran a hand furiously through his hair. 'That woman in there could have *died*, Cassie. Do you not see the seriousness of what you did? If you'd acknowledged that Liam was Josh's, none of this would have happened.'

Gulping back a sob, Cassie looked away.

'*Talk* to me,' Adam demanded. '*Make* me understand. For pity's sake, just tell—'

'He's his brother!' Cassie cried. 'Ryan and Josh are brothers! They didn't *know*.'

'*What?*' Adam choked the word out.

'They didn't know of each other's existence,' Cassie went on unsteadily. 'Ryan was brought up in care.'

Adam studied her intently. Did he know this woman at all? he wondered. Had he ever?

'Jemma said she was going to tell him, now that Josh was no longer…' Cassie kept her eyes fixed down. 'She must have. I tried to stop her. I tried to tell her she would lose him.'

Stopping, she gasped out a breath. 'I robbed Josh of his brother. I *stole* him. How was I supposed to tell him that? That the woman he'd fallen in love with, made a child with, was his brother's *wife*?'

Emitting a tortured moan, Cassie buried her face in her hands. 'He would never have forgiven me. Not ever. How could he have?'

CHAPTER SIXTY

Cassandra

'Ryan and Josh…?' His expression thunderstruck, Adam could barely get the words out.

Why hadn't she told him? Why had she done this to him? To Jemma? Poor Ryan, his heart had been utterly broken. She hadn't considered what the consequences might be. She'd been furious with Jemma for what she'd done to Josh, but she had understood why, after losing her baby, she would have behaved uncharacteristically. Suffering a similar loss herself, Cassie hadn't been able to see anything beyond her own precious baby's little body. She pictured him as she'd cradled him, saying her last heartbroken goodbye. Blue, he'd been blue… but entirely perfect. His eyelashes, his tiny fingers and toes, all perfect. And then there had been Joshua. Beautiful. Vulnerable. Lonely and helpless. Born to a woman who would put him at risk. A woman who'd barely looked at him since he'd arrived in the special care unit. Cassie swallowed hard, trying to will the tears back. Adam wouldn't comfort her, dry them for her. How could he?

She felt Adam's eyes burning into her. 'You're telling me that Josh wasn't yours?'

Cassie bowed her head. 'I lost my child,' she tried to explain, an impossible, unbelievable explanation after all this time. 'He was stillborn. He would have been Josh's age. Exactly Josh's age.'

Adam sucked in a sharp breath.

Cassie looked over at him. She saw the agonised look in his eyes, the flash of sympathy. And then his face hardened. 'You need to explain,' he said, his voice gruff.

Lowering her gaze, Cassie nodded, defeated. 'I knew his mother,' she said, knowing she had to tell him now. She didn't dare hope he might understand. *She* didn't understand why she'd perpetuated the lie. Lied to hide her lies. Lies that had led to Josh's death. There could never be any forgiveness.

'I first met her when I did an article for a magazine,' she went on tremulously. 'It called for some research into drug dependency. Her name was Susan Anderson. She was an addict, incapable of looking after her children. Josh was born with neonatal abstinence syndrome. Drug dependency,' she clarified, when Adam looked at her in bewildered confusion. 'He had to be weaned off the drugs.'

'*Jesus.*' Adam ran his hands over his face.

'I left the hospital with her. I could already see she was struggling to cope. I… offered to help her look after the children. Eventually I suggested that Josh stay with me permanently.'

'Suggested?'

'I offered to pay her.' Shame burned Cassie's cheeks.

'I don't fucking believe this.' Adam laughed cynically. 'And Ryan?'

'His father was involved in his life then. The two boys were by different fathers. Josh had no one but her. I thought…' Cassie swallowed again. 'She knew I would provide him with a good home, all that he needed.' She forced herself on, knowing that each word was sealing her fate. Karma catching up with her.

'So you basically provided her with drug money.'

Hearing the scorn in his voice, Cassie didn't dare look at him. She hadn't done that in the end, but that didn't make what she had done any better. 'I was thinking of Josh,' she blundered on. 'I couldn't let him stay with her. He was so tiny, so vulnerable. I thought I was doing the right thing. I…' She stopped. She had thought she was doing the right thing at the time. Everything she'd done since, though… *so* wrong. So, so wrong.

'And the paperwork?' Adam asked shortly.

'I gave her an upfront payment, just a small sum, persuaded her to sign the paperwork, but…' Again Cassie faltered. He would think she truly was a monster now. He would be right. 'I never made the subsequent payment. I wanted to,' she said quickly, 'but the paper I had articles lined up with folded. I had no more money. No way of obtaining any. I'd given her everything I had. I couldn't let Josh go back to her. What kind of future would he have had?'

'And she didn't pursue you?' Adam sounded sceptical.

Cassie hesitated. 'I moved house. Changed my name.'

'From Smith to Tyler, because you wanted something zappier.' Adam emitted a hollow laugh. 'And Josh never knew,' he said flatly.

'No.' Cassie wiped at the tears that were falling freely, despite her best efforts not to let them.

'But…' Adam was clearly struggling, 'how the hell did you… His birth certificate… How…?'

'I wasn't sure what I would do,' Cassie admitted with a hopeless shrug. 'Then, after a while, I realised his mother had never registered his birth, so…'

'You did,' Adam finished, sounding sick to his stomach. 'So *many* fucking lies.' His voice cracked. 'How did you live with yourself, Cassie?'

'I don't *know*,' Cassie sobbed. 'I didn't know how to undo it. I thought it might all come out when Josh insisted on being involved in the baby's life. I thought Jemma might claim that Ryan was the father. That they might go the DNA route and that the link might be made that Ryan *or* Josh could be the father. I know now it wasn't likely unless they were searching for the link, but I was desperate. All I could think was that if Josh found out what

I'd done, I would lose him. You. Everything.' She looked at him. There was nothing in his eyes now but absolute disillusionment.

Adam nodded slowly. And then, after an excruciating silence, he asked her the question she'd most feared. 'Were you involved, Cassie? In trying to keep all this from being found out, were you responsible for Josh's death?'

She kept her gaze fixed down, her heart fracturing – for him, for her son. 'I loved him,' she murmured eventually.

'Were you there, at the station?' Adam spoke quietly. 'Look at me, Cassie.'

Hearing the desperation in his voice, she closed her eyes. 'It was an accident,' she whispered. 'I tripped. I—'

'*No!*' Adam tore his gaze away, banged his head back against his headrest. 'Jesus Christ… No.'

'It was an accident,' Cassie repeated hoarsely.

CHAPTER SIXTY-ONE

Joshua

July 2019

'Josh! *Josh!*' Hearing Kim's frantic tones drifting from his phone, Josh might have smiled ironically had he not been so petrified. She did give a damn about him then. It took a second for him to comprehend through his terror who it was standing above him.

'Why did you do it, Josh?' Ryan asked, his voice choked. 'You could have had your pick of any number of women. You always did, you good-looking… *stupid* bastard. Why did you have to sleep with my *wife?*'

His heart hammering in time with the vibrations rumbling below him, Josh moaned deep in his throat. *Please help me*, he pleaded silently. *I'm sorry. Please don't leave me here.*

'Why did you have to sweet-talk her into sleeping with you?' Ryan stifled a sob.

I didn't. I… A stark image flashed through Josh's mind. *You forced me. Coercion is a crime, Josh!* Kim, screeching with fury, accusing him of something he'd never done, would never dream of doing. All eyes turning towards him. Why was this happening?

Ryan's voice rose, filled with pain and naked rage. 'She would *never* have cheated on me if you hadn't come to her fucking rescue with your concern and your sympathy. Your dazzling fucking smile and broad shoulders that every deluded girl in college wanted to cry on.'

Girls. A few girls after Jemma had left him for Ryan. The ghosts of Josh's youth blew through his mind like the cold wind forced ahead of the train that hurtled towards him. He'd never loved any of them. Only her.

'Why did you have to be standing so close to the edge?' Ryan's voice was hoarse, desperate. 'Why won't you move? Get *up*, will you, for fuck's—'

His mother's voice, frantic, screaming over Ryan's. 'Ryan! *Josh*! Where is…? Oh my God! *No!*'

The tracks hissed and spat, white heat burning into him, blistering his skin.

'Help him! He's your brother!' were the last confusing words he heard before the raucous metallic shriek of the brakes drowned his mother out. A blinding white light the last thing he saw before his vision exploded.

EPILOGUE

Twelve months later

Cassie had been relieved that Adam had allowed her to stay in their beautiful house. He'd been confused when she'd said she wanted to live in it with her memories. He'd probably imagined it was the last thing she wanted. They couldn't continue as a couple, that was clear, although Adam hadn't become involved with anyone else. He'd said he wouldn't. Ever. Cassie couldn't quite believe that. He was a good-looking man. A good man at the core. He'd been reluctant to report her. She'd felt his anguish as she'd watched him doing battle with his conflicting emotions. She'd taken the decision away from him. She'd hoped that going to the police herself might help assuage her guilty conscience. It hadn't. They'd charged her with involuntary manslaughter, adjourned the hearing before sentencing for medical reports. It had helped that she'd sought counselling through her doctor. Adam had been there every day. She'd been glad he had, but part of her wished he hadn't. That he could walk away. He seemed reluctant to do that too. He was relieved and surprised, as she was, when she received a suspended sentence, subject to meeting certain requirements, unpaid work being one of them, the other to seek mental health treatment with a psychologist. She was happy to do that, finally, though she could never tell all of it.

She was sure Adam suspected there was more to what happened at the station than she'd told him. She couldn't confide in him either, though, not everything. Ryan had suffered enough. He would live with what had happened for the rest of his life. Jemma too had suffered enough. She needed Ryan in her life, a man who loved her, wanted to look after her. He was a good man too, fundamentally. It really had been an accident. Ryan had attempted to climb down on the tracks as the train approached. It was too close. There might have been two deaths that night.

There'd been no way to recount all the details to Adam or anyone else without implicating Ryan. Her stomach tightening, as it did every time she replayed the scene, Cassie recalled how, hurrying across the bridge, she'd seen Ryan walking towards Josh. Josh hadn't been aware he was there. He'd been on his phone, oblivious, alive.

She squeezed her eyes closed. She'd known Ryan had found out about the baby. If only she'd managed to park her car more quickly, to reach Josh on his phone. She'd watched helplessly as the black cat had darted in front of Ryan, causing him to stumble. Her petrified scream when he'd lurched into Josh had been lost against the thunderous clatter of the train shaking the ground beneath her, blowing her world into a million pieces. How ironic was it that Josh had been speaking to Kim, a woman whose obsessive love, twisted need to protect him, and complete inability to accept that Josh didn't love her had ultimately destroyed him?

She clamped down hard on the memory. She would revisit it later. It would creep back to haunt her in the bleak, lonely hours. It always did.

Breathing in the rich smell of the earth, she looked around her garden, grateful for this small oasis of tranquillity, where sometimes her memories were less painful. Adam had levelled the overgrown leylandii trees at the back to make sure her view of the countryside wouldn't be obscured. That had been thoughtful. He'd always been that.

Turning her face to the sun, she smiled sadly, and then went back to her digging. She didn't rejoice too much in her freedom.

She didn't really have any. She didn't crave it. She was in prison in a way, she supposed, a self-imposed prison. She preferred it that way. Enjoyed the solitude.

She glanced up at the fragrant pale yellow roses climbing the trellis. She'd done a good job, even if she did say so herself, creating the pretty roses-around-the-door garden she'd had planned.

Adam had admired it. He came every weekend without fail, bringing her anything she might need from the shops, though Cassie did most of her shopping online. He would fill her in about Samuel, who was growing into a sturdy little toddler, living happily with Ryan and Jemma. She'd done something right at least, Cassie consoled herself. She missed seeing Samuel, almost as much as she missed Josh, but that was her pain to bear for the hurt that she'd caused. Adam showed her photographs when he came, looking at her occasionally with quiet sorrow in his eyes. Cassie hated that she'd put that there.

He'd wondered again where Kim was when she'd mentioned her, speculating as to whether she'd ever been pregnant. Cassie thought not. The woman had so badly wanted her deluded fantasy, it had become her reality. She truly had thought that Josh and she were destined to be together, that he belonged to her.

She'd last been seen boarding a train heading for Wales, according to a witness who'd come forward. They police had been slightly baffled when they'd found out she didn't have a sister living there. They'd registered her as a missing person. She never had been traced. Her disgusting father eloquently telling them that it was likely she'd 'pissed off with some bloke' had led to them scaling the search down.

Utilising the anger that still simmered inside her whenever she thought about Kimberley Summers and the darkness she'd brought into her son's life, Cassie attempted to dig a deep-rooted dandelion root from the ground.

Leaning back on her haunches, her eyes grew wide as she plucked up a shoot that she realised wouldn't easily be extracted.

She glanced quickly over her shoulder, and then looked back at it. They would probably never find Kim. Sighing sadly, she went back to her labours, tucking the tendril of red hair back under the soil and compacting the earth neatly around it.

It was cosier here in her little garden, at least, than it was in the dank, forbidding woods.

A LETTER FROM SHERYL

Thank you so much for choosing to read *The New Girlfriend*. I really hope you enjoy it.

If you would like to keep up to date with my latest book news, please do sign up at the link below. We will never share your details and you can unsubscribe at any time.

www.bookouture.com/sheryl-browne

The story looks at loss and regret, touching on emotional issues caused perhaps by the depressive phase of bereavement, which might not always be obvious because the sufferer might be too embarrassed to admit to what they see as a personal failure, the inability to cope even with everyday simple tasks. Sometimes all we need to do is reach out to realise there is a hand to hold, someone there to support us. That, I think, has never been more obvious than in the challenging times we are living through just now. There are so many people offering help, sympathy and support to those who need it, both within our communities and through social media, and it's a lovely reminder of the kinder side of humanity.

The New Girlfriend also looks at the power of love, which can inspire us to great things but which also, when it is obsessive or unrequited, might drive us to great acts of despair. It explores the tangled web we weave when we set out to deceive. I love to look at how the past, our perception of ourselves, our failures, strengths and flaws, might shape our future. There are some parts of our past that, through a sense of unworthiness or shame, or some dreadful deed perhaps, we might choose to hide because of what we imagine other people's opinions of us will be. And so that first lie is told. Some little white lies might make no difference to our lives. Others might have a devastating impact on us and on the people around us – friends, children spouses or lovers, sisters or brothers. To keep a secret from being found out, we might bury it under another intricate lie, and then another, until the web becomes so tangled we can't find a way to extract ourselves. Thus begins the snowball effect: each lie building on itself to become larger, more dangerous, gathering momentum, until it crashes into the walls we build around ourselves and shakes the foundations beneath us. That, then, is the premise of *The New Girlfriend*. We look at a seemingly perfectly normal family, whose lives begin to unravel as untruths unfold. How far will someone go to keep their secret safe?

As I pen this last little section of the book, I would again like to thank those people around me who are always there to offer support (when I remember to reach out); those people who believed in me even when I didn't quite believe in myself.

To all of you, thank you for helping me make my dream come true.

If you have enjoyed the book, I would love it if you could share your thoughts and write a brief review. Reviews mean the world to an author and will help a book find its wings. I would also love to hear from you via Facebook or Twitter or my website.

Stay safe, everyone, and happy reading.

Sheryl x

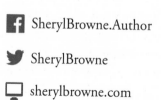

SherylBrowne.Author

SherylBrowne

sherylbrowne.com

ACKNOWLEDGEMENTS

Massive thanks to the fabulous team at Bookouture whose support of their authors through these extraordinary times has been amazing. Special thanks to Helen Jenner, without whom *The New Girlfriend* would definitely not have been all that it could be. Huge thanks also to head of publicity Kim Nash and publicity and social media manager Noelle Holten, who are always there to offer unstinting support. Thanks too to Alex Crow, Bookouture's head of digital marketing, for the brilliant graphics, and also to the fantastic cover artists. I adore my book covers! To all the other super-supportive authors at Bookouture, I love you. Thank you for cheering me on.

I owe a huge debt of gratitude to all the fantastically hard-working bloggers and reviewers who have taken time to read and review my books and shout them out to the world. Your passion leaves me in awe.

Finally, thanks to every single reader out there for buying and reading my books. Knowing you have enjoyed my stories and care enough about my characters to want to share them with other readers is the best incentive ever for me to keep writing.